Strictly
Murder

To Michael
Lynda.

LYNDA WILCOX

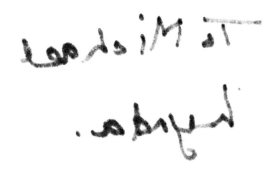

Strictly Murder

Cover design by Katie Stewart: www.magicowldesign.com

This book is dedicated to David Gaughran, who showed me the way. And to Richard, always.

Chapter 1

I HAD BEEN IN THE job only six months when my employer pulled a gun on me.

"You do see that you have to die, don't you Verity? That I can't allow you to live?"

She sat on the opposite side of the desk, perfectly composed, perfectly groomed, not a dyed black hair out of place, her glossy red fingernails curled around the weapon she pointed directly and steadily at my heart.

"I know my typing speeds haven't been so hot lately," I began, my voice surprisingly calm though my mouth felt as dry as a sandpaper sandwich.

She smiled grimly. Using the hand that wasn't engaged in threatening my life, she removed a cigarette from a packet on the desk in front of her and placed it between her red-painted lips. She tilted her head to one side, her eyes never leaving mine. Then she pulled the trigger.

I jumped in my chair, hand clutched to my chest, eyes closed, anticipating the bang, the searing pain and the ensuing darkness. Instead I smelled smoke—cigarette smoke. I opened my eyes.

She still had one end of the cigarette pressed between her lips but now the other protruded into the flame of the novelty lighter she held in her hand.

"Really, Kathleen. You nearly gave me a heart attack. If that's your idea of a joke I don't find it at all funny."

"I'm sorry, Verity, I thought you'd realise the gun wasn't real."

She dropped it on the blotter. I picked it up, turning it over in my hand, giving it closer inspection. A clever little piece of work.

"Where did this delightful bauble come from?"

"Hmm?" She drew on the cigarette. "Oh, it's just some toy of my ex–husband's."

I got up and crossed to my own desk on the other side of the room where I dropped the 'gun' into my bag. I'd dispose of it later.

"And what's this about not allowing me to live?"

"Ah yes." She became animated, stubbing out the cigarette in an ashtray and wafting away the cloud of smoke with her free hand. "It's my new idea for a story."

It is my joy, I use the word loosely, to work for the famous author Kathleen Davenport, writer of crime stories featuring the massively popular detective, Agnes Merryweather, a Church of England vicar. Her books sell in shedloads but KD had written nothing in the last two months, claiming writer's block. In reality we hadn't found a case meaty enough for KD to get her teeth into. My role in this was to discover and research old cases, spending most of my time in libraries, dusty newspaper archives, or trawling the internet. KD would then take the bare bones and basic facts of an old real life crime and, changing names, locations, genders and dates, work her magic to weave them into a new piece of fiction. In some cases she had been known to change even the guilty party, making it the butcher, rather than the baker, whodunit, as it were. As a system it worked and worked well, earning KD a lot of money and giving me an interesting, well-paid job with the added bonus of the occasional cardiac arrest. What more could a working girl ask for?

"Is this from an old case or an original idea?" I asked.

"Oh, it's an original idea." Her eyes gleamed with excitement. "Where an employer, a financier perhaps, shoots his secretary because she knows too much about his dodgy dealings. I thought you might be pleased if I modelled the secretary on you."

"Not if I end up dead, I won't be."

I poured myself more coffee from the percolator on a table by the door. Putting the jug back on the hotplate I went on,

"Besides, if you start having original ideas, I could be out of a job."

"Unlikely, Verity, dear. I employ you for more than your skills as a researcher, you know."

"Really? What skills might these be?"

I resumed my seat as she rose from hers.

"Well, obviously, they don't include anticipating my need for caffeine at the same time as your own," she laughed, making a beeline for the coffee machine.

"But other than that," I prompted. Getting praise out of KD was akin to drawing teeth.

"Your main skill, as far as I'm concerned, is coping with me. I'm aware that not everyone can do that, Verity, but you do it very well."

I nodded. My two predecessors in the role of PA had lasted a mere six weeks—between them.

KD took the coffee mug to the circular table placed between two easy chairs in the conservatory that formed an open extension to the large office. She sat down gracefully and reached out a hand for the morning paper.

"I see they've still not found her."

"Who?" I asked, still pondering how my ability to cope made me so attractive to my boss.

"Jaynee Johnson."

She turned the paper round to face me and I crossed to the table for a closer look. Splashed across the front page in large banner headlines were the words "JayJay still missing!" Underneath a grainy photograph of a buxom woman took up nearly the rest of the page, with just enough room left below for the words 'Full Story Page 4'. I didn't bother to read it.

"Who the hell is JayJay?" I asked, taking the newspaper from KD's outstretched hand.

"Oh, come on, Verity, you must know who JayJay is. She's a celebrity, the star of *Star Steps*." She caught my blank look. "With Greg Ferrari."

"Nope. Never heard of either of them."

"Don't you watch television?"

"Not the rubbish that passes for light entertainment these days, I don't, no. When I was a girl cream rose to the top while dross sank to the bottom. These days it's the other way round."

She gave me a glance that implied I must live in a cave.

"Oh but you should. It's a massive hit; people are queuing up to take part in the show."

I wasn't listening, I was studying the photo; it showed an averagely pretty face with a big mouth full of white teeth surrounded by a profusion of wavy hair. Blonde obviously—if not naturally.

"So what's this show about then?" I asked, throwing the paper back onto the table.

"It's a dance programme, on every Saturday," KD told me. "Contestants, members of the public, are teamed with celebrities and they have one week to learn and practice a dance routine before they are filmed in a dance-off to decide the winners."

"A dance-off?" Already I'd decided I didn't like it. Any programme that could so butcher the English language in a quest for tabloid ratings was not for me.

KD nodded.

"It's the same celebrities every week but a new member of the public and, at the end of the series there is a finale where the winners have a…"

"Dance-off?"

"Right. To find the overall winner."

"And where do this Jaynee Johnson and Greg Whatsisname come in?"

"Oh, they're the presenters. Greg Ferrari used to be a professional dancer and Jaynee Johnson is a celebrity."

"A professional celebrity, I assume?"

My sarcasm brought me a glare from KD who probably never missed a programme.

"They do their own routine at the beginning of the show before they introduce the contestants. They're really good," she assured me before adding, wistfully, "it's like watching Fred Astaire and Ginger Rogers."

Bless her! Bloody *Star Steps* must have been the highlight of her week.

"So how long has the bimbo been missing?"

"Really, Verity, if you've never watched the show how can you judge her a bimbo?"

I shrugged. I knew the type.

"Maybe she's in a secret love nest, somewhere," I suggested. "Or having a facelift in a private clinic. Or a brain implant in Switzerland."

"She disappeared about a week ago, I believe," said KD in her frostiest tone, getting up and going to her desk. Opening a drawer she took out a DVD case. "I've got a recording here of the show that I made for a friend. You might like to watch it. You know, to bring yourself into the 21st century."

I took it from her and put it in my bag.

"How's the house hunting going?" KD asked, leaning back in her chair at the computer, the subject of the disappearing JayJay closed for now.

"OK. I spotted a likely place at the weekend and I'm hoping to go and view it this afternoon when I've finished here."

"I've told you, you're more than welcome to move in here with me. There's oodles of space, Bishop Lea is a huge house with five bedrooms and even I don't need that many."

"Yes, I know, KD. It's a kind offer and I am grateful, but the reason for moving out of Sutton Harcourt, apart from my dreadful landlord and the poor state of repair, is to be closer to the centre of Crofterton."

"Closer to the action eh? To the night life?"

I smiled at her.

"Hardly. Not at my age."

"Nonsense, you're a spring chicken just like me."

I was thirty two and, at a guess, KD was about twenty five years older. Neither of us bore any resemblance to spring chickens. Broilers, maybe. I changed the subject.

"I was thinking of going to the library tomorrow or the day after, KD, to have a rummage through the old newspaper archives there. I might find some local crime reports of cases we could use."

"Good idea." She swung round to face me. "Are you going to call that friend of yours?"

She meant Jim Hamilton, chief crime reporter on the Crofterton Gazette.

"Yes, I'll need to use his library card."

"Go ahead. Give him a call now if you like."

She swung back to the keyboard while I picked up the phone.

By the time I quit work for the day—I work hours and times to suit both KD and myself—and arrived in Crofterton the warm, early June sunshine made me glad of my light summer clothes. I was still in time for a late lunch in Valentino's and strolled along the High Street looking forward to a baguette and a glass of wine. The promise of summer had brought out the shoppers who, unusually for a Monday, crammed the pedestrian High Street wearing too few clothes and showing far too much flesh. I popped into the stationer's for a new writer's notebook having left my old, nearly full one in the office. It would come in useful this afternoon and I would certainly need it at the library. Jim had been delighted to oblige when I'd phoned with my request and agreed to meet me on Wednesday morning.

"Lovely day," observed the girl in the stationery shop, sliding my purchase into a paper bag.

"Indeed." I smiled my agreement. They were always friendly in here which is why I gave it my custom rather than the larger Smith's down the street.

Once back outside, my stomach rumbled like some active volcano about to erupt. It was nearly two o'clock and hours since I'd had breakfast. I opened the plate glass doors of Val's place with relief. Inside cooler air greeted me and the wine bar was virtually empty apart from a couple, dawdling over coffee, at one of the small, circular tables. I made my way to the 'L' shaped counter and perched on a bar stool.

"*Bonjour, Verity, tu veux manger?*"

Yes I did want to eat and soon. I settled on a ham baguette and a small glass of wine. While Val disappeared to order the baguette from the kitchens, I sipped gratefully at the cool, fruity wine and pondered KD's decision to write an Agnes Merryweather story entirely out of thin air. That she was capable of it I didn't doubt and most of her work had been written that way but, about five years ago, she had been struck down—in her words—with a bad case of writer's block. She had worked her way through it, though maybe round it would be a better description, by hitting on the idea of using genuine crimes from the past, whether solved or unsolved, as the basis for her stories. That's why I spent more time researching than I did answering the phone, typing letters, dealing with autograph requests and the mounting fan mail as well as making salon and other appointments. My duties could undergo a dramatic change if she no longer required any research and wrote everything from thin air again and I wasn't altogether sure that I liked the idea. I didn't relish being only a secretary and I might find myself looking for a new job as well as a new place to live. I didn't want that. I enjoyed the job I currently had, the work was both interesting and varied, and I needed the sort of money KD was prepared to pay me.

"Your baguette, *chérie*."

"Thanks, Val," I said before almost snatching it from the plate and falling on it like some underfed mongrel who'd found an unattended butcher's shop.

"You were hungry, yes?"

Val smiled as I brushed away the last of the crumbs from around my mouth.

"Oh, yes. Boy, I needed that."

I had been friends with Val and his brother Jacques for over ten years, ever since I'd met them on holiday in France. I wouldn't have minded him making some pointed comment about the piggish speed with which I'd disposed of the delicious, thickly cut ham and soft bread, I knew many an English person who would have done so, but Valentino had always shown me typical Gallic courtesy.

"Are you going so soon?" he asked as I reached for my bag on the bar stool beside me. "It is bad for the digestion, that."

I glanced at my watch. It was barely three o'clock and there was plenty of time before I needed to be at the estate agent's, I didn't have any appointment, but I knew that if I stayed I would be tempted to have more wine and I needed a clear head.

"Yes, sorry Val. I'm house hunting this afternoon." I got down from the stool.

"You are buying a house? That is good."

"Oh no, I can't afford that. I'm just looking for a new one to rent, that's all. I want to move out of Sutton Harcourt and closer to Crofterton."

"Ah yes, I see. Well, *bonne chance mon amie*." He blew me a kiss as I went out the door.

Knight's estate agents had boasted a discreet presence on the High Street for as long as I could remember. It offered its upwardly mobile dreams, to those who could afford them, from behind freshly painted dark green woodwork and an expanse of plate-glass that was only ever filled with the most select of properties. And why not? After all, the Knights themselves lived in the largest, most opulent house in the area although the founding Knight, as it were, had long since departed for a more bijou residence in the sky. His grandson now carried on the business without ever setting foot in the premises that bore his name, content behind the walls that surrounded his home and the layer of managers that protected him from doing a day's work. I didn't bother to read the current crop of beautifully typed and illustrated cards intended to entice the wealthy into parting with more in monthly mortgage payments than I earned in a year. I just kept my head down and walked past. Then I took a deep breath before putting my hand to the door and going in.

None of the heads lifted as the jangling of the door bell announced my arrival, not a single pair of eyes raised themselves to meet mine, no lips curved in a welcoming, albeit insincere, smile. The five occupants of the outer office had obviously sussed me out as a waste of their precious, busy time when I'd passed the window. I glanced around, looking for any indication of a lettings department or any desk with such a sign on but could see nothing. Nearly a minute passed with me standing in the middle of the plush carpet like some unwanted piece of lost property. Either that or I had put on my superhero's cloak of invisibility that morning without realising it. If I'd been in a better mood I would simply have turned round and walked back out of the door. Instead I spoke loudly and clearly, in the kind of voice I normally reserve for naughty children.

"I apologise for interrupting you at a busy time but would it be too much to ask if you have a lettings department, please?"

For a moment I thought even this simple request would be too much. Then, just when I had decided to throw in the towel and go elsewhere, a tall, dark haired man in a sharp suit appeared from an office at the rear.

He weaved his way towards me through the desks, a task made easier by the sheer oiliness of his manner. He aimed a condescending smile loosely in my direction.

"Good morning. John Adams, office manager. How may we help you today?"

"I'm interested in a house you have to let."

"House lets. Ah, that would be Tom. If you'd just come this way."

He oozed his way back between the desks towards a partition at the far end of the room. Here, behind the screen, shoved in a corner and hidden from sight like an ageing and incontinent relative one nurses but doesn't quite like admitting to, lay what constituted Knight's Estate Agents Lettings Department. A boy, a table and a filing cabinet.

"Tom, this lady is interested in a house let." Mister Oily introduced me to his colleague. "I'll leave you in Tom's hands."

His departure back into the inner sanctum he had sprung from left a moment of silence. The shrill note of a telephone from the main office finally roused the youth looking curiously up at me.

"Take a seat Mrs…?"

"Miss. Miss Long."

"Ah, right. I'm Tom Powell, Miss Long. Did you have a particular property in mind?"

"Yes, 27 Willow Drive."

"Um, Willow Drive, Willow Drive," he muttered, finally standing up and taking a step to the filing cabinet, his part of the office being so small that a step was all that was needed.

"Yes, it's in that maze of streets off the Bellhurst Road. Down Old Church Street and turn left."

"Ah, yes." He nodded as though my directions had filled in some gap in his mental road map. "Just give me a moment."

While he flicked through the files in one of the drawers I gave him a closer look. To my more advanced years and, admittedly jaundiced, eyes he appeared about twelve years old but was probably nearer to twenty five. He would have left school with a media studies A-level and become a car salesman before trying tele-sales and finally settling on a career in estate agency because he got to wear a smart suit— though the one he wore today probably cost him less than a hundred quid and came from Next.

"Here we are. 27 Willow Drive." He brandished a pile of papers in his left hand as he manoeuvred himself back round the desk to his seat.

"Well now, the property is an attractive period building with some interesting original features," he began chirpily and my heart sank. Knowing how estate agents love to manipulate and mangle the language, that meant it was a late Victorian villa that had had no renovation since it was built in 1900.

I couldn't resist the temptation of asking, "Is it deceptively spacious?" which is estate agent speak for the size of a rabbit hutch, but the irony was lost on young Tom.

"It's ideal for city living," he enthused.

So, a rabbit hutch with no parking, then. I gave a mental sigh. Oh well.

"What is the monthly rental?"

He flicked through the papers.

"Hmm…the landlord is seeking a figure of 650 pounds per calendar month."

Six hundred and fifty quid! That's not a landlord, that's a robber baron. There was little to be gained by pointing that out to young Tom, even assuming he'd ever heard the term. He was dealing with silly figures like this all the time. I'd just have to ask KD for a rise.

"Would you like to view the property?"

He pulled a large desk diary towards him and looked at me enquiringly.

"Could I just look at the particulars for a moment, please?"

He had been so busy reading them himself he'd forgotten to give me a copy.

"Oh, yes. Of course."

He took a sheet from the bundle he'd been holding and passed it to me. It was the usual thing, full of estate agent speak and therefore not a lot of use. It told me nothing but I folded it and put it in my bag anyway. A visit was definitely called for.

"Is there any chance we could go now?"

He gave a quick glance down.

"Yes, I don't see why not. I'm free until four o'clock and my next appointment is out that way so that should fit in nicely. I'll just pick up the key on the way out."

We drove there in separate cars. Fortunately Willow Drive was almost empty and there was plenty of space to park.

"Here we are," said young Tom cheerily, clipboard in hand, as he put the key to the lock. He jiggled it around for a moment.

"That's odd," he muttered. "Must be the wrong key."

He looked at the bunch in his hand and selected a different one.

"That's better."

This time the key slid straight in. He pushed open the door and I followed him in. We stood in a hallway, stairs going up in front of us and with doors off to right and left. A passage ran down the left hand side of the staircase leading, no doubt, to the kitchen and the back door. Young Tom showed me round. It didn't take long to view the downstairs part of the house. Although unfurnished the general state of repair was actually quite good. There were modern fittings in the kitchen, the two front rooms were of a reasonable enough size and, for the moment, I could live with the carpets and wallpaper. We returned to the hallway. So far, so good.

"Upstairs, now?" asked Tom turning over a page on his clipboard.

"Well, yes. Please." He'd made it sound like a question and I wondered if he expected me to leave without having seen all of the house. His phone rang just as he put his foot on the bottom stair.

"You go up and have a look round. I shouldn't be long. Hello, Tom Powell."

I left him with his mobile to his ear and continued up the stairs. The carpet was worn in places and one of the newel posts was missing on the left hand side. At the top, a door in the facing wall led to a bathroom and toilet which, if the irregular join in the tiles was anything to go by, had once been separate rooms. The suite looked relatively new and recently cleaned. Tiles, missing from behind the bath, were of the plain white variety readily found in any DIY store so I shouldn't have trouble replacing them. A shower attachment hung over the bath with a rather disgusting curtain around it but once again that was something I could easily deal with myself. Close to the toilet and wash basin I detected a faint but heavy aroma. As smells often do it stirred a vague memory. I looked in vain for an air freshener.

Coming out of the 'usual offices' a further door along the same wall opened into a small box room with a larger bedroom opposite, above the downstairs dining room. Here, I decided, I would set up my home office. This only left what the particulars had described as 'the master bedroom' so, with Tom still busy talking downstairs, I retraced my steps and opened the door at the far end of the landing.

My first reaction when I got in there was to say "Oh, I'm sorry", for a bed stood under the window facing the street and on it lay a woman wearing a long evening dress and a pair of high-heeled shoes. My initial surprise gave way to anger and I stepped closer, ready to make a fuss and ask what the hell she thought she was doing. The woman's face, surrounded by blonde hair that spread out across the pillow, was composed and peaceful. I took a step or two closer to the bottom of the bed, all set to let fly and give her the rough edge of my tongue, but the words of reproach died on my lips. This woman would never again hear any reprimand from me or from anyone else for that matter. I had no doubt that she was dead, she was too pale and too still. No whisper of breath escaped the full lips.

Of course, what really clinched it was the dagger sticking out of her chest. I took a closer look at the white, drained face. Well, I thought, one thing is certain. Jaynee Johnson isn't missing any more.

Chapter 2

T HE POLICE HAD ARRIVED QUICKLY after I called them on the mobile. Once I had done so I took a closer look at the woman (I tried not to think of her as a body) on the bed. I worked quickly; the police would not be long and Tom Powell could appear at any moment. JayJay lay on her back, arms straight down by her sides and dressed for an evening out. The white gown was shot through with silvery threads matching the solid silver snake around her neck, the crossed head and tail resting on her collar bone, the eyes picked out in precious stones. Judging from the peaceful look on her face death had come quickly, without struggle. Her platinum dyed hair spread out across the pillow. I glanced at her hands; palms down, no cuts or grazes on the soft, unblemished skin, the red painted finger nails undamaged, untorn. I forced my gaze upwards to her chest. The dagger had been thrust in until only the white, enamelled handle, that from a distance had camouflaged it against the dress, protruded from between her breasts. It pointed upwards like an accusing finger and I wondered how long it was. Not much blood, I thought with some surprise, though whether that implied she was dead before the vicious strike that had embedded the dagger in her chest, I would leave to the police and the forensics lab.

Poor Jaynee Johnson. I scoffed at the modern cult of celebrity, but Jaynee had, in her own talentless way, brought pleasure to the millions of people who watched her show. I couldn't help but feel sorry for her now. I made a last appraisal of the otherwise empty room, went out and closed the door on JayJay's death bed.

Now I waited alone in the kitchen, while the police swarmed over the house like an army of soldier ants. Tom Powell had gone, dismissed after leaving his name and contact details, once the police discovered that he hadn't set foot upstairs. Poor lad, he'd looked very pale as he'd scurried off down the steps, warned by the police to say nothing until they had issued a press statement. I hadn't given him the name of the victim when I'd rejoined him and told him what I'd found and that the police were on their way, nor had I been surprised that he didn't want to go up and see for himself.

"Miss Long? I'm Detective Inspector Farish and this is Sergeant Stott. Sorry to have kept you waiting."

I shook the offered hand. Behind the Inspector his younger sergeant smiled softly at me. If it was an attempt to reassure me it failed.

"Please sit down." The Inspector was curt.

I was glad to. My legs were shaking.

"Round up the usual suspects," I muttered to myself.

"But Major Strasser hasn't been shot, has he?"

I gaped at him.

"It's one of my favourite films, *Casablanca*." He smiled and the knot of tension worming around in my stomach eased. Slightly.

"No, this was as neat a stabbing as I've ever seen." He looked serious again. "Did you know the victim?"

"Jaynee Johnson?"

He nodded.

"No. I'd never even heard of her before she went missing and her name and picture were splashed all over the papers."

He raised an eyebrow.

"You don't watch television?"

"I don't watch LCD television, no."

"LCD?" queried Stott who, until now, had been doing a good job of blending with the background while he took notes.

"Lowest common denominator," supplied Farish. "So you were simply here to view the house?"

"Yes. I was just in the wrong place at the wrong time." I grimaced at the cliché.

"But you didn't call for an ambulance before you called the police?"

"It was too late for that," I replied, sadly. "She was obviously dead."

"Did you touch anything in the room?"

I was sure I hadn't but gave the question a moment's thought.

"No. Only the door handle, I think."

"You didn't, for example, touch the body?"

I shuddered at the thought. "No."

"Or remove anything from the room?"

"No." My denial this time was more vehement. "I know better than that. Why do you ask?"

He ignored the question.

"Not as a souvenir, perhaps?" he asked in a silky voice.

"No!" I snapped. "I'm not a ghoul!"

"So, you would have no objection to Sergeant Stott searching your bag?"

I'd hardly begun to say, "No, that's all right," before his minion had whipped my bag off the table and rummaged through its contents. I didn't miss the shake of the head he gave his boss before he replaced it.

"What time did you get here, Miss Long?" The Inspector went on with his relentless interrogation.

"Sometime around half past two, at a guess."

"And you had no difficulty getting in?"

"Oh!"

Of course, Tom would have told him about the business with the key. I had been too occupied with wondering why there was a dead celebrity in a room upstairs to consider how she had got there.

"Miss Long?" The Inspector's stern face and voice demanded my answer.

"Mr Powell did have a problem with the key," I recalled. "He said it was the wrong one."

"And did you notice anything particular while you were alone upstairs?"

"What? Other than a dead body, you mean?"

His mouth twitched briefly at my sarcasm before he got it under control.

"In any of the other rooms?"

"No, I don't think so. Oh, wait."

There had been something. What was it?

"There was a smell." I struggled with the memory. "A faint smell in the bathroom."

I prevented him from making the obvious interruption by holding up my hand. I was almost there, I'd almost got it.

"Perfume."

"Perfume?"

"Mmm. Estée Lauder's 'Youth Dew'."

Inspector Farish raised an eyebrow while behind me Sergeant Stott's pen scratched rapidly across the pad.

"You're sure?"

"Umm?" I dragged my attention back from considerations of perfume to the man across the table. "Not a hundred percent, no, but fairly sure."

"Anything else you noticed?"

I shook my head.

"What do you do, Miss Long?" He changed tack.

"I work for Kathleen Davenport."

Sergeant Stott looked up quickly from his notebook.

"The writer?" he asked.

"Yes. Have you read her books?" I swivelled in my chair to look at him but it was his boss who replied.

"I'm too busy dealing with crime fact, Miss Long, to have time for crime fiction."

Maybe, I thought. He still knew KD was a crime writer, though.

"What is it you do for Kathleen Davenport? Secretary?"

"Yes, I'm her PA and researcher."

He nodded as Stott made an entry on his pad.

"All right, Miss Long. I think that's it for now though we may need to question you again. If you think of anything in the meantime please get in touch. Leave your name and contact details with Sergeant Stott, will you?"

He rose and strode to the door.

"Oh and by the way …" He paused in the doorway.

"Yes?"

"Given your job, please don't be tempted to try a bit of amateur sleuthing. Leave it to the professionals."

"I'm a PA, not a private detective," I snapped back.

"Yes, please remember that. The last thing I need is some star-struck typist getting under my feet because she thinks that working for a crime writer qualifies her to do so. It doesn't. Stay out of this."

I was so stunned that by the time I thought of an answer, he had already gone.

I drove home in cold fury. Slamming the door shut behind me, I headed straight for the wine rack. Bloody Inspector Farish. I unscrewed the top off a bottle of red as if I were unscrewing his head from his neck and grabbed a glass. Bloody, rotten, stinking Inspector

Farish. My hand shook so much I overfilled the glass, wine spilling onto the table. I cursed. What about me? I'd found her, for goodness sake. I'd found the body but did Farish care? Did he hell. I lowered my head to the glass, slurping at the wine until the level dropped. I was almost tempted to lick the spillage off the table. Damn Farish. I reached for a cloth. Damn all policemen. I felt like kicking the wall.

Instead, I marched through to the living room, swept the books and paper work off the settee and plonked myself down in the cleared space, then took another good swig of wine, and promptly went to pieces. I sobbed for twenty minutes, probably as much in shock as in anger. I might work for a crime writer but finding real corpses was hardly part of my job description. I sobbed for myself and for the luck of the Longs that dictated I'd been the one to find her. I'd been the one on the end of the Inspector's grilling, his callous, thoughtless treatment. Then I cried for JayJay. For a young life, a life that already held fame and wealth, cut short so brutally.

When my tears finally stopped, I traipsed through to the bathroom and splashed water over my face. My fit of the vapours had ravaged my make-up. I repaired the damage as best as I could then went back to the kitchen, picking up my wine en-route.

It was nearly seven o'clock, my baguette was a distant memory and my stomach was starting to complain. I took a pizza from the freezer and threw it into the oven while I prepared a small green salad and sat at the kitchen table to eat. Normally I would cook for myself and read whilst I was eating but I needed a calm mind to do both those things and calm was the last thing I felt at the moment. I spent the entire meal thinking about Jaynee Johnson.

What had she been doing in a three up three down Victorian villa? Why had she gone there? And in evening clothes? How had she, and her killer, got in? Was there any significance to the smell of Estée Lauder in the bathroom? I'll bet Inspector bleeding Farish is asking himself exactly the same questions, I thought, as I carried my empty plate to the draining board. Despite the Inspector's parting shot, I couldn't help but be interested, given my involvement so far in what the press would soon be calling 'the JayJay murder'.

I poured more wine and fetched my notebook then, for an hour or so, I wrote down everything that had happened since young Tom and I had left the estate agent's office. I made lists. Lists of people, lists of known 'facts' and most importantly, lists of questions. This alone covered two pages. I leaned back in my chair, arching my back, arms stretched above my head.

Only then did I think of Inspector Farish's questions to me and what lay behind them. Why had he asked if I'd removed anything? Why search my bag? Did he think … Of course! Realization hit me like a house brick. Where was Jaynee's handbag? It would be a flimsy affair, made of fabric to match her dress or, maybe, white leather and holding no more than a lipstick, comb and mobile phone and, yes, it would be small enough to fit inside my voluminous carry-all. As I worked through the implications of this the Inspector's questions began to make more sense—not that I liked him any better for it.

Suddenly, feeling bone weary and ready for bed, I thought of KD. I ought to call her, let her know what had happened. For all I knew, the police might have called her to check my story by now and she would know already. I gave this idea a moment's thought before dismissing it. No, KD would have phoned me if that were the case.

With a sigh I walked through to the living room and picked up the phone.

"You should stay out of it, Verity. Leave investigating JayJay's death to the police. Don't get involved," said KD the next morning when I got into the office and informed her of my decision to do a little sleuthing.

"But I am involved," I cried. "I found her body."

"That's no reason for you to get any deeper in than you already are. The police won't thank you."

No, they wouldn't. Which was one of the main reasons for doing it, of course.

"Why don't you take up a hobby? Embroidery? Or knitting perhaps?"

"A tad too sedentary for me, I think."

She thought about this, her head tilted.

"Hmm. You may be right. After all, you don't want to be sitting around at home all evening when you've been doing that here all day."

What cheek! She made it sound as if I didn't do a stroke of work. I glared at her.

"Any more bright ideas?"

"How about amateur photography?"

No, the only thing I wanted to take a shot at was solving this case. I shook my head.

"Sorry."

I turned back to my computer, but my employer knows me too well.

"How could you investigate anyway?" she asked now.

I swung round to face her and pulled my notebook from my bag. I'd been considering this very question since I'd got into bed last night.

"Well, it strikes me there are three main questions." I counted them off on my fingers. "Firstly, what was she doing there? Secondly, how did she get in? And finally, who did she know that would want to kill her?"

"Hmm, means, motive and opportunity."

KD always put things so much more succinctly than I did.

"Actually, there are several questions you haven't thought of."

"Very probably," I agreed.

She got up and paced back and forth behind her desk.

"Still, for the moment, let's consider the questions you have identified. Why was she there? We can't say much about that at the moment."

'We', I thought. What's this 'we' business all of a sudden?

"She was hardly likely to be at the house with a view to renting it," KD went on, "so, she either went there to meet someone or was taken there by someone."

"Agreed."

"Unfortunately we don't have enough to go on to answer that question at the moment. So, let's turn to your second point."

I glanced down at my scribbled notes.

"How did she get in?"

"Yes. To me this is a far more interesting point. And it's the one question that, with a bit of judicious ferreting, we might actually be able to answer."

"Judicious ferreting? Really KD, you do have a way with words."

I was laughing but she stopped tramping up and down the carpet, looking at me sternly.

"Naturally, dear. I'm a writer. Now, if you really want to get involved, I suggest you pump your spotty young estate agent friend…"

"He's not spotty and he's not my friend."

"Whatever." KD ignored this protest. "Ask to view another property with him and then pump him hard about those keys. Where are they kept, who has access to them and so on. That's the best option, Verity. Because without knowing more about her private life we have absolutely no way of answering question three."

No we hadn't but, unknown to KD, I had phoned Silverton Studios before I left home that morning and made an appointment to see JayJay's producer later that afternoon. I'd meant to tell KD when I arrived for work but there had been so much else to impart I had forgotten that bit. Her negative response to my sleuthing idea deterred me from doing so now.

Still, her suggestion about talking to Tom Powell was a good one and I said I'd give him a call.

"Good. Now where are you with your current workload? When are you going to the library with your reporter friend?"

"Tomorrow morning, so I probably won't be in until after lunch time."

She nodded acceptance. Working time was always flexible with KD.

"How many possible cases do you think you'll need?" I asked.

"How long is a piece of string? If you start, say twenty five years ago and work forward a few years, that should be enough. It really depends on how many usable crimes you find, of course."

I nodded, I knew what KD meant by 'usable crimes'. She had a preference for something nice and domestic, no big business, no robberies and no drug related crimes. At times it was a tall order. People aren't constantly bumping each other off in quaint English villages, for all you might think so from the bookstore shelves, but so far I'd always managed to find something KD could work with.

"Don't bother looking at anything within the last twenty years," she instructed. "I've been here that long and remember nothing of note."

I wrote all this down on my pad.

"Right. Can you call my agent and see if she's in, now, please. I've had an idea."

She turned back to the keyboard without elaborating. I picked up the phone and dialled.

"Emma Lawrence Associates."

"Good morning, Crispy Bacon Sandwich, please."

I heard a giggle in my ear.

"Oh, I'm so sorry," Mortified by my gaffe I hastened to apologise.

"Don't worry. We all call her that," the chirpy voice of the receptionist laughed back at me.

Well, with a name like Kristy Baker Sanders, what else could you expect?

"I'm sorry but she won't be in until three o'clock. Can I ask her to call you back?"

I relayed this information to KD, who mouthed 'yes' back at me without stopping the rapid flow of fingers over the keyboard.

I gave the receptionist KD's name and put the phone down.

Silverton Studios sprawled over several acres alongside the road between Crofterton and Bellhurst. I spent the journey going over the cover story I had concocted. It had more holes than a string vest, and I hoped I could brazen things out if it became necessary. Ten minutes after leaving KD's I pulled into the car park, at the same time as a large Mercedes. I followed the occupant, a portly, broad-shouldered man with receding grey hair, towards the main entrance at the top of a broad flight of steps. A commissionaire in a fancy, dark green uniform manned the door and sprang into action as the older man reached the top of the stairs.

"Good afternoon, Mr Brackett."

"Afternoon, Ray."

This individual continued to hold open the door, murmuring a greeting as I passed through.

Inside the spacious lobby I headed straight for the reception desk.

"Good afternoon, Mr Brackett," the receptionist called out to the man from the Mercedes who had made a beeline for the smaller of two lifts to the left of her desk and now stood waiting for its arrival.

I gave my name and appointment time with JayJay's producer, Candida Clark, while wondering what might inspire parents to name their daughter after an embarrassing fungal infection. Her secretary soon came to collect me and we walked across to the lifts.

"What's the 'P' for?"

"Hmm?"

"The 'P'." I indicated the single button on the left hand lift.

"Oh, that's for the Penthouse suite. It's John Brackett's office on the top floor."

"He has a whole floor to himself, does he?" I smiled.

"Well, he is the CEO."

Deposited in her office some few minutes later, I found the producer of *Star Steps* was just as I had pictured her. Stiletto-heeled shoes made more of her medium height and build—she would probably run to fat in her later years—and her honey-blonde hair was swept up in a neat French pleat. She wore an expensive, pale grey business suit over a pastel silk blouse.

"Candy Clark."

Candy, now, eh? Well, that was hardly surprising. Not that I was going to let her get away with it.

"Candida. That's a pretty name," I said, innocently.

"Yes. It's from a Tony Orlando song of the same name. And you are?"

It was a bare five minutes since the receptionist had announced me. Ms Clark must have a very short memory.

"Oh, I'm Verity Long, *Oh Hi!* magazine." I might as well start as I meant to carry on—lying through my teeth.

She looked blank, as well she might seeing as it was an invention of my own, made up in the car on the drive to the studios.

"I don't think I've heard of that one."

"It's like *Hello*, only for the blind."

I mentally crossed my fingers and prayed that blind people everywhere would a) forgive me and b) miraculously be blessed by the gift of sight.

Candida, however, didn't bat an eyelid. She returned to her desk and waved me to a chair.

"Hold all calls, please, Jenny, and if that old trout Kathleen Davenport calls, tell her I'm evaluating her proposal and I'll get back to her, OK?"

She slammed the phone down.

My ears pricked up at the mention of KD. What proposal was this and how dare this woman call her an old trout? I added it to my list of reasons not to like Ms Clark.

"Kathleen Davenport?" I tried to make it sound as if the name was vaguely familiar instead of one I uttered every time I answered the phone in the morning.

"Yes, she's some crime novelist who wants me to make a series out of her books, pfft."

Did she indeed? I ignored Candida's dismissive tone. This was news to me and I thought it a brilliant idea. I was just about to say so when I remembered why I was there and my stupid cover story.

"Anyway, er, Miss Long." She checked my name on a scrap of paper. "I can give you ten minutes before an executive meeting. What can I do for you?"

"I'm writing a piece about Jaynee Johnson," I began in my best professional air and with what I hoped was a winning smile. "Her life and work, her rise to fame, that sort of thing."

"Well! You're certainly quick off the mark, I must say." She threw me a suspicious glance before adding, "and what's the point? The woman's dead, isn't she?"

Maybe Jaynee's producer had never heard of eulogies. She gave me an icy stare.

"Yes, but I'm taking the line that a popular and much loved celebrity, who brought so much joy to so many people, especially our readers, has been taken from us far too early."

Her eyebrows were nearly under her hairline and I felt like gagging on my own hypocrisy but I was in full flow now and gushed on.

"We have lost a shining star from the television firmament, a star burnt out far too soon, too young, with the world at her feet and..."

"Yes, yes. I get the idea."

Luckily Candida Clark interrupted this load of unmitigated tosh before I went too far overboard and turned a talentless slapper into a modern saint.

"Well, what can I tell you?" Her gaze drifted to a point above my head. "JayJay was a much loved friend and colleague, easy to work with, who got on with everybody. She was warm-hearted, full of praise and encouragement for the contestants on *Star Steps*. JayJay was a perfectionist who worked hard to get things just right whilst making things as easy as possible for others. Her current fame was just reward for her natural talent and all the hard work she put in."

Ye gods! I looked up from my notebook where I was making a good show of writing all this down. I had to hand it to her. I thought I'd been over the top but this woman was better at fiction than KD.

"She will be a sad, sad loss," she went on, bringing her gaze down from the ceiling, her voice growing mournful as she dabbed at dry eyes with a tissue. "It was a pleasure and a privilege to work with her. I shall miss her so much."

The business-like tone returned.

"There. Will that do?" She dropped the unused tissue in the waste basket.

The hypothetical readers of *Oh Hi!* might have lapped it up but it didn't help me to understand why someone had hated JayJay that much they'd put a dagger in her heart. I nodded before I said, "I'm sure our readers will appreciate that. What did you think of Jaynee, personally?"

"Personally? Harrumph. Well, personally what I thought about Jaynee Johnson isn't fit for publication."

This was more like it. Now how did I get her to talk? She saved me the trouble.

"Not fit for publication at all," she looked at me pointedly.

"OK."

I put the notebook away. I could take a hint and she wasn't to know I had a very good memory.

"Jaynee Johnson was a bitch. A scheming, conniving little bitch who would use anybody and anything to further her career."

"Anything?" Just what was she implying?

"Oh yes." She smiled grimly before answering my unasked question. "Including her body, of course, though she did have considerable brains."

"She did? She always seemed like an air-head to me."

Candida Clark gave a bark of laughter.

"Oh, she was certainly clever enough to give that impression." She looked down at her desk for a moment. "It is just so typical of Jaynee to mess everyone about by getting herself killed before the end of the run."

This seemed a little harsh even by the bitchy standards I assumed prevalent in TV and Theatre circles.

"How long is the run?"

"Usually eighteen weeks."

"As long as that?"

Hell's teeth! No wonder people talked of little else but *Star Steps*. They couldn't get away from it.

"Yes," Candida said. "It's a gruelling schedule. We are all feeling pretty exhausted by now. It's just a shame that JayJay's death means we won't get to record the final few programmes."

"Thank you. Our readers will appreciate a bit of background on the making of *Star Steps*," I lied. A sudden thought occurred to me and I tried one more question. "The public like to think of JayJay and Greg as a couple. Were they romantically linked, do you know?"

"I believe so, for a while at least, but I think that all ended about the middle of April."

She gave a grunt and looked at her watch. I'd had well more than my allotted ten minutes.

"Now, if you want to know more, especially about her personal life, you'd do well to speak to Holly." She picked up the phone and punched in a number.

"Holly?" I asked.

"Holly Danvers, her secretary." She spoke into the phone. "Hi, Holly. It's Candy. Are you free to see a magazine reporter who's writing a piece about JayJay? Yes. She's here with me now. Good. I'll send her along."

The redoubtable Candy Clark rose, our interview over.

"Nice to meet you, Miss Long. Holly's office is down the corridor, third on the left."

I smiled and closed the door behind me.

Jaynee Johnson's producer obviously had no love for the dead woman, I reflected as I headed down the corridor, but whether she'd killed her or not remained to be seen.

Chapter 3

I LIKED HOLLY DANVERS ALMOST as soon as I set foot in her office. She was a total, and welcome, contrast to the brassy producer I'd just left, in age, in looks, in style. Her genuine smile greeted me warmly as she offered me a seat. I trotted out the lies about my fictional magazine and its non-existent readers, ashamed to be deceiving this girl—she couldn't be more than twenty—with her clear, fresh skin unadorned by any make up except for a flicker of mascara and her childlike gaze.

"Candida tells me that JayJay was clever. Would you agree?"

"Oh, she was. Very clever. She had been to university and had a degree, you know."

The thought of Jaynee Johnson dancing through the halls of academia was a new one.

"Really? What in? Media studies?"

"No. She had an MA in English from Durham."

So, maybe not the air head I'd presumed her to be, then.

"What was she like to work for?"

"She was lovely," came the unexpected reply—I'd hardly pictured JayJay as a model employer. "She was really nice to me. She bought me a lovely silk scarf for my birthday, and … and…"

Suddenly she was in floods of tears. Real tears, not the crocodile variety employed by Candida Clark.

"I'm sorry, Miss."

She opened a drawer and pulled out a box of tissues.

"No." Instinctively, I reached a hand across the desk to offer comfort. "I'm sorry to upset you."

I waited until the weeping abated, unsure whether to go round the desk to her or stay where I was.

"She was so kind." Holly dabbed at her streaming eyes. "I really liked her. Why would anyone want to kill her?"

She gazed at me, beseechingly, but I had no answer to give her.

"I don't know, Holly, but I'd like to find out."

Uneasy at my own deceit in the face of her real grief, I thought it time to live up to my name. It was time for honesty.

"Holly," I began. "I'm not a magazine reporter."

"You're not?" Baffled, her fingers worked on the bundle of wet tissues, scrunching them into a ball.

"No. I'm a PA, like you. I work for Kathleen Davenport."

"Really?" She perked up. "I've read all her books."

"And well, you see, it's just that I found the…" I had been about to say 'body' but thought better of it, no need to set her crying again. "I found JayJay."

Her eyes widened.

"You mean you …? In that house?"

I nodded.

"Oooh. How awful."

"So, I feel involved, you see."

"And so you're going to investigate. Just like Agnes Merryweather."

I groaned inwardly.

"Well, that's the police's job. I just wanted to find out more about her. Talk to her friends, her colleagues. Build up a picture of JayJay."

She nodded enthusiastically from the opposite side of the desk.

"Oh, I see. Like a detective, building up your case till you uncover the killer."

This kid's innocence was remarkable. Did she really think I could beat the police at their own game?

"Holly, this isn't a book. This isn't a story—it's real life. There really is a killer out there. JayJay is really dead." Her face threatened to crumble again. I hurried on. "So all I'm doing is trying to find out information that will help the police, without putting me, or anyone else, in danger. Do you understand?"

"Yes."

"So, what can you tell me about Jaynee? Was she popular?"

"Oh yes. Everyone liked her. She got on well with everybody."

"Including her producer?"

Holly's viewpoint certainly didn't tally with what I'd heard from Candy Clark.

"Yes. I remember once in the canteen, somebody spilt vinegar and it went on Candida's dress. JayJay was really sympathetic and said how disfiguring the acid could be, but then she looked at the mark and said it would all come out in the wash."

I wasn't as sure as Holly seemed to be that this was a mere girl-to-girl chat about laundry but I let it pass.

"And what about her co-star?"

"Mr Ferrari? He's gorgeous, really nice." Her eyes looked wistful for a moment though I hadn't missed the formality. "My friend Lauren, in make-up, says he hardly needs to spend any time in her chair before recording the show."

"Did he and JayJay get on?"

"Oh yes. They got on really well together. She always said that as a presenter he made an excellent dancer."

My head shot up from my notebook. That hardly tallied with what Candida had told me. The producer had reckoned the two stars had had a romance.

"Really? Were they seeing each other?"

Fleetingly, a pinched look crossed Holly's face, though whether in distaste or disapproval, I couldn't tell.

"I think they might have gone out on a date a couple of times but I don't think it was serious." She dismissed the idea with a wave of her hand. "JayJay had lots of admirers."

Hmmm. Holly was either too young or too innocent to be a good observer of human nature and the people around her, by the sound of it. Time to change tack.

"Did anyone ever threaten her?"

"What, here?" She sounded aghast. "Oh no."

"She didn't, for example, receive threatening letters or hate mail?" Holly shook her head.

"No, just loads of fan mail. She was really popular."

I began to think I was wasting my time. Holly's sunshine view of the world offered no clues to the dead woman's real personality, what she truly thought about others, or what her colleagues felt about her. Once again I moved on.

"Can you tell me more about the show, Holly? I got the general gist of things from Candida but it would help if I had more details."

At least, I hoped it would help. Just at the moment I felt totally in the dark, floundering around in unknown names and an unfamiliar subject.

"Sure. What do you want to know?"

"I understand that the series lasted eighteen weeks? When did they start?"

She flicked through a large upright calendar on her desk.

"The programmes were recorded every Monday afternoon and the first one of this series was on..."

I waited while she found the right place.

"...Monday 22nd February."

I wrote this down before asking, "What about rehearsals?"

"There was a meeting here every Tuesday morning when the new contestants would be paired with the professionals," Holly explained clearly. "They then rehearsed for three hours every weekday morning. There would then be a full rehearsal, including the presenters and the judges, the following Monday morning before recording, in front of a studio audience, later that afternoon."

Tempting though it was to ask if that was 'a live studio audience'—you don't, after all, get dead ones—I refrained. I didn't think Holly would get the joke so I merely nodded.

"What about the first week's recording? Did they meet the Tuesday before that?"

Holly looked at me witheringly.

"Of course. The very first contestants would need a week to practice, too."

"Did JayJay and Greg rehearse this often?"

"Oh no," Holly laughed at the idea, "they're professionals. The contestants wouldn't get to meet the stars until the full rehearsal on Monday morning, prior to the recording which could go on until late in the evening. JayJay and Greg practiced their routine for the next week on Tuesday, Wednesday and Thursday before returning the following Monday. They were never here after Thursday or before Monday morning."

I frantically scribbled all this down whist trying to get it clear in my head. One full day and three mornings' work a week hardly amounted to the gruelling schedule Candida Clark had claimed.

"Thanks, Holly. I think I understand it better now. Did the two stars stay in hotels?"

"No, they both rented out houses during the run. They could be up here for nearly six months. JayJay had a house on the Golden View estate."

I knew of the place. Only for people on celebrity salaries.

"I don't know where Mr Ferrari stayed."

Again, I noted the formality whilst wondering why she would know where one star lived but not the other.

"Golden View is a long way from Willow Drive. I wonder why

she went there?"

Holly shrugged but said nothing. I felt I was getting nowhere fast. I tried one last question, one angle I'd not touched on yet.

"And JayJay was happy in her work here at the studios?"

She pulled at her lower lip.

"Well…"

"Yes?"

"I did once hear her say, 'I shall be glad when I'm out of this place', but I think she just meant she was ready to go home, you know, to the house she rented when she was up here doing the show."

It didn't sound like it to me but perhaps Holly was right. She'd certainly given me plenty to think about.

"Well, if you can think of anything else will you give me a call? Here's my home number."

I scrawled my name and number on the back of one of KD's business cards and passed it across the desk. She looked at it briefly and slid it into a drawer.

"And, Holly, I think it would be best if we kept all this to ourselves."

She gave me a conspiratorial wink, out of place on her guileless face.

"Don't worry, Miss Long. Mum's the word."

I sighed and left the office.

I'd put it off for as long as I could—in truth, I'd largely forgotten it— but now there was no way round it. It was time to watch the DVD of *Star Steps*. I slipped the recording KD had given me into the slot in the machine, grabbed the remote control and made myself comfortable on the settee, coffee and a bar of chocolate to hand on the small table in front of me. Gritting my teeth, I pressed the 'play' button.

"Welcome to *Star Steps*, your Date with the Stars," screamed a voice.

The screen showed a wide flight of stairs with garishly clad couples posing at the edges of each tread.

"Ladies and Gentlemen, please greet your hostess," the same voice went on in a rapturous tone. "Here she is. It's JayJay!"

The unseen audience whooped, hooted and applauded in a cacophony of sound as a celluloid version of the woman I had last seen dead, shimmied and twirled onto the stage. The skirt of her silver lamé dress flared around her hips as she pirouetted in silver dance shoes to centre screen coming to rest, legs spread wide, arms stretched out above her head, all hair, mouth and teeth.

"And here is your co-host, Greg Ferrari."

Now, the camera panned upwards past the wide, white-toothed smile of Jaynee to the top of the stairs as, once again, the audience erupted into whistles and cheers.

With a balletic leap that might have put Baryshnikov to shame, a figure in black appeared at the top of the steps. To the accompaniment of applause and the plastic grins of the dance pairs to either side, Greg Ferrari tapped and spiralled his way downwards. Even I had to admit that the man could dance. His long legs moved swiftly, elegantly in a variety of steps and complex movements that dazzled the eyes and, whilst I would love to say that I never took those same eyes off his feet, in fact they were transfixed by his face. Gorgeous, Holly had called him and I could see what she meant. Quite simply, he was the most massively handsome man I had ever seen.

When he reached the bottom of the stairs, he took Jaynee's hands and twirled her around so fast her blonde hair flew out behind her and swayed in its own slipstream, then he pulled her to him, lifting her as if she were no heavier than thistledown, before flipping her over and gently setting her down.

He sashayed to the left of her, then to the right. He twirled all the way round her before catching her hand, reeling her in towards him, then unwinding her out again, like some horizontal yo-yo. In all of this time, JayJay had hardly taken two steps under her own steam and their routine had clearly been designed to highlight his talents over hers. She was no Ginger Rogers that's for sure, I thought as, with a final twirl, they came to rest taking their bows in front of audience and camera. The whole thing had lasted six minutes and the crowd hadn't shut up once. It reminded me of a magic show where the illusion is all done with mirrors. Or as Shakespeare put it, 'full of sound and fury, signifying nothing'.

Their performance having finished, the camera moved from the two presenters to focus on the contestants. In swirls of jewel-coloured satin and chiffon the dancers on the stairs descended to take their turn in the spotlight, circling the stage, their acrobatic and frenzied gyrations bringing gasps from the appreciative audience but only groans from me. The sheer fakery of their rictus smiles together with the doll-like make-up, the skimpy and ridiculous costumes of the women, the black frock coats and glossy gelled hair of the men all left me entirely unmoved. I paused the disc, appalled at the fatuousness of it all.

I heaved a sigh and took my mug through to the kitchen to refresh my coffee. My problem, I thought, standing at the sink looking out at the brick wall as the kettle boiled, was that I was an anachronism, born in the wrong era, out of my natural time and out of step with the modern world. I enjoyed things that made me old enough to be Holly Danvers' grandmother, not a mere twelve years her senior. I liked old films from the heyday of Hollywood in the 1940s and the music of the 60s; not modern movies filled with graphic sex and violence or the current crop of chart toppers - all girl bands and rap artists. KD would no doubt say I was simply old-fashioned, I reflected, sipping at my coffee and sitting back down. Whatever, I was too old to change now. I picked up the remote control and forwarded the disc past the still-grinning faces of the contestants. Jaynee and Greg came into shot, smiling and talking to each other. I turned up the sound.

"Wow, Greg, what a dazzling line-up." Jaynee Johnson's voice rang with an amazement that gave all the appearance of being sincere. "It looks as if we have a bumper crop of fabulous dancers tonight."

"You're right, JayJay. The judges are really going to have their work cut out."

Hell's teeth! Did somebody write this? Were the prize pair following a script or did they just make it up as they went along? I shook my head in sheer disbelief that hundreds of thousands of people watched this drivel every week and, apparently, found it entertaining. I pressed the mute button. The couple continued to mouth soundlessly at each other as I watched. This served two purposes, I discovered. Firstly, I was no longer distracted by the banalities and secondly, I could concentrate on the body language of the two stars which was telling me far, far more. I'm no psychologist but if Greg and JayJay had ever been an item, they certainly weren't now. I rewound the disc and watched those last few seconds again. They stood just a fraction too far apart as if one or the other wanted to maintain some distance between them and their heads were tilted fractionally away—even allowing for the clichéd drivel they were uttering, this couple were talking at, not to, each other. I paused the disc again while I found my notebook and made a list of questions.

When I'd done that I sat back and surveyed the page. One thing was becoming increasingly clear. If I was going to delve any deeper into the mystery of JayJay's death then I needed to talk to Greg Ferrari—and soon.

Chapter 4

*A*S HE'D PROMISED, JIM WAS waiting in the entrance to the Central Library when I got there. He gave me a grin and a peck on the cheek before pushing open the double doors and letting me through.

"Is this going to be a regular date, then, Ver?"

"Regular date?" I looked at him blankly.

His eyes smiled at me from under a mop of sandy hair.

"It's not the first time you've asked me to come digging into the bowels of the library with you," he pointed out as we crossed to the enquiry desk.

I laughed at his choice of words.

"That's an interesting way of putting it. It's hardly the most glamorous, or tempting, description for a date."

"Well, if you won't go on a proper date with me, I have to take my chances when I can."

I was well aware that Jim had carried a candle for me ever since, at the age of eighteen, I had fallen madly in love with his flatmate, Robert Hastings. Rob with his good looks, intelligence and personality had swept me off my feet. Add to that the fact that he could wear the tattiest jeans and tee-shirt as if they'd been designed for him, he was brilliant in bed and he drove a sports car and what more could a girl want? Well, for this girl, nothing. He was my ideal man and I loved him passionately and with total abandon. Unfortunately, I wasn't his ideal woman and, when he'd dumped me after a few short months, I was devastated. For a while I went out of my mind. I slept with almost every man that asked me and flung myself at a fair few that didn't, then I shut myself away and lived like a hermit, not wanting to see anyone, or to eat, or to live. Rob was my life and without him my life was over. I contemplated suicide but, as one of my favourite writers, Dorothy Parker, pointed out, all the options were either too painful or too difficult to achieve. So I lived. By the time I'd come out of this spiral of misery and self-loathing, Rob had moved away, back to University in Salterton, and I had never set eyes on him since. Fourteen years since I had seen the man I still considered I loved. I didn't think of him often these days, except perhaps to wonder what he had made of his life, and, when I did, the pain in my heart was still there, a huge block that stopped me moving on, stopped me loving again. Poor Jim, what chance had he got when I compared all men to the one I'd lost and they all came out wanting?

"Verity? Are you all right, Verity?"

"Hmm?" I looked at Jim's concerned face and took a deep breath.

"Are you OK? You disappeared there for a minute."

"Yes, thanks Jim." I breathed out. I had been so far gone in my memories I'd almost forgotten where I was.

"Shall we carry on?"

"Of course," I smiled. "We'd better, there's a lot to do."

We'd reached the desk by now and the librarian looked up at us, evidently relieved to have something to do.

"Good morning. How may I help you?"

"We'd like to see the newspaper archives please. In the basement." Jim took out his newspaper identity card and flashed it in front of her.

"If you could hang on a minute, I'll have to get the key."

We nodded and she wandered off to an office somewhere.

"So what is it this time?" Jim asked when she'd gone.

"Just general research, really. KD is looking for more ideas for her next book."

"So why doesn't she just make it up? Isn't that what writers are supposed to do? Fiction writers, I mean."

He grinned. Jim called himself a writer but his official job description was crime reporter for the Crofterton Gazette. If you write for a newspaper you're not supposed to 'make it up'.

"Well, she does in a sense. She will change all the names, obviously, and the locations, the dates and so on."

"And you do all the research do you?"

"Yes, to start with. Later on, once KD's into the plotting and planning stage of the novel then we'll discuss things, throw ideas around and try and work out whodunit. If we don't know that already, of course."

"It sounds as if you both write it."

"Oh, no. KD does all the writing. I just do the research, offer ideas and usually come up with the solution, that's all."

"So you're the detective and she's the writer."

I laughed, but after the events of the last twenty four hours Jim's throwaway comment came a little too close to home. Besides, given the way KD and I worked, his observation was largely accurate. Not that I would admit it. KD liked to think of herself as the real life version of her fictional hero, Agnes Merryweather. I was just her sounding board.

"My official title is Personal Assistant and I don't claim to be anything else."

"Are you enjoying it?"

"Yes, I am. Apart from the research work there's the regular PA stuff - booking hair appointments, book signing tours, interviews and appointments with her agent. So it's varied and interesting enough for me not to get bored."

The librarian returned with the key. Jim signed for it with a flourish before leading me through the silent tiers of books and downstairs to the door to the archives.

"I can't stay long, Verity," he said, opening the door. "I'm working on the Jaynee Johnson murder case and supposed to be tracking down the estate agent who found her."

"Umm …"

"What?"

"The estate agent didn't find her."

"Oh? How would you know that?"

I took a deep breath. I felt I owed Jim and could trust him not to splash my name all over the Gazette.

"Because I did."

"What? Found her? My God! What an exclusive!"

Jim's face lit up before assuming a baffled look.

"But I thought it was an estate agent."

"Where did you get that idea from?"

"The police, I suppose. I think it was in their press release."

I took a chair at the wooden table in the centre of the room, waiting for Jim to join me while I digested the fact that Inspector Farish had, thankfully, withheld my name.

"I was viewing the house, Jim, with a member of staff from Knight's. He stayed downstairs taking a phone call. I was the one who actually made the discovery."

"Oh, Verity, how awful. I'm sorry for that comment about an exclusive. You probably don't want to talk about it."

He tried to look contrite but couldn't quite mask his disappointment. I took pity on him.

"It's OK, Jim. Though I'd rather my name isn't splashed all over your paper."

"Absolutely, Verity." He ran a hand through his pale hair. "You have my word on that."

So I told him everything I could about my unwelcome discovery of Jaynee Johnson's body. I only gave him the facts and drew the line at the 'human interest' side of things.

"No, sorry, Jim. 'How did I feel?' is not a question I'm prepared to discuss with the readers of the Crofterton Gazette. What business is it of theirs how I feel? Besides, it's a stupid question."

His eyebrows shot up in surprise but I was in full rant mode now and carried on regardless.

"How do you think I felt? How would you have felt?" I jabbed a finger in his direction.

"Gosh! Well, nice to know that age hasn't mellowed you any, Verity."

He laughed and, realising how I must have sounded, I laughed with him.

"Be sensible, Jim. Anyway, I've given you what I can."

"Thanks, Verity, and I'm no end grateful. My editor is going to love me for this."

He grinned boyishly before leaving me to go back to the office with his story, promising to return as soon as possible in order to lock up.

For the next hour or so I worked feverishly through the archives, searching out the cases that I thought would interest KD. I'd just finished when he reappeared.

"That's good timing," I said, arching my back after so long poring over microfiches and the computer terminal.

He gave my shoulders a friendly rub.

"All set?"

"Yes, thanks, Jim. I've got what I need. Now I'm ready for some fresh air."

We parted as we'd met, on the library steps and promised to keep in touch.

I turned into the drive leading up to KD's house, Bishop Lea, well pleased with my morning's work. I had only found two cases between 1985 and 1990 that I considered would be of interest to KD—a murder in 1986 and the disappearance of a schoolgirl during the summer of 1990—but the news reports of the time had supplied enough facts and figures, as well as acres of righteous editorial, to allow my employer to put some fictional flesh on these few remains.

I let myself in with my key, dropped my bag and notebook on my desk in the empty office then ambled through to the kitchen to make a cup of tea and a sandwich. KD's kitchen was so vast you could die of starvation between the fridge and the sink. I reckoned it covered the same square footage as my entire flat. The same might be said of the rest of the house. There wasn't a small room in the place, even the loo could accommodate a cocktail party for twenty five people.

KD allowed me free run of the place, including the kitchen and its contents so, while I waited for the kettle to boil, I buttered a couple of slices of bread—fortunately my boss hated imitation butter, those spreads that claim a taste they don't possess, as much as I did—slapped a thick piece of ham between them and dropped a tea bag into a mug.

I'd just finished when her dark head appeared round the door.

"So you're back, are you? Thought I heard you. How did you get on this morning?"

"Not bad," I replied, brushing crumbs from my mouth. "I think I've found a couple of things that you could use. The details are on my pad in the office."

When I'd eaten my lunch and we were both at our desks, I gave her the gist of my morning's work.

"The first involves a local farmer who killed his wife and fed her to the pigs."

KD made a moue of distaste—for a crime writer she can be remarkably squeamish.

"And the second is the case of a disappearing schoolgirl, though that mystery remains unsolved."

KD's eyes lit up.

"Excellent. I can have Agnes solve it any way I like. Tell me more."

I looked down at my pad.

"Charlotte Neal, a fourteen year old from Darrington, disappeared in broad daylight on a summer's evening in 1990 whilst returning home from a friend's house."

"And she was never found?"

"No. Full police investigation, TV and poster appeals, searches, the lot. Nothing. No trace of her, whether alive or dead, ever found."

"Excellent!" KD said again, clapping her hands together. "That's the one we go for."

"OK. So, what do you want me to do?"

She thought for a moment, leaning back in the chair and swivelling from side to side.

"I'll need you to go out to Darrington and get me a feel for the place. The sort of area it is, the house the girl lived in and so on. Also, what facilities were provided for youngsters, you know, playgrounds, youth clubs, all that stuff. When did you say this happened?"

"1990."

"Only twenty years ago, so there may still be people around who remember it, remember the girl and what she was like. See if you can find any and talk to them. Neighbours perhaps, or shopkeepers. What did they think of the family or the girl herself—and don't forget the friend and her family, ask about them too—and what did everybody think happened."

I scribbled all this down.

"Then check with the police. See if you can find out who was in charge of the investigation."

"Detective Chief Inspector George Plover," I supplied. The Crofterton Gazette had named and quoted him several times, to start with in full page articles under hyperbolic headlines such as 'How Could This Happen?' and 'Agony of the Waiting Parents', before they'd lost interest in a vanishing girl and a case going nowhere and turned their attention elsewhere.

"Right." The ideas and questions were still pouring out of KD as she went on, "Find out if he's still alive and go and interview him. It would be helpful to have the police's take on this. You know the sort of thing; did they think she'd been murdered, kidnapped or … or,"

"Went of her own accord?" I suggested.

KD smiled.

"Precisely. But first, type up your notes and let me have them, please."

I spent the rest of the afternoon doing just that, as well as checking through the phone book for the Neals and the family of Charlotte's friend, Kimberley Hughes. I found no trace of the Neals at their former address, hardly surprising perhaps, but there was an A. Hughes still listed at 122 Conway Drive. I tried the number but got no reply. Turning my attention to the policeman, I found a G. Plover on Main Street in Harcourt and dialled again. Bingo! Right first time. Mr Plover, who had reached the heights of Detective Chief Superintendent before he retired, or so he told me, was more than happy to see me once I'd explained who I was and what I wanted. Arranging to call on him the following morning, I replaced the receiver then returned the directory to the bookcase of reference works that stood beside the door and took down the map of the Crofterton area. Mr Plover's address was easy to find—he lived in the next village to mine and had a cottage on the main road. The two addresses in Darrington I located quickly from the gazetteer. Then, with no little difficulty and a lot of bad language on my part, together with shouted instructions from the far side of KD's desk, which were totally inaccurate and no use at all, I battled with refolding the map.

"Right. That's me finished for the day unless there's anything else you want me to do?"

It was nearly six o'clock already.

"Did I hear you make an appointment with the Inspector chappie?"

"Plover, yes. Ten o'clock tomorrow morning. Is that OK?"

"Fine. I'll see you when you get here. Have a good evening."

"You too. 'Bye."

Perched on my favourite stool in the wine bar that evening, I decided it was time to go home; I could do with an early night and the place was beginning to fill up. I glanced around at the crowd and suddenly changed my mind. Stepping out of one of the booths at the back of the room came Greg Ferrari! The first thing I noticed about him was his height. He was about a head taller than anyone else in the place and seemed to tower over them as if on stilts. I had a momentary flight of fancy at the idea of him dancing on giant platform boots, before glancing down at his footwear. Even at this distance they appeared to be made of hand-tooled leather. Ten to one they were Italian and specially made and shipped over for him. Given how much money he must be making out of *Star Steps* no doubt he could afford to buy them by the boat-load. The suit, too, looked Italian, superbly tailored with sharp lapels, waist darts and buttons that were probably hand-crafted on the banks of the Arno by some dark haired, oval-eyed maiden. He filled it immaculately from broad shoulders to narrow hips. Now, don't get me wrong, I'm no expert on men's fashions—or even women's for that matter—but Greg Ferrari just oozed class, style and money. He moved, not unnaturally, like a dancer with a lithe cat-like grace. He was on the prowl, that was for sure. More surprisingly he was prowling in my direction.

"Hello. Didn't I see you at the studios yesterday afternoon?"

Had he? I hadn't seen him—and believe me I would have noticed him, if I'd done so.

I could have jet-skied off the plane of his cheek bones, his eyes were like molten chocolate. I wanted to dive right in and lap it all up. I held his deep brown gaze for a moment, wishing I was ten years younger, before I snapped out of my fantasies.

"Well I was there." I admitted. "So, perhaps you did."

"Greg Ferrari," he said, as if it wasn't a household name and held out a smooth well manicured hand. Still, I thought, as I shook it, up until a few days ago I'd never heard of him so it was possible there were others like me. Monks in a silent order perhaps or hermits in some cell in a valley in deepest Wales.

"Verity Long."

"Can I get you a drink, Verity?"

He smiled, lines showing at the corner of his eyes. He wasn't as young as I'd first thought him to be and I found his stare somewhat disquieting. Suddenly, I was on my guard.

"I'll have an apple juice, please."

Val raised a surprised eyebrow at this change to my usual order of a glass of Merlot but then gave an almost imperceptible nod, perhaps in acknowledgement of the wisdom of my choice. I would need all my wits about me dealing with Mr Ferrari.

"We don't see you in here very often, Mr Ferrari," I said.

"I don't often get into the city centre. Is this a favourite watering hole for you?"

"Me? Oh I'm a habitué," I laughed.

"So what were you doing out at the studios, Verity?"

Is that what he's after, I wondered? Is he going to start pumping me for information? Well, two can play at that game.

"I interviewed Candida Clark for a magazine article about Jaynee Johnson."

I caught a momentary flash in his eyes. Anger? Fear, perhaps? Hard to tell, but this was getting more interesting by the moment.

"Really? Which magazine?"

The question was casually put, but again I became wary.

"I'm freelance. There are lots of magazines interested in JayJay right now."

"Of course. She will be a sad, sad loss," he said, echoing Candida's false sentiments word for word. And with the same amount of conviction. This man was not mourning the death of his co-star.

"It must be awful for you. So distressing." I sounded suitably sympathetic.

"Indeed. I shall miss her so much."

Yeah! Like you'll miss a hole in the head, I thought.

"What will happen now?"

"That rather depends on the studio." He shrugged.

"Will the show continue? It's very popular, I've heard."

His eyebrows shot up. "You've heard? You mean you don't watch the show?"

Heaven forfend! I'd rather have my teeth drilled than watch a bunch of talentless twerps prancing around in the name of entertainment.

"I'm usually busy on a Saturday," I said with total dishonesty. "Hadn't you nearly finished the run, though?"

"Yes, it's an eighteen week season and we had three more programmes to record. I've suggested Kaylee Blake would make an excellent replacement. Should the studio heads decide they want the show to continue, of course."

Of course. And your career too, I thought nastily.

"Greg! Darling!"

A woman's high pitched shriek shattered my eardrums.

"Hello, Babs."

He turned towards the newcomer and I slipped from my stool.

"I've got to go. Nice meeting you, Greg."

"Wait."

He laid a hand on my arm, bedroom eyes gazing into mine.

"Dinner next week?"

"Oh!" Surprised at his quick work, I agreed. It fitted in nicely with my plans, too. "Yes. OK."

"Great. Next Tuesday?"

I nodded.

"I'll meet you here, say seven thirty? We'll go next door, shall we?"

"Sounds good to me." I never refused dinner at *Chez Jacques*—especially if someone else was paying. "See you then."

I left them to it, turning and blowing a kiss to Valentino as I passed.

My flat in Sutton Harcourt occupied the ground floor of what had been a substantial two-storey brick cottage. It had once possessed a large garden, but during the last property boom the land had been bought by an enterprising builder who'd thrown up a couple of boxes, called them 'bijou residences' and sold them for a fortune. Instead of sitting outside in the evening and admiring trim lawns and flower filled borders, I had four slabs and the side of a house to look at.

I finished wiping the last of my supper pots, stacking them away in the few cupboards that made up my fitted kitchen, and poured myself a glass of wine. It was nearly nine o'clock and, if I couldn't sit out in a garden then I would have to make do with the lounge. I was half way there, wine in hand, when the doorbell rang. I sighed and carried my glass back to the kitchen. The original front door now served the flat upstairs while I made do with the back door re-sited to the side wall when the cottage was divided.

"Hello, Miss Long. I hope I'm not disturbing you?"

"Not at all. Come in, and please call me Verity. I was just about to have some wine," I waved the glass in my hand, "would you like one?"

Holly Danvers refused but asked for a soft drink.

"Do you like 'Youth Dew', Holly?" I asked on a whim when we sat down in the lounge.

"Youth what?" She looked blank. "Is it a drink?"

I shook my head.

"'Youth Dew'. It's a perfume."

"Oh, I can't wear perfumes. They give me a headache."

No, Holly Danvers wasn't the sort to suit perfume—certainly not a heavy fragrance like Estée Lauder's classic. Candida Clark, on the other hand ... I kicked myself for not having asked her when I'd had the opportunity.

"So, what can I do for you, Holly?"

I took a small sip of wine before putting the glass on the table. For the sake of the precious contents, it was a good job I did so because Holly said, "I've got JayJay's diary."

"What? Here?"

She nodded, reaching down to her bag out of which she drew a fancy leather bound book with a metal clasp. Just in case there was any doubt it had the word 'diary' picked out in gold on the front.

She passed it to me.

"Where did you get hold of this?"

Holly coloured slightly.

"There's an office next to mine with a connecting door. JayJay always used it for the thirteen weeks when she was recording *Star Steps.*"

"But haven't the police already searched that?"

"Oh, yes. A nice young sergeant came and went through JayJay's desk." This time a more pronounced blush appeared on her cheeks. "But I'd got it."

Whether the blush was for the sergeant, probably D.I. Farish's sidekick Stott, or her failure to hand over what could be a vital piece of evidence, was hard to tell.

"You see," Holly went on, anxious to explain herself, "JayJay kept the diary in a drawer. She didn't carry it round with her."

Easy to see why, I thought. It had the dimensions and weight of a medium sized paperback and wouldn't fit in the type of small, flimsy handbags so favoured by celebrities.

"Anyway, one day she phoned me from outside and asked me to check up on an appointment, so I went and fetched the diary and didn't take it back. I was busy, um ..." She faltered to a stop.

"So you put the diary in your drawer and forgot about it?"

"Yes. It got pushed to the back and, and ..."

"Well, no harm done. Don't blame yourself," I said in an attempt to console her. The poor kid had guilt written all over her face. "The police will need to have this, though."

"Oh yes, I know, but I thought, as you are investigating, you might like to see it first."

I nearly sprayed the mouthful of Merlot I'd just taken all over the carpet.

"Me! Investigating?"

"Yes. And then you could give it to the police, couldn't you?"

"If that was a hint, Holly, it was about as subtle as a train crash," I informed her. "Anyway, what makes you think I'm investigating?"

"Well, you found her and when you came to the studios yesterday, I rather got the impression you wanted to do a bit of detecting, yourself."

"Hmmm, maybe I did but that was before everyone started telling me to stay out of it and leave it to the police."

I thought bitterly of my conversation with Inspector Farish and KD's pronouncements.

"Oh." She looked disappointed. "I thought you'd be pleased to have the diary."

I was, of course, but I still didn't want to give her any unnecessary encouragement to think of me as Agnes Merryweather.

"I suppose it won't do any harm to have a look. Are there any secrets or racy details inside?"

If I'd thought to catch her out I didn't succeed.

"I don't know, I've not looked."

"But you looked when JayJay called you."

"Yes, but I just went straight to the date and it said '12.30, lunch,

KC."

"Do you know who KC is?" I asked, taking another sip of wine before sliding the clasp undone and opening the diary.

"I don't think so," said Holly, shaking her head.

I flicked through the pages until I got to June. There was only one entry and that was for Tuesday 8th June when she'd had, but never kept, a hairdresser's appointment at 10.30. I turned back a page to the previous week. JayJay had had no appointments between Monday 31st May and Sunday 6th June. I went back another week.

"Do you know who Dawn is?" I asked Holly. "Only, JayJay has written that name and 3.30pm against Tuesday 25th June."

She shrugged and shook her head.

"I didn't know much about her personal life, sorry."

"Don't worry." I smiled, leafing quickly through the months from January to June. There was certainly nothing here to set any biographer's pulses racing. No intimate secrets, no lurid love life retold in sweaty detail.

"This is really just a list of dates, times, and names, mostly just initials," I said to Holly.

I fetched my notepad and pen.

"Right, let's go through them and you can let me know if you recognise any of the names."

"OK."

It didn't take too long. The last entry was for Saturday July 10th and after that nothing but blank pages that would never now be filled with the round, almost schoolgirlish handwriting.

Most of the entries meant nothing to Holly who recognised only the initials 'JB' as belonging to John Brackett, the head of Silverton Studios who, going by the diary listings had had several meetings with his dead star in April and May. For the rest, it appeared that JayJay used code words. I sighed. There would be a lot of head scratching if I was to make anything out of this.

"Will you take it to the police?" Holly asked, as I closed the diary at last and slid the clasp back into place.

"Would you rather I did?"

She nodded.

"I'd be grateful if you would, please, Verity." She rose to go.

"Very well. If you can think of anything else that would be useful …" I had been about to say 'take it to the police' but she interrupted me.

"Oh, I'll let you know, of course."

I gave a resigned smile as I opened the door and said goodnight.

Chapter 5

WISTERIA COTTAGE, WHEN I REACHED it, turned out to be a low stone building sheltering under a thatched roof. The newly whitewashed walls were barely visible behind the riot of roses and climbers scrambling over them. And, sure enough, an elderly wisteria drooped like some Mexican moustache above and around the door. Definitely jigsaw puzzle material, I thought as I lifted the heavy iron door knocker and let it fall.

It took a while before the door was opened by a small, white haired woman wearing an old fashioned pinafore over her cotton dress.

"Mrs Plover? I'm Verity Long."

"Oh, yes. Do come in. George is expecting you."

Deep blue eyes in a homely face assessed me briefly before she turned and led the way down a stone-flagged passage towards the rear of the house.

"Mind your head."

She reached up to point out a low roof beam before descending the two steps into a spacious and comfortable living room. I gazed about in frank curiosity as I followed her across to the French window.

"George, your visitor has arrived."

She stepped back to let me through.

"Go on out, dear. I'll make some coffee."

"Oh this is beautiful," I exclaimed as I stepped out onto the patio. Opposite me an elderly man was tying-in roses against a wooden trellis, whistling happily as he worked. In the border at his feet oriental poppies waved their pink and purple heads above coral-coloured London Pride and deep blue hardy geraniums. To my right a circular rose bed was filled with hybrid teas, their delicious scent wafting me back to my childhood, whilst on my left a matching bed held dahlias and chrysanthemums that would flower later in the summer. I could think of few places I'd rather be on a gloriously sunny, June morning. Out here it would be so easy to leave the world and its cares behind. No wonder the gardener seemed so contented.

"Chief Superintendent Plover? Hello, I'm Verity Long."

"Ex-Chief Superintendent, Miss Long. I retired ten years ago and please call me George."

Kindly grey eyes twinkled in a round, lined face as he pulled off his gardening gloves and dropped them into a wicker basket before shaking my hand.

"Only if you call me Verity." I smiled back, before looking away to take in more of the garden.

"You like it?"

"It's wonderful. This is like heaven with the gates thrown open." I breathed in deeply, taking in the scents all around me. I waved a hand in the direction of the circular bed. "I'm glad to see you grow the old roses too. Ena Harkness, Josephine Bruce, Peace."

"Yes, they're not much grown nowadays," Plover remarked as we ambled towards the bed. "I'm impressed that you know them."

Well, impressing an ex-police Superintendent was no bad thing, I thought, as I buried my nose in a particularly fine specimen, inhaling memories as well as the fragrance.

"My father grew them when I was a little girl. We had a bed

similar to this in the front lawn."

I hastily brushed a speck of pollen from the end of my nose.

"My wife wants me to grow more modern varieties," Plover commented somewhat sadly. "I might try a few next year."

"I wish I had space and time to grow anything," I remarked. "Even a window-box would be a luxury at the moment."

I thought of the four slabs that made up my patio, the only outside area I had. Intending that spring to plant up some tubs so that I had something other than a brick wall to look at from my kitchen window I had, as usual, never got round to it.

"Coffee's ready."

As if on cue, Mrs Plover's shout from the French window ended the gardening talk and I followed the ex-Super back across the lawn and into the house.

"So what did you want to talk to me about?" asked Plover when we were settled either side of the stone fireplace, a small tray with a pot of coffee and a plate of biscuits between us. "You mentioned something about being a writer."

I explained that I worked for Kathleen Davenport and we were interested in an old case of his.

He nibbled on a chocolate digestive, waving his hand to show I should help myself. I reached for a garibaldi.

"My wife reads her books. Personally, I'm more into biographies." He made it sound like a secret vice, like sharing porn magazines behind the bike sheds. "I don't know that I'd be too happy at you writing up one of my cases. Which one is it?"

Briefly, I described how we worked and how the sex, ages and locations would all be changed in the writing.

"You probably wouldn't recognise it as the same case. If you were to read it, that is."

"Hmm, so you do all the researching and leg work, the hard work in other words, and she just does the writing?" He smiled.

I warmed to this man.

"Something like that," I admitted.

"You still haven't told me which case."

I took a sip of coffee. Now came the hard part. How would this man react to the mention of a case that remained unsolved?

"It was twenty years ago. The disappearance of a schoolgirl. Charlotte Neal."

He glanced at me sharply, finishing his coffee and putting the cup back down on the tray before he replied.

"Not one of our successes. She was never found, you know?"

I nodded.

"So how much do you know about the case?"

I filled him in with what I had learnt from the Crofterton Gazette, referring now and again to my notebook.

"It seems incredible that a child could just disappear in broad daylight," I said when I had finished my recital.

"Not really. It happens more often than you think. Charlotte left her friend's house between eight o'clock and half past eight at night and you forget the date."

"The date? How was that relevant?"

"July 4th, 1990. It was during the World Cup and England were playing West Germany in the semi-finals. Every bloke in the country was glued to the damned television. The score was 1-1 and it went to penalties. We lost."

I wondered if he'd watched the match himself.

"The only chap we found who didn't claim to have watched the entire match was the other girl's father. What was his name?" He frowned in thought.

"Hughes," I supplied. "Roger Hughes."

"That was him."

"Did you suspect him?"

"Of what? This wasn't a murder case, Verity." He pulled at his lip as he thought back. "We had no evidence that the girl had been harmed. She could have gone off for any number of reasons. She might have had a boyfriend, been unhappy at home or bullied at school. Not that we found evidence for any of that, either. She might have had an accident. We checked with all the hospitals, it's the first thing we do, but we found no trace."

"So what did the friend," I checked my notebook, "Kimberley, have to say?"

"Nothing much. Nothing that helped us anyway. Charlotte had turned up at the house in the late afternoon and stayed for tea. Then the two of them had gone upstairs and listened to music. All very innocent, the sort of thing girls of that age do, at least if they are as well brought up as those two were. And yet …"

He paused, a crease appearing between his brows as he sifted through the memories of twenty years ago.

"And yet …" I prompted.

"Well, Kimberley was first interviewed by my sergeant, Delia Rees, and Delia was convinced she was holding something back."

She was probably right, I thought. Most middle-aged men could have the wool pulled over their eyes by a sweet little girl. Trust another woman not to be so easily fooled. I wasn't about to say that, though. Instead I asked, "Such as?"

"Oh, nothing important, I'm sure of that and I interviewed her enough times myself trying to discover what it was she wasn't saying. Girls of that age have their little secrets." He laughed, ruefully. "And what they think is of consequence is often of little or no concern to their elders. But you'll know that."

I nodded as if I were an authority on young teenage girls. On reflection maybe I was, after all I'd been there. Once. A long time ago. Twenty years ago I would have been almost a contemporary of Charlotte and Kimberley.

"It could simply have been that they didn't do the homework they were supposed to do," Plover went on, "or they'd leant out of the window for an illicit cigarette, something of that nature. Anyway, Delia was an experienced officer and she was sure there was something Kimberley wasn't telling us. Whatever it might have been, we never did get to the bottom of it."

I changed tack.

"And Roger Hughes? Why wasn't he watching the football?"

"Oh, he's your candidate for villain of the piece is he?"

Plover smiled as he reached for the coffee pot and re-filled both our cups. I returned the smile but said nothing, merely taking the milk jug from his proffered hand.

"Well, Hughes had an alibi, of sorts. He had spent the earlier part of the evening at a meeting of the local business club in the centre of Crofterton. According to him, and his wife confirmed it, he didn't arrive home until nearly nine, by which time Charlotte was long gone."

"His wife confirmed it?" I tried to keep the incredulity out of my voice. Of course his wife would have confirmed it, she would have backed him to the hilt even if she'd known he was lying through his teeth. Still, Plover and his team weren't fools. They'd have double-checked this.

"Oh, I know what you're thinking, but we did have corroboration. A neighbour putting milk bottles out during a break in the football saw him drive up."

"What time would that be?"

"Nearly nine o'clock as Hughes said."

I hastily scribbled a note. I was still suspicious of Hughes and he would certainly serve KD's needs when she came to write the story. It would depend on how much would change; how much of the truth, if any, would be retained in the final telling of the tale. KD wrote fiction, after all, and my job was simply to gather the facts that made that fiction possible.

"What about DNA testing?" I looked up from my writing.

"What about it? It was in its infancy then and we didn't, thankfully, have a body against which to test it."

I gave a defeated sigh.

"Oh, well. KD will just have to magic this one out of thin air."

"I'm sorry. I don't seem to have been much help to you, Miss Long."

His eyes smiled at me over the rim of his cup until a sudden frown appeared on his forehead. Absently, he replaced the cup on its saucer.

"You know, there is something."

"Something else about Charlotte Neal?"

I leaned forward eagerly, pen poised.

"Yes." He snapped his fingers. "Got it!"

I waited.

"It may not be much use to you, it was just a strange coincidence."

"Coincidence?"

"Yes, that's probably why it's stuck in my mind. There was another case involving a girl called Charlotte Neal at the same time."

"That is odd," I agreed. "Were you in charge of both cases?"

"No, no. This other case happened up north somewhere." The crease returned, wrinkling his brow. "A hit and run accident in which the girl was killed. I don't think that one was ever solved, either."

He gave me a rueful look.

"Well, thank you, Mr Plover. It was good of you to give up your time to see me."

I picked up my bag and rose to go.

"My pleasure, Verity. If I remember anything else about the case, I'll give you a call."

"Please."

I took one of KD's cards out of my bag and handed it over.

I said goodbye and walked to the car thinking wistfully of Wisteria Cottage's beautiful garden and longing for one of my own. Still, I now had plenty to pass on to KD on my return.

Bishop Lea was a modern house built to resemble a Palladian villa on land once owned by the Bishop of Crofterton. Constructed to satisfy the pretensions of some flash-in-the-pan 1970s rock musician, it had been sold to pay the taxman his overdue revenues when said musician had plummeted earthwards like a latter day Icarus, along with the pilot of his private plane. It was certainly big enough to host the sprawling booze- and drug-fuelled parties rumoured to accompany the rock star lifestyle, possessed as it was of five bedrooms, living room, drawing room, dining room, cloakrooms and more bathrooms than you could shake a stick at. The kitchen alone would have housed a shouting match of celebrity chefs, complete with camera crews and sound men, and still have room for the two fat ladies. Our office—OK, KD's office, my workplace—had been made from one of these cloakroom conversions when KD had bought the place eight years previously.

There was no sign of my employer when I walked in, though the conservatory door stood wide open and, for the second time that morning, I stepped out into a flower filled garden. Two belligerent blackbirds, sitting on branches in the chestnut tree, warred against each other to see whose song could be the loudest and a chirpy robin added his sweet voice to the medley.

At my approach KD stood up from the bed where she had been dead-heading roses.

"Ah! There you are."

KD advanced towards me from the rose bed brandishing a pair of secateurs like a deadly weapon.

"Come over here and tell me how you've got on." She led me to a picnic table and bench, its gay parasol ready to shield us from the glare of the sun. It was barely midday but already the heat was intense.

"I've got some chilled wine and some sandwiches waiting."

"An alfresco lunch!" I exclaimed, delighted at the spread revealed as she removed the table cloth that had covered and protected it. "What a wonderful idea, KD. Thank you."

She really could be so thoughtful, I reflected, as I sat down. Her face, round as an apple, smiled back at me and I was conscious, not for the first time, of what a good job I had landed in working as her PA.

"Well, it's a lovely day. We should take advantage of it while we have the opportunity," she said, pouring the chilled wine into two glasses. "Now, what have you to report?"

"Naturally, I've a great deal on the police view of the case but not a lot else." I raised my glass. "Cheers!"

KD munched away as I filled her in on my visit to Mr Plover, nodding her head from time to time in recognition of salient points. When I'd finished and helped myself to another smoked salmon sandwich she thought for a moment two.

"What's your gut feeling, Verity?"

"Oh, the friend's father," I replied without hesitation. "And yours?"

"I'm not so sure that this was murder. From our point of view, the disappearance itself is far more interesting."

As was KD's use of the word 'our'. It made the finished story sound more of a collaboration than I felt it warranted, though it was nice to think she valued my contribution. I loved these sessions at the start of a new book where we thrashed things out between us, throwing ideas around like confetti. Though in the end, much as I might like to think I'd been helpful, it was KD who wrote it.

She was twirling the stem of the glass round and round between her fingers. Fiddling with something, anything—a pencil, paper clip or a wine glass—is a sure sign of deep thought and concentration on KD's part. I didn't interrupt her.

"You know," she said finally, "I've a feeling that female sergeant's comment about the friend is going to turn out to be worth its weight in gold."

"Oh? How so?"

"Well, I'm a great believer, as you know, in women's intuition. I think that she picked up on something her male colleagues missed."

"To be fair, George Plover did acknowledge that," I pointed out. "Besides even she," I glanced down at my book, "Delia Rees, couldn't discover what the girl was hiding."

KD waved this aside.

"Yes, yes, I know, but what I mean is, if the female suspected something, it would be a female thing."

"Eh?"

She had lost me completely.

"Look, the friend was hiding something feminine, something girly. Like make-up, a boyfriend, that sort of thing. That's what the sergeant was subconsciously getting."

"Oh, I see! You could be right."

"And it's perfect for our purposes, of course. Instead of the sergeant we have Agnes Merryweather to divine the girls' secret."

I let the outrageous pun go.

"Clever. That's really very clever."

I sat back, surveying my boss with admiration.

"I'll bet it's not far from the truth. In any case it will do for our purposes. After all, we aren't intending to solve the original case."

Well, maybe not. Nevertheless I was intrigued now and wanted to know what had become of Charlotte Neal.

"Do you still want me to go out to Darrington?"

"Oh yes. Tomorrow morning, if that's OK with you?"

"Yes, fine."

I grabbed another sandwich before she could whisk the plate off the table. She had started to gather the remains of our meal together.

"I'll go and wash up. You type up your notes from this morning,"

She was halfway to the conservatory door, a tray full of used plates and cutlery in her hands, when she dropped her bombshell.

"Oh, and don't worry about coming in tomorrow after you've been to Darrington. Whatever you find can wait until Monday and I'm going to be working on the dodgy financier story all day. I shan't need you for that."

I was slumped on the settee mulling over KD's words and wondering whether I would soon be out of a job when the doorbell rang. What now? I was in no mood for visitors, I decided, walking through to the kitchen, the high heeled black mules I used as slippers clacking on the slabs in the passage that linked it to the living room. This had better not be my landlord demanding his rent a week early. It wasn't.

"Good evening, Miss Long. Sorry to call so late but I wonder if you could spare me a minute?"

"Come in."

Detective Inspector Farish smiled his thanks and followed me into the kitchen. There was no sign of his sidekick.

"I was just enjoying a glass of wine." I indicated the three-quarters full bottle on the table. "Would you care to join me?"

"No, thanks."

"Are you on duty? Is this an official visit? Perhaps you'd prefer coffee?"

"No, sort of, and no thank you." He answered my Spanish Inquisition with a soft smile that reached his eyes as well as curving his mouth. The smile definitely improved him.

"Well, come on through, then."

I led the way into the living room, offering him a chair as I sat back down on the settee. This time I perched rather than lounged.

"So what can I do for you, Inspector?"

"Well, firstly, I've come to apologise."

A pink tinge crept up his cheeks. He looked remarkably uncomfortable.

"For what?"

"For being so abrupt with you on Monday. You must have had a considerable shock ..."

I bowed my head in agreement for a moment. It's not every day you find a dead body.

"… and my sergeant tells me I was fairly brutal with you."

His sergeant told him? Hell's teeth! If he needed his sidekick to point out his appalling treatment then the man was a machine. I took a sip of wine and waited. I wasn't going to let him off that easily. I watched with malicious pleasure as the man squirmed on his chair.

"It's just that, well," he paused, searching for the right words, the silvery hairs at his temple evident in the light from the table lamp. "This is, as I'm sure you're aware, a high profile case."

"Press giving you a bad time, are they?" I asked nastily.

The public too, no doubt. Detective Inspector Farish and his team must be under considerable pressure to find JayJay's killer. After all, the Crofterton Gazette had apparently lost all sense of proportion and gone so far as to call her a National Treasure. The police didn't need allegations of callous treatment of vital witnesses on top of everything else.

Surprisingly, Farish relaxed, leaning back in the chair, crossing one corduroy clad leg over the other. I didn't want him relaxed, not in my lounge anyway. What I wanted was for him to grovel. I took another mouthful of wine - which I nearly sprayed all over him at his next words.

"We can offer you counselling, of course."

Counselling? Bloody counselling? Oh, don't get me started. I swallowed my wine, clenched my jaw and uttered a firm "No."

"You don't want counselling?"

"No thank you, I don't. Shit happens. That's life. I deal with it."

He raised an eyebrow.

"You don't mince your words, do you, Miss Long?"

I shrugged.

"And secondly?"

"Your statement. Would you read and sign it, please? That is if you agree with what my sergeant has typed up from the notes he took at our interview."

I ignored the sarcasm in his voice as I took the proffered sheets, though I made sure I took my time in going through them. He said nothing while he waited. Finally I appended my name to the bottom and handed them back.

"Anything else?"

"Umm? Oh, yes, this question of the smell in the bathroom." He bent towards me, forearms on his thighs. "You are sure about it?"

"Oh, yes."

"And it was definitely 'Youth Dew'?"

I eased myself back on the sofa, elbow resting on the arm, my legs curled to the side.

"Yes. It's an unmistakeable fragrance, very heavy and pervasive. I had a friend who used to wear it."

"So the smell would hang around for a while?"

"Oh, easily. She spilt some in my car, once. It was like driving around in a Persian brothel for months afterwards."

His lips quirked with the beginnings of a smile. I went on as casually as I could.

"Of course, what makes it really interesting, is that JayJay wasn't wearing it?"

He became serious again.

"Ah! You noticed that, did you?"

I nodded without saying anything, reaching for the glass on the table between us.

"And what did your perfumier's nose detect on the vic... Jaynee Johnson?"

I caught the sarcasm again, and the hurried correction, but replied honestly.

"Nothing at all."

I'd been within a few feet of the dead woman; if she'd worn 'Youth Dew' I would have known it. She might have used a different fragrance, of course, but my ability to smell it would depend on when she'd applied it—and how long she'd been dead.

"OK, thank you. Well, I think that's all."

"There is one other thing," I said, uncurling myself from the settee and padding across to the desk.

"You've thought of something else?" His tone was eager.

"No, I've been given something else."

I dropped JayJay's diary into his hand and resumed my seat, watching him closely. If he was surprised he hid it very well.

"Where did you get this?"

"As I said, I was given it. By Holly Danvers."

"Johnson's secretary? But ..."

"It was in her desk drawer and she'd forgotten she had it when Sergeant Stott called," I explained hurriedly. I didn't want him blaming either Holly or his underling for what had been merely an oversight.

"How long have you had it?"

Dark eyes bored accusingly into mine as he undid the clasp.

"Only twenty four hours. You'll need to get your cryptographers to work on it."

"Hmm?" He glanced down at the book on his lap, long fingers turning the pages.

"There's not a lot in it and what there is, is written in code."

He closed it quickly.

"And neither you nor Miss Danvers thought to bring it to us?"

Unmoved by the anger in his tone, I shrugged.

"Holly was too scared to and I was going to drop it in tomorrow. I haven't had time today. I'm a working girl."

"Yes, you are. You work as a PA, not a detective."

I controlled myself with some difficulty. This man was making a habit of rubbing me up the wrong way. In an attempt to mollify him, I said "I'm not trying to be a detective ..." which wasn't true but I hoped sounded suitably apologetic.

"But you've looked at it." He lifted the diary.

"Of course. I was intrigued. Wouldn't you be curious about a dead woman's diary?"

"Yes, but then I'm paid to be."

The retort came quickly, hitting me like a slap in the face. Well, I thought sourly, I walked straight into that one. I lowered my gaze.

"I'm sorry."

My voice sounded suitably contrite.

"Miss Long. Please."

I looked up quickly at the pleading note in his voice.

"You didn't mince your words earlier, so I won't do so now. Stay out of this. You must have realised that there's a very clever killer responsible for JayJay's death."

I nodded. That was becoming clear. Getting JayJay to a downmarket, empty house, the business with the keys; it all indicated a carefully thought out crime.

"I don't want ..." He turned his head away briefly, his profile revealing the strong line of his jaw. "I don't want to investigate your death at the same time as Jaynee Johnson's."

"I'll do my best," was my only answer, but I did take his concern seriously. He was right and I would have to watch my back if I was to take my interest in the case any further.

"Good."

He got up to leave and I walked him to the door.

"Er...there is one other thing." He smiled rather sheepishly, turning to face me, one foot already out of the door.

What now, I wondered, suddenly wary.

"Ye-es?"

"Will you have dinner with me on Saturday night?"

Stap me! Whatever I'd been expecting, it wasn't that.

"Erm ... erm," I stammered like a schoolgirl asked out on her first date. "Yes. OK. Thank you," I finally got out.

"Great. I'll pick you up about seven thirty?"

I nodded, too dumbstruck to speak, wondering what on earth I was getting myself into.

"I'll see you then. Good night, Miss Long."

And he was gone, pulling the door shut behind him.

Chapter 6

T HE SUBURB OF DARRINGTON RUNS like a ribbon along the
eastern edge of town. Although on the opposite side of
Crofterton from my flat in Sutton, the opening of the
northern bypass would make the journey easier. Even so I didn't set
off until after nine, when the morning rush hour had passed,
determined to get a good look at the area where, on a bright
summer's evening twenty years ago, a young girl had simply vanished.
The sun hung high in a cloudless blue sky, offering the promise of
another perfect June day and I made good time to Conway Drive on
the edge of the estate. I parked up in a lay-by in front of a parade of
shops and took my notebook and digital camera from the glove box.
KD liked to have photographs as a visual aid to her work; a few
pictures of the two houses and some shots of the surrounding area
should do it.

I checked my notes and the street map I had brought with me.
Kimberley Hughes and her family had lived at number 122 while
Charlotte Neal had been just round the corner at 17 Rhyl Close. On
the map the two streets were very close, but it gave no indication of

house numbers so one of my tasks this morning was to check out the distance on foot between the two, then time how long it took to walk between them.

Once out of the car I slung the camera strap over my shoulder and headed for the small row of shops. Facing me from left to right stood a newsagents, a chemist, Patel's Mini Supermarket, a hair salon called Curl Up and Dye—I nearly did—and Chan's Cottage Chinese Take-away. For the moment I resisted the temptation to go in and buy a newspaper, bottle of pills, bar of chocolate or have my hair done and Chan's was closed, so I passed them all and carried on along Conway Drive. Before the houses began, a strip of unmown grass, waving in knee-high drifts, fronted a belt of undergrowth and trees. A couple of paths, beaten down by the constant passage of feet, ran across this mini meadow towards the trees. A large black labrador, old and fat, waddled through it in my direction. His owner, equally old but thin and wiry, walked behind.

"Sit, Blackie! Sit!"

What an imaginative piece of naming, I thought before, to my surprise, the dog did just that. It sat down on its haunches a foot or so from where I stood and gazed solemnly up at me.

"Good boy, Blackie." His master's approval followed instantly.

"Hello, Blackie."

I put forward an open palm for inspection before scratching the top of its head.

"Good morning, Miss." The man touched the front of his cap in an old-fashioned gesture. "He won't hurt you."

"I'm sure he won't," I replied. Apart from a ripple of pleasure running down its flanks as I stroked the silky head, the dog hadn't moved an inch. "He's too well trained for that."

Having thus earned the approval of both man and beast, I attempted to make best use of it while I could.

"Have the shops been there long?"

"About ten years or so, I guess. They took away some of your playground, didn't they, boy?" He looked down at the dog, scratching it lazily behind the ears. As if in answer, the dog put its head against the man's leg and gazed up with big, sorrowful eyes.

"Playground?"

"Yes, there were more woods and open land here, then. We'd not had him long as a pup," he nodded towards the dog, "and we used to walk all over here, regular like, until the developers moved in."

He looked as sad as his labrador.

"I'm surprised they've not built on what's left," I said. "Do the trees go back far?"

"Oh, a fair way. Half a mile or so till you reach a stream. There's a bomb hole in the middle. A crater, like," he explained seeing my blank look, "where a bomb exploded during the war. It's all covered over now, nature reclaims its own, and farmer's fields beyond that. At one time they had planned to extend, to build more houses here," he pointed towards the woods, "but fortunately for Blackie and me, and the local kids, the property crash put paid to that."

So twenty years ago there had been quite a stretch of woods and common land close to where the Hughes family lived. I glanced across to the trees. It was hard to see anything behind them. At this time of year the grass and undergrowth were high and straggling. If it stretched back for half a mile as the old man thought, well … it might be possible to hide a body there, perhaps at the bottom of the crater. I had a sudden vision of a girl, struggling to break free from her captor as he dragged her into the trees. I shook myself and brought my thoughts back to the present and the old man now looking curiously at me.

"Memories, eh?" He suggested.

More like an over-active imagination, I thought.

"Ah, well. Better be off home for some breakfast. Nice talking to you, Miss." He touched his cap again. "Come on, Blackie."

"Goodbye. Goodbye Blackie."

I watched them go for a moment, the dog obediently walking a few paces behind his master, before I carried on up Conway Drive.

I passed the end of Rhyl Close before I reached my objective. Kimberley Hughes's old home was a typical 1980s detached house with a small, neatly kept front garden and a curved tarmac drive. Somebody had been spending money on the place, for it had recently been fitted with new UPVC windows and fascia boards that shone brightly in the sun. Other than that, nothing distinguished it from the identical little boxes that stretched away on either side. I took a couple of photographs from different angles to give KD some idea of the house when she got round to working on the story. There was every probability that the four bedroomed bow-fronted property would metamorphose into something completely different by the time she had finished, but that, she had often told me, was the joy of writing fiction.

In contrast, Charlotte Neal's house when I reached it some twelve minutes later, looked unkempt and uncared for. The garden was a wasteland of grass and dandelion intersected by a path of broken concrete slabs leading to a faded and peeling front door. I wondered how long ago Charlotte's family had moved out and who lived in it now—there was no listing for a Neal at this address in the phone book. I needed a nosy, and talkative, neighbour but there didn't seem to be anyone around and my job description didn't involve ringing doorbells, asking prying and unwelcome questions. I crossed to the opposite pavement for a better angle and nearly dropped the camera when a voice behind me said,

"Excuse me."

I spun round. Leaning on the gate of the house behind me, a small, elderly woman looked suspiciously up at me.

"What are you doing?"

What did she think I was doing? I was stood there with a camera in my hands, for goodness' sake.

"I'm just taking some photographs."

"Are they moving, then? The Joneses?"

Manna from heaven! I seized my chance.

"Yes. Or at least, I've been told by my boss to come and take some photos."

Which was no word of a lie. She didn't need to know my boss wasn't an estate agent.

"Unlucky house that," she offered.

"Unlucky? In what way? It certainly looks an eyesore."

"Oh, it's never been cared for. Been let go to rack and ruin."

"How does that make it unlucky?"

"It was the Neal house, that. Their little girl disappeared, you know, about twenty year ago or more. All over the papers it was"

"Did she? Were you here then? What happened?" I asked as casually as I could, though my eagerness was beginning to make me sound like a police interrogation.

"Oh, I've been here since these houses were built, love. Back in the eighties that were. The Neals moved in shortly after and it were their daughter that vanished coming back from a friend's house."

"How awful. What do you think happened?"

"No idea. No more idea than the police had anyways, and they were swarming all over the place for nigh on a week. House to house they come, asking if we'd seen anything. Well, of course, we 'adn't." She sounded rather regretful at this as if she longed to be someone who gave the police vital information. "But then nobody 'ad. At least, no one admitted 'aving seen the girl."

The more excited she got the more her aitches disappeared, I noticed, but at least she was talking.

"I suppose the police did a thorough search of the area?"

"Oh yes. And of the house," she pointed across the road to number 17. "They even dug up the garden."

"Did they find anything?"

"Nah. Nothing. There's some around here that reckoned she'd gone off with a feller, but she were a nice girl, Charlotte. I'd known her since she were two years old. Watched her grow up, I did."

She nodded in satisfaction as if watching a child grow up gave you a deep insight into their character. Perhaps it did, but not if the watching had only been from across the road.

"Not like modern teenagers then? Covered in make-up and wearing clothes that reveal far too much."

"Oh, I know, shockin' it is nowadays but Charlotte weren't like that." She paused. "I did see her wearing make-up a time or two, though."

"Did her mother approve?"

"Carol? I wouldn't 'ave thought so. She were quite strict and so were Charlotte's dad. She always had to be home by a certain time. Not like today with kids roamin' the streets at all hours."

I was about to ask her who lived in the house now but remembered just in time that she had already told me. Besides, my supposed employer would have known.

"When did the Neals move out?"

She thought for a moment.

"Oh, about a year after, I'd say. Carol reckoned there were too many memories. They were going down south somewhere to make a fresh start, she said. It's been sold about five times since then. None of 'em 'ave looked after it nor cared for it much. As you can tell."

I nodded. It was time I wrapped this up. I'd got about as much out of her as I was going to get, though she had given me one possible pointer.

"Well, I must get on. Nice talking to you."

"And to you. Good morning." She turned and shuffled back down the path while I strode off towards Conway Drive and the patch of woodland near the shops.

I had the place pretty much to myself when I got there. There were no dog walkers about and the children were in school so I wandered at will, stopping now and again to take a few photos. I found the 'bomb hole' easily enough and stood on the rim for a few minutes while I thought about the missing girl. If the police had scoured the area and found nothing then there was probably nothing to find. Surely Blackie and his mates would have unearthed anything hidden here in the twenty years since Charlotte's disappearance, so this was probably a wild goose chase on my part. Still, KD might find it useful as she weaved the few meagre facts I had been able to gather into a plausible story.

I looked at my watch. Half past twelve, time to return to Crofterton and get some lunch at the ABC.

On a whim, I called in at Knight's Estate Agents on the way to Valentino's. I still needed a place to live and I might as well kill two birds with one stone. Mr Oily was in the outer office and came across as soon as I'd shut the door.

"Good morning. How may we help?"

No sign that he remembered me, I noticed. Good. It avoided any potentially difficult comments or questions.

"I'd like your lettings department, please."

He accompanied me through to the boxed in space behind the screen.

"Client for you, Mr Powell."

The smile Tom directed upwards died on his face as soon as he recognised me.

"Hello, Tom," I said taking the chair at the end of his desk. "Can you let me have some more details, please. I've decided against the last property you showed me."

I smiled in what I hoped was a friendly way but Tom merely threw me a black look as he got up and slid open the top drawer in his filing cabinet.

"Any particular property in mind?"

"Not this time, no."

He rifled through the contents for a moment before sitting back down clutching a handful of papers which he thrust towards me.

"Have the police been giving you a hard time too?" I asked, hoping to inspire a feeling of solidarity. It seemed to work for he relaxed and turned towards me, almost eagerly.

"I'll say," he replied, voice barely above a whisper. Fortunately there was a lot of noise coming from the main office. I thought it unlikely we'd be overheard.

"Anyone would think I killed her."

I widened my eyes in mock horror and incredulity that they could think such a thing and tried to look sympathetic.

"Then, yesterday, they came in and confiscated the appointments diary." He indicated a blank space on the desk.

"Really? I suppose they wanted to know who'd viewed the place last? Before me, I mean."

"Yes."

"And?" I prompted, I didn't want Tom going all monosyllabic on me. He stayed silent, so I applied a little flattery.

"Naturally, they'd come to you. You'd be the best person to tell them. After all, you must be a good judge of character by now. Meeting so many people, showing them round. You could probably recognise a dodgy character a mile off."

Was it my imagination, or did young Mr Powell sit up a little straighter and taller in his chair as he considered this?

"Well, there is that, of course."

"They'd rely on that," I assured him. "Your assessment would be important to them."

"There was only an old lady, Mrs Smith, about a fortnight ago," Tom finally admitted.

Mrs Smith? Oh great! It was going to be fun trying to find her, then. For a moment I indulged in the malicious pleasure of imagining the attempts of Inspector Farish and his team in doing so before re-focusing my attention on the lad in front of me.

"An old lady? I can't see her killing JayJay, can you?"

"Hardly. She wouldn't have had the strength. All grey hair and wrinkles, she was."

Thus, in Tom's view, obviously incapable of doing anything more strenuous than sitting in a rocking chair and knitting.

"Oh well, the police will find her, no doubt, and give her the same third degree treatment as us. I suppose they've asked you about the keys, too?"

He drew back a fraction. Fearing I'd lost him and he might clam up, I went on in a confidential tone,

"They seemed to think I'd had them but I told them they were never out of your pocket."

Strictly speaking they'd merely asked me if I recalled Tom having trouble opening the door but he wasn't to know that. Fortunately, this blatant lie bore fruit.

"Me too." He was eager to talk again. "And where they were kept, who had access to them, if I'd ever lost them or given them to anybody."

"Ridiculous," I agreed as he enumerated these points on stubby fingers.

"Or whether I'd put them down where someone could get at them."

"Well, of course you hadn't."

He had. He'd left them on the kitchen worktop—for a short while at least. Still, I wasn't going to point that out. I smiled encouragement.

"Well, no."

A shifty look appeared in his eyes for a moment. Was it merely the memory of putting the keys down that worried him or something else, I wondered.

"And I suppose they've taken the keys as well?"

"Oh, yes," he nodded. "Took them off me before they let me go on Monday."

I heard the faint, muffled noise of a phone ringing.

"Excuse me a moment."

He opened a desk drawer and lifted out a mobile. While he took the call I dropped my gaze to the pile of particulars he'd given me, pretending to read them but, in reality, my brain was working furiously. If taking calls on his mobile was a regular occurrence—he'd certainly done so that Monday—and he'd left the keys lying about, then it was possible the key to Willow Drive had been switched whilst he was thus distracted. Everything would have to fall just right though, for me to feel totally happy with this idea.

"Sorry, about that. My next appointment."

Leaving the phone on the top of the desk, he stepped to the filing cabinet and pulled out a folder and a set of keys which he set down next to the mobile. In a flash I picked up the keys.

"If you don't mind." He sounded cross as he shut the drawer and held out his hand.

"I was just looking at the fob," I lied, dropping the bundle into his open palm. "Clever idea that. The logo, I mean."

It was. The words 'Knight's Estate Agents' were engraved on one side of a heavy, metal fob that had been fashioned in the shape of a knight on horseback. However, the ring itself held far greater interest. It wasn't, as I'd expected, a thin double circle of wire but a single ring with a depressible clip. Much easier and quicker to use than twiddling key and wire round and round in circles, pinching your fingers and breaking your nails. Very interesting.

"Anyway Tom, thanks for these." I got up, waving the sheaf of particulars in my hand. "I'll be in touch."

He nodded. "OK. Goodbye."

Well, I thought once I was back on the High Street, he may not know it but Tom Powell has definitely given me plenty to think about.

The ABC lunchtime crowd had hardly thinned out at all; it seemed particularly heavy even for a Friday. The wine bar was growing increasingly popular with local businessmen and it pleased me to see the place so busy. When I arrived most of the tables were still occupied but, fortunately, my usual bar stool was vacant and I hurried across to claim it. While I waited for my *croque monsieur* I read through the estate agent's particulars, turning the pages over in a listless fashion. I didn't enjoy house hunting, I decided. It was fast becoming a ceaseless trawl around one drab, poorly maintained and overpriced property after another. I could paper my current flat with the fistfuls of A4 sheets I'd collected from all the letting agents I'd visited. (Despite Knight's claim to be 'the' estate agent, there existed half a dozen more in Crofterton alone and two others in the nearby town of Bellhurst—I know, I had trudged into every single one over the past couple of months.) I sipped at my white wine spritzer dejectedly. Of the four sets of details Tom Powell had given me, I dismissed two out of hand. The first was way over my budget - £1600 a month! That was more than I earned working for KD in that time and twice what I paid in Sutton Harcourt—and the second too far from the centre. I nibbled at my hot sandwich while considering the remaining pair. I liked the sound of 'a modern town house in a pleasant thoroughfare close to city centre and all amenities', so that was a possibility. The other I wasn't quite so keen on but, what the hell! Both were probably worth a look. I folded the sheets and stuffed them in my bag.

"How is the house hunt, Verity? *Ça va?*"

I wiped melted cheese from my mouth and chin before replying.

"It goes, Val, but not very far and not very fast."

"My poor Verity." His sensuous mouth twisted in a sympathetic grimace. "You know, Verity, there is a flat above here that you are most welcome to have."

I did know. It wasn't the first time the offer had been made. I just didn't fancy living over the wine bar. It would only encourage me to spend more time in the place—I treated it as a second home as it was—and I wanted to put a greater distance between me and my bed than a stagger up a flight of stairs every night. Besides, I might be tempted to drag him up the stairs with me.

"Thanks, Val. I might take you up on that if I get any more grief from my landlord."

"*C'est bon.*"

He gave a Gallic shrug, his handsome face creasing in a smile. Once, I'd considered taking him as a lover, an idea he had actively encouraged, but sleeping with a man is a sure fire way to ruin a good friendship, I've found, and so far I'd always managed to resist.

As if reading my thoughts his eyes twinkled. I changed the subject hastily.

"Business is good?" I indicated the groups of diners with a wave of my hand.

"Oh, yes, very good. And you? You are working hard for your writer of novels?"

"Certainly am." I sounded confident enough but in truth felt rather less sanguine about my prospects of working for KD for too much longer. Her comment about not needing me while she worked on the new book did not bode well for the future. My future, anyway. Not that I was going to confess my concerns to Val, bless him, he'd only offer me a job. He moved away to serve coffee to his customers, leaving me to continue fretting over KD's words. I thought of the agents' particulars in my bag. I wouldn't be able to move out of my flat if I lost my job. With a sigh I slid off my stool and moved across to one of the now empty tables. Taking my notebook from my bag, I proceeded to write down all the reasons I could think of to persuade my employer that we should carry on the way we were. Val brought me a cappuccino but said nothing and left me to it. When I'd done I sat back and looked at my meagre list. The problem was, I could think of any number of reasons for KD to write new, original material, but hardly any for her to pay a PA cum researcher. I heaved a frustrated sigh and threw my pad and pen back in my bag.

"You are not going back to work, Verity?"

I glanced at my watch - nearly half past two already. I got up and walked towards the bar.

"No, I've got the afternoon off. I'm going to go home and spend it working on my report."

"Your report?"

"Yes. KD and I are working on a twenty year old case. It's one involving a schoolgirl called Charlotte Neal."

"Ah, *bon*." Val leaned towards me over the counter just as the phone began to ring.

"Now I must fly. Thanks Val."

We touched cheeks and I made for the door as he turned away and picked up the phone.

I strode back down the crowded pavement towards the car park. This continued spell of warm weather certainly brought out the shoppers, I reflected, as I skirted the dawdlers and dodged the kids on skateboards. At the junction where the High Street met All Saints, I joined the queue waiting at the pedestrian lights. With all the various filter lanes this crossing nearly always involved a long wait. I stood patiently, deep in thought, shifting forward from time to time as people moved around and about me. Suddenly the whole world was spinning towards me, my arms flapped wildly like some demented flat-footed booby desperately trying to get airborne. I struggled to stay upright. Something big and red filled my vision and there was a scream followed by a gasp, though that might have been me. An arm shot out like a safety barrier in front of me, hands clutched at my sleeves and pulled me back. Back from pitching head first into the roaring traffic and under the thundering wheels of a number 29 bus.

"Are you all right, love?" asked an elderly gentleman to my left. "I thought we'd lost you there."

"Yes, yes, I'm OK, thank you," I replied, my heart racing.

I looked round wildly, but didn't recognise anyone I knew in the sea of faces gathered at the kerbside. The lights changed and we surged across. When we reached the far side I turned and looked back, scanning the pavements opposite. No one was running off or lurking inconspicuously in a shop doorway. Everything seemed placid and normal but I was as sure as eggs is eggs that some bastard had deliberately pushed me in the back, fully intending me to fall to my death beneath the rush of oncoming traffic.

Chapter 7

I HATE HOUSEWORK. IT'S IN my genes, a trait inherited from my mother who claimed that a tidy house was the sign of an empty life. She led a full existence did my mother. She was also replete with a maxim for every occasion so I would often be admonished with 'never a borrower nor a lender be' or 'a place for everything and everything in its place.' Which explained why I grew up in a house piled high with books, knick-knacks and mementos of every description. She didn't have a place for any of them.

I finished vacuuming and dusting and gave the living room a quick blast from a can of furniture spray—it works just as well as elbow grease when you are in a hurry. All right, it doesn't polish the wood but it does make the room smell nice. Then I tackled the kitchen sink.

At half past eleven, exhausted after my morning's efforts, I flopped on the settee with a mug of coffee and the intention of going through my notes from Jaynee Johnson's diary. Then the phone rang.

"Good morning, Verity, it's KD."

"Morning, boss. What can I do for you?" I asked, my heart in my mouth, my fingers crossed as I prayed fervently she was going to ask me to do some new research or anything that would save my job.

"Are you doing anything this afternoon?"

"No, I don't think so. Why?"

"Oh, good." Her voice sounded relieved and I wondered what my admission of an empty Saturday afternoon had let me in for. "I meant to ask you on Thursday if you would come with me this afternoon."

This sounded ominous.

"Come with you? To what, exactly?"

"I'm presenting the prizes at the Crofterton dog show."

"You're what?"

I failed to keep the incredulity out of my voice and KD sounded faintly hurt when she replied.

"It's all part of the job, dear."

"Part of being a writer or a dog lover?"

"Don't be so dense, Verity. It's all part of being a local celebrity."

"Oh! That job!"

KD looked on being a famous face as a necessary evil but it remained the one aspect of her work she liked least.

"Anyway, please say you'll come."

"Well, I am out this evening," I murmured.

"Ooh. A hot date, eh?"

I'd hardly describe dinner with Inspector Farish in that fashion so I ignored the comment.

"Go on. Where is it and what's the dress code?"

"Crofterton racecourse and posh frocks."

"OK. Where and when do you want me to meet you?"

"Thanks, Verity, I really appreciate it. Shall we say two thirty-ish in the VIP lounge at the top of the grandstand?"

"The VIP lounge? Will I be able to get in? I don't want to be thrown out for impersonating somebody important."

KD barked with laughter at the other end of the line.

"Oh yes, you'll be all right. As long as you're dressed decently and not in jeans and a tee-shirt, they'll let anybody in."

"Oh, I can impersonate an anybody," I assured her. "I do it all the time. OK, I'll see you there."

I returned to studying my notes on JayJay's diary. Besides appointments with the dentist, the gym, her beautician and her mum, all of which I'd noted but now dismissed, there were six further entries. Assuming Holly Danvers' suggestion that 'JB' stood for John Brackett was correct, that still left five others unaccounted for. Thrush, Mr Smith, Spaniel, Dawn and Xmas Wreath. I fetched a fresh sheet of paper from the desk, making a separate list of these names and the dates they appeared. Despite having told Inspector Farish that the diary had been written in code, it was clear that this was no cipher. Surely, I thought, scratching my head with the end of my pen, JayJay had made the same connection I had and Thrush referred to Candida Clark. I felt hampered by not knowing the dead woman, not knowing how her mind worked. Without that knowledge, figuring out who she'd meant was well nigh impossible. I reached for my coffee in frustration. I had originally wondered if the entries were the dates JayJay had made with her lovers, but that idea went out the window with the inclusion of her producer. Unless she was bisexual, of course.

"Yes!"

I bounded off the settee, galvanised by a sudden bolt of inspiration. Could Xmas Wreath be Holly Danvers? Now I might be getting somewhere. I picked up the sheet of paper that had leapt to the floor at the same time I did. There was only one date for this entry, January 7th. I grabbed the phone, checked my notebook and dialled.

"Holly? Hello, it's Verity Long."

"Oh, hello, Miss Long. I was just about to go out."

The secretary's small voice, made tinny by the wires, came back at me.

"I shan't keep you, I just wanted to know when you started working for JayJay."

"Umm … it was in January, sometime in early January. I can't remember when exactly. Is it important?"

"I don't know. I'm just working through the diary you brought me."

"Haven't you given it to the police?"

"Oh, yes, they've got it," I assured her. "But I made a few notes before I handed it over."

"I understand," replied Holly knowingly, before she added, "to help with your enquiries," which proved she didn't.

"Did you have a job interview beforehand?"

"Sorry?"

"Did you go to an interview with Jaynee, before you began to work for her?"

"Yes, that's right. I did."

"And can you remember when that was?"

"Oh, only the week before. She wanted someone who could start immediately, so I saw her on the Wednesday, or the Thursday I think it was, and started the following Monday."

"Would Thursday the seventh sound about right?"

A brief silence while she considered this.

"Yes, I think so."

I thanked her and put the phone down, then wrote 'Holly Danvers' next to 'Xmas Wreath' on my pad. I was making progress. Of a sort. I'd accounted for two names on my list, or three if I pushed the list up to the six I'd had originally and included John Brackett. Pleased with myself, I ticked them off. Only three to go: Mr Smith, Spaniel and Dawn. Spaniel! Hell's teeth! I was due to meet KD for her wretched dog show in under two hours and here I sat, bedraggled, covered in dust and grime, giving a damned good impression of a mongrel myself. I raced for the shower.

As well as the dog show there were several races on the card that afternoon and spectators were pouring into the course. A swirling sea of people ebbed and flowed around the new grandstand, like survivors of a maritime disaster desperately trying to reach the safety of the ship sent to rescue them. Rising concrete tiers with blue painted railings looked for all the world like decks on an ocean-going cruise liner that should be plying the warm waters of the Caribbean, not stuck in dry dock at Crofterton Racecourse. The distorted metallic voice of a Tannoy informed us that judging would shortly take place in the Gun Dog class before going on to announce the runners and riders in the next race.

How the hell was I going to find KD in this seething mob? Hemmed in on all sides, I turned quickly, narrowly avoiding stepping on a Yorkshire Terrier masquerading as a mobile toupee. Sod this for a game of soldiers, I thought, as I engaged 'elbow mode'. Using these extremities as deadly weapons I forced my way through the crush much as Boadicea's chariot scythed through the Romans, eventually reaching the main doors at the base of the stand. I smiled briefly at the man on the door and stepped into a haven of coolness and calm.

"You took your time getting here," snapped KD irritably, when I finally stood, glass in hand, at her side in the VIP lounge on the top floor. The circular room with its floor to ceiling, plate glass, folding doors gave panoramic views over the course and the surrounding countryside.

"Where on earth have you been? I've had to listen to that dreadful woman droning on for hours."

"Which dreadful woman?" I asked, looking around.

They all looked pretty awful to me, face-lifted matrons showing far too much flesh, their over-applied make-up already beginning to run in the afternoon heat.

"Lavinia Drew-Steignton. She's a Kennel Club judge who breeds Borzois."

"Doesn't everybody?" I muttered as KD pointed out a woman in a pale pink dress and jacket leaning against the bar, talking to a dark haired man incongruously dressed amidst all the finery in a Barbour and brogues.

"And her breath reeks of gin."

"The same could be said of everybody in here, KD," I pointed out.

She laughed. "Too true."

There was certainly enough booze being swilled to fill an Olympic sized swimming pool. Suddenly I jumped at a loud bang directly behind me. I twirled round in time to see champagne frothing out of a bottle held in the pudgy hand of John Brackett. He was pouring the golden flow into the firmly gripped glass of Candida Clark. I turned back quickly, for some reason unwilling to let her see me.

"Stop being so jumpy, Verity. What's the matter, did you think it was a gunshot?"

I grinned weakly.

"Just nervous, I guess. One corpse a week is enough for anybody."

"Verity." KD drew out the last syllable of my name in admonishment. "Enough. You're here to have fun."

"OK," I said. "So what's your fancy in the next race?"

"Starlight Dancer. The filly's a dead cert. Oh!"

She stared at me in horror while I gazed steadily back over the rim of my glass.

"How unfortunate," she muttered.

"A poor choice of words, certainly" I agreed, thinking, as we both were, of Jaynee Johnson. "But apposite as usual, KD."

She glared at me.

"Stop it."

"So, when do you do your bit?" I sipped at my massively overpriced glass of wine and hoped KD would pay out for the next one.

"From four o'clock. The dog show is out the back, the other side of the grandstand."

We gravitated towards the far side of the bar area just as a surge of people swept past us in the opposite direction. The 3.15 race was under way. The volume of noise swelled as the race progressed. Finding it impossible to talk over the yells, the shouts of encouragement, the screams of excitement as the crowd urged on its favourites, KD and I waited until a final roar signalled the end of the race.

"Starlight Dancer, by half a length." The commentary was piped into the lounge but the place had been so noisy I hadn't noticed it before. The crowd surged back, gathering urgently around the bar, clamouring for attention, eager to celebrate or to drown sorrows and disappointment as the case may be.

"Did you have any money on it?" I asked KD.

"Me? I never bet."

She buried her nose in her glass, sleek, dark head lowered. So she had.

"How much?"

"Fifty quid." She grinned.

Fifty pounds? I wished I could afford to risk that much.

"Buns for tea, then?"

"Hardly. The odds weren't *that* good."

I nodded absently, gazing about me at the gaily underdressed women and the loudly overdressed men.

"Another blonde? He does like to collect them, doesn't he?"

"Who?" I asked.

KD nodded towards the door where the head of Silverton Studios, followed by Candy Clark, shouldered his way out.

"John Brackett."

"That's Candy Clark, the producer, he's got with him. I wonder where they're going?"

"The Studios are joint sponsors of the dog show. They've also put the money up for the race so he's probably off to award the prizes."

"Are they sleeping together, do you think?"

Had he also been sleeping with Jaynee Johnson? Did that explain the entries in her diary? For all I knew, the whole book was a list of her conquests. No, I reminded myself, that wouldn't work. Not with both Candida Clark and Holly Danvers in there.

"What?" I hadn't caught KD's reply.

"I said, 'do bears crap in the wood?' JB will sleep with anything in a skirt. Except his wife of course."

For one wild moment I pictured KD and JB together in the throes of passion. I shook my head quickly to dispel the frightful thought.

"What's the matter?" KD asked suspiciously.

"Oh, nothing." I gave her my sweetest, most innocent smile.

"Come on," said KD, putting her glass back on the bar. "The dog show calls."

A large marquee had been erected for the show on the far side of the grandstand. So big you could have fitted the entire population of Wales—and half that of Belgium—comfortably inside, it now played host to every canine in Crofterton. Except the mongrels, of course. Nor did I expect to see Blackie, the Darrington labrador there, either. A young girl at the entrance handed KD a programme.

"God! What a racket," said KD, to the accompaniment of assorted yelps, growls, barks and whines. "Here, take this, will you? My bag's too small."

I snatched the programme from her and stuffed it in my bag. There are times I think KD only takes me to functions to act as her pack-horse.

We worked our way around the parade ring, where a selection of topiaried poodles and their similarly clipped owners attempted to catch the judge's eye, to a roped-off area at the back. Inside this, seated at trestle tables, were the clerks, recording the results and filling in certificates.

"Kathleen Davenport." My employer announced herself to an elderly chap busy aligning rosettes. "Is Tom around?"

"He's at the back of the podium," the official told her, making it sound on a par with 'the back of the bike sheds'.

"Thank you."

KD sailed off in search of Tom, whoever he was, and I trailed in her wake.

"KD! So kind of you to come."

A large man with mutton chop whiskers stuck out a hand.

"Hello, Tom. May I introduce Verity, my assistant?"

"How do you do? Tom Cheeveley Hall."

"Pleased to meet you." Was this just his name or did it also include his residence? I shook the proffered hand.

With KD's permission, I left her to it and wandered around. Unsurprisingly the place was full of dogs. Short ones, tall ones, fat ones, thin ones, sleek dogs, hairy dogs, long tailed, short eared, long eared, short tailed. Brown ones, black ones, white ones, red ones, golden ones and beige ones. And all of them with absurd names. An Afghan, rejoicing in the ridiculously silly title of 'Plantagenet Cumbria the Third' won the hound class and an adorable little Cairn Terrier, who was probably called 'Bobby' at home but for today's purposes went under the alias of 'Vogel Bridie of Brunswick', took first prize in the terrier section.

I like dogs - but you can have too much of a good thing.

I watched KD graciously perform her duties and then returned to the back of the podium.

"Home time," announced KD as we left the marquee and made for the car park.

"Verity!"

An unmistakeable figure approached us.

"Hello, Greg. And ..."

"And your mother. Hello, Mrs Long."

I stifled a laugh. KD's glare would have frozen a coal fire at twenty paces.

Oblivious, Greg Ferrari raised her hand to his lips. "I can see now where your beautiful daughter gets her good looks from," he smarmed.

KD smiled—a rictus spreading from jaw to eyes. Really, I thought, it's like watching a man with a match trying to melt a glacier. Fortunately he turned his attention back to me.

"Still on for next week, Verity?"

"Yes, of course." I started to move away. "I'll see you there."

"Next week?" asked KD, through still clenched teeth once we were out of earshot.

"Yes." I kept my voice casual, "He's taking me for dinner at *Chez Jacques*."

"Be careful, Verity," she urged. "That man is trouble. I can smell it."

All I'd detected was Calvin Klein. I should have heeded her warning.

"I've booked a table at *Chez Jacques*," said Jerry Farish, sitting next to me in the taxi that sped us towards Crofterton.

"Is that all right with you?"

"Yes, fine thanks," I replied, hoping I didn't sound as nervous as I felt.

Still unsure why he'd asked me out, I stole a glance across at him. Relaxed, he leant back in his seat, forearms along his thighs, hands loose on his knees, thick brown hair beginning to curl over the collar of his pale grey suit.

"So is tonight business or pleasure?" I asked.

He laughed. "Oh purely pleasure, I assure you," he said, turning his face towards me with eyes and lips smiling. "Even policemen are allowed a night off, you know, and a private life."

Was it my imagination or had the taxi driver lifted his foot from the accelerator on mention of the word 'policemen'?

Despite the honesty in his voice I remained unconvinced. Life has taught me that I possess neither the looks nor the intellect to appeal to the type of intelligent, good-looking man that I, in return, am attracted to. Like Jerry Farish for instance.

"Besides," he went on, as if reading my thoughts and anxious to give the lie to them, "why shouldn't I want to spend time with an attractive, clever woman?"

I smiled politely, robbed of words for once.

It's possible, I thought. Possible, that is, that he wanted a break from work, from murder and death and the inevitable pressure that must come from being in charge of such a high profile case as the Jaynee Johnson slaying, as one headline had put it. Desperately as I wanted to know what progress they had made, what clues they'd uncovered, and the list of suspects—while fervently hoping I wasn't on it—tonight was not the right time to demand my curiosity be satisfied. Give him a break, Verity, I thought, noticing for the first time that the light from the lowering sun illuminated lines of tiredness around his eyes. A tightness to his lips and jaw revealed him not to be as relaxed as I'd thought. I resolved to make the evening a pleasure for both of us.

Jacques was his usual urbane, welcoming self when we reached the restaurant.

"*Mademoiselle* Verity," he greeted me, bowing over my hand occasioning a raised eyebrow from my companion.

"I didn't realise you knew this place," he whispered as Jacques showed us to a table and helped us get seated.

"Oh yes, Jacques is an old friend. I've known him and his brother Val, next door, for years." I smiled across the glassware at him whilst taking the proffered menu from the maître d's hand.

"What's next door?"

"The ABC wine bar."

"Ah," he nodded, "yes, of course. It's always struck me as a funny name for a wine bar."

"It's Val's idea of a joke," I told him. "We were going to call it Valentino's and decorate it with photographs of silent movie stars from the 1920's. I still think it was a great idea."

"And the joke?" he reminded me.

"Oh, yes. Val says it stands for 'Anything But Chardonnay'."

He chuckled, a rich, throaty sound. "Very good."

For the next few minutes we were silent, scanning through the menu. I made my choice fairly quickly and put the menu down.

"Have you decided already? There's so much to choose from, I'm struggling."

He wasn't to know how familiar I was with the dishes in this restaurant and I saw no reason to enlighten him.

"Yes, I'm going for the wild chanterelles followed by the duck."

"Duck?" He looked back down at the menu. "Ah yes, the *Confit de Canard*. Hmm."

Jacques reappeared at the table.

"Are you ready to order, sir?" he murmured.

"Yes, I think so," said Farish, giving my choices and ordering smoked salmon followed by an individual beef Wellington for himself.

Jacques gathered up our menus and then stood there, the wine list in his hand, looking at me as though undecided which one of us to give it to. A rare lapse. I nodded in my companion's direction—he was paying for the meal, or I hoped he was, and therefore had the right to choose. I'd soon put him right if he ordered a bottle of 'Blue Nun', though this was unlikely since it wasn't on offer.

Farish wasn't a detective for nothing, his sharp eyes had obviously noticed the unspoken interplay between Jacques and myself.

"What would you suggest?"

"Hmm, the Beaune, I think, or, if you are feeling flush, the

Brunello di Montalcino."

He studied the list again for a moment.

"And which would you prefer?"

"The Beaune," I said, without hesitation.

"Then the Beaune it is."

He closed the wine list and handed it back. Jacques glided silently away.

The Inspector looked around, taking in the surroundings. The restaurant had twenty tables and a maximum of eighty covers, most of them full this evening—as on most Saturdays.

"It's the first time I've been here, though I've heard good reports about it."

"The food is excellent," I assured him.

"So I understand. It came highly recommended by the Assistant Chief Constable, no less."

I made a face to show that I was suitably impressed, before saying, "He's a man of taste, then, obviously."

"Oh, obviously." He laughed back.

"And if you haven't been before, then you are in for a treat."

"Well, if the company's anything to go by then I'm sure I am."

His hazel eyes twinkled at me, as he tasted the small amount of wine Jacques had just poured into his glass. Then they widened as his eyebrows raised.

"That's fine, thank you," he said to Jacques before looking at me and adding, "Good choice, Verity."

Stupidly, I found myself basking in his praise. Stay on your guard, I told myself. You still don't know what he is after.

"So, how come you know so much about wine?"

I swallowed the forkful of chanterelle I'd just put in my mouth and wiped a trace of cream sauce from my lips before replying.

"I worked for a wine exporter in the Burgundy region once—a long time ago—and then later, when I'd moved back to England, I worked for a wine importer."

"Did you enjoy the job?"

"I certainly enjoyed their products." I laughed. "And learned a fair bit about wine in the process."

"Is that where you met Jacques and ..." He paused, searching for the name.

"Valentino," I supplied, "usually shortened to Val and no, it's not his real name. I don't know what that is. Anyway, I met them in 1999 when I took a French holiday. They ran a small bar cum bistro. Look, it's a long story. Are you sure you want to hear this?"

He finished the last of his salmon and pushed the plate away. "Yes, please." He looked genuinely interested. "Frankly, I'm fascinated."

"By what?" I asked sharply, aware of his eyes on me.

"You," he said, simply. "Besides, I've never met a wine importer before."

"You haven't met one now," I pointed out. "I only worked for one."

"Whatever. Go on."

Encouraged by his smile, I gave him the bare bones of the story.

"For various reasons the boys were thinking of moving to England. When they mentioned this to me I said that a wine bar and bistro was just what Crofterton needed. So they looked into it from their end, I did the same over here and *voilà!* as they say, here they are."

"Just like that?"

"Well no, hardly," I laughed, leaning back in my chair as a large plate of duck on top of sauteed potatoes was placed in front of me.

We ate in silence for a while. Was he really that interested in the life and works of Verity Long, I wondered, or was it a ploy to keep off the subject that had thrown us together? Pleasure, Verity, I reminded myself. Tonight is about enjoying yourself, remember. Besides, the JayJay case was hardly a suitable topic for discussion over an excellent meal and damned fine wine. Maybe there would be an opportunity later to raise the subject.

"So, are you into old films or do you just like quoting lines from *Casablanca*?" he asked.

He put down his knife and fork and raised his glass, looking at me over the rim.

"Yes, I like old films," I told him. "They're less violent, less overtly sexual and in your face than modern ones." I sounded remarkably prim.

"You don't approve of sex and violence?"

"In the right place. I certainly don't want to watch it in a cinema with hundreds of others." Fearing that this made me sound like a secret voyeur I hurried on, "or on television in my own living room."

Goodness! I'd made a right hash of explaining that.

"What I mean is …"

"I know what you mean." He smiled to put me at ease. "So what is your favourite film?"

I speared a piece of potato while I considered this.

"Do I have to choose just one?"

"Well," he glanced at his watch, "the night is young. I don't mind a long list."

If he was laughing at me, I didn't care. I laughed back.

"I think I could narrow it down to three."

"And they are?"

"Apart from *Casablanca* I would also include *Singin' in the Rain* and *Some Like It Hot* on my list."

"Yes, they'd probably be on mine too. What about *It's a Wonderful Life*?"

"It's OK. A bit too sentimental and schmaltzy, though, for my liking."

He nodded as if this list of films had revealed some hidden aspect of my personality. He put the last piece of fillet into his mouth.

"And what about you? Do you prefer more modern movies?"

"I hardly get the chance to watch them."

Jacques removed our plates and offered us dessert. We settled on coffee and liqueurs.

"Thank you, Verity," he said later, savouring his Calvados. "Your taste in restaurants is as excellent as your taste in films."

"Don't thank me. It was your ACC's recommendation," I pointed out. "I merely approved of it."

I finished my *Tia Maria* and went to the ladies while he settled the bill. I re-applied my lipstick and brushed my hair, chiding myself for my vanity whilst admitting that Jerry Farish was a damned attractive man—especially when he set out to be as charming and entertaining as he had been that evening. I stared at my face in the mirror, inwardly laughing at myself. I'd no idea where I was heading. I just hoped I could control the ride.

"You've been very good," he said. We sat side by side on my settee drinking the coffee I'd made, the taxi driver that had brought us home agreeing to come back for him in an hour.

"Good?" My eyes flashed. "I do know how to behave in public, you know. Did you expect me to strip off and dance on the tables?"

"Hardly, though I would have been interested in watching the performance." He caught the warning glint and hurried on, "I meant that you hadn't mentioned the Jaynee Johnson case all night."

"Oh well, I decided you deserved a break."

He smiled, relaxing, putting his arm along the back of the settee.

"Thank you. You'll never know how much I appreciate that."

A wicked voice inside my head said 'Show me'. I leaned towards him.

The arm came down around my shoulder, pulling me closer still. My head was almost on his chest.

"Jerry," I began, looking up at him.

His lips were on mine. I felt their warmth, their softness as I responded. Eventually I pulled away. Thank goodness he had a taxi coming.

"Jerry, I'm sorry but I must talk to you. How did JayJay die?"

"She was stabbed. Obviously."

I waved a hand to dismiss the obvious.

"Yes, but there would have been blood all over the place if she'd just been stabbed. Was she drugged first?"

"Possibly. We're still waiting for the coroner's report."

"Oh. Now, about JayJay's diary."

He sighed.

"I just wanted to tell you that I think I've worked out one of the names."

"Which one?"

He sat up, retrieving his arm which had slipped to my waist. Stupidly, I felt bereft.

"I think Xmas Wreath refers to Holly Danvers, JayJay's secretary. There's only one entry in the diary with that name, January 7th, when Holly had an interview with her at Silverton Studios. So Holly, Christmas, it all fits."

He nodded.

"Yes, I think you're right. I'll pass that on to Emma."

"Emma?" Why did I suddenly sound jealous?

"Sergeant Emma Harrison. I've given the diary to her on the assumption that it takes a woman to get inside another woman's mind."

I laughed at his logic.

"I'm still going to work on it and the rest of the names," I informed him.

"I wish you'd stay out of it."

"I can't, Jerry. I have to be honest with you. I'm intrigued, curious, involved."

"Curiosity killed the cat," he warned me. "I can see that I'll have to keep a close eye on you."

He smiled as he said it. If he meant what I hoped he meant, then I would raise no objections.

A ring at the doorbell announced his imminent departure. So soon? I reluctantly walked him through to the kitchen and opened the door to the driver.

"Right you are, guv, I'll wait in the car."

"Verity, thank you for a lovely evening. Can we do it again?" His arms slid round my waist holding me close.

"Yes, please. I'd like that."

This time, I offered my lips up for his kiss, yielding to him, to his gentleness and the warm firm pressure of his mouth on mine.

"Good night, Verity." His voice sounded husky in my ear.

Then he was gone, into the night.

Chapter 8

A S USUAL ON A SUNDAY, I allowed myself the luxury of a lie-in. Curled up in bed, warm and drowsy with the last vestiges of sleep still clinging to my mind, I thought about my date the previous night and wriggled my toes in pleasure at the memory. My earlier dislike of the Inspector had gone, replaced by a growing sense of attraction, a sexual pull that I found hard to resist. For a while I daydreamed, imagining what it would be like to surrender myself to him, to give in to my desires. Then I took a cold shower.

After breakfast of bacon and scrambled eggs I fetched my notes, eager to get my thoughts on the JayJay case into some kind of order. I'd no sooner started when the doorbell rang. My heart leapt in the hope that it might be Jerry again and I gave myself a mental slap for such girlish enthusiasm—then hid my disappointment.

"Oh, hello, Barbara. Come in."

I stood back to let my neighbour into the kitchen. A trim 70 year old, she and her husband John lived in the flat above mine and although friendly, it was unusual for either of them to call. I wondered what was wrong.

"I'm sorry to disturb you, Verity."

"That's all right. Would you like coffee?"

"No, I won't, thanks. I've only popped in to tell you we are moving."

"Oh! I'm sorry to hear that."

I was. The Lawsons were good neighbours. Quiet and unobtrusive, keeping themselves to themselves yet willing to offer help when needed. They had no children - at least not young ones - no pets and didn't hold rowdy parties. An ideal couple to have living in the flat upstairs.

"Well, we felt it was about time we moved to a bungalow. John finds the stairs increasingly difficult, with his arthritis you know, and we've decided to move closer to our daughter and the grandchildren."

"So, you are moving out of Sutton Harcourt altogether?"

She nodded. "Yes, at the end of the month. We just wanted to let you know."

"Thank you, Barbara. I shall be sorry to see you and John go but I wish you all the best."

"Thanks, dear. Now I must go. I've left John packing my best china."

I appreciated her sense of urgency as she smiled and said goodbye. Never leave a man in charge of packing. You'll end up on your week's holiday with enough dresses to clad a hen party and no shoes or underwear. As for delicate crockery, Barbara might as well go out now and stock up on paper plates. I laughed at the thought but felt depressed after she had gone, my earlier pleasurable mood dispelled. Knowing my luck, my landlord would house a young couple with a screaming baby or a constantly barking Doberman over my head. Yet another reason to get out of this place. Still, there was nothing I could do about it for the moment so, as a consolation, I decided to treat myself to Sunday lunch at the Fox Inn. Then, as an added distraction, I returned to worrying over Jaynee Johnson's murder. I fetched a new pad from the front room and compiled yet another list.

1. The keys

2. Who was 'Mrs Smith'?

3. Why had Jaynee gone there?

4. Where was her handbag? And her mobile phone?

5. The diary

I made fresh coffee while I mulled over these questions. Given the type of keyring used by Knight's, it would be easy enough to slip the key from the ring and substitute one of your own. There would be an element of risk involved but nevertheless I was convinced this was how it had been done, so I wrote 'Easy. Substitution' next to item one.

Mrs Smith might well be a harder problem to solve. An old woman, according to Tom Powell, and the name was likely to be an alias.

I left this for the time being and moved on to question three. Jaynee must have gone willingly to the house; there would have been signs of a struggle otherwise and the chance that somebody—a neighbour or a passerby—might have seen or heard something. And why? The answer stared me in the face. She went to view it! Her killer invited her there on the pretext that they were thinking of renting it and moving in. Well, that let out John Brackett and I couldn't see Candy Clark or Greg Ferrari in a Victorian villa so I could strike them off my list of suspects as well. Or could I? There might be other reasons, besides the obvious one, for JayJay to have gone to Willow Close, so that still left the producer and the co-star in the picture. Damn.

I walked around the kitchen while I pondered what I'd got so far—unlike KD I don't fiddle while I'm thinking, I walk—and wished I'd pumped Jerry Farish for more information last night. How much of this did the police already know? How much brain work could the man have saved me? Maybe, as our relationship developed— relationship? What relationship? Did one dinner together constitute an affair?—he might be prepared to discuss his work with me. For one wild moment I wondered if he talked in his sleep and then laughed uproariously at my own lascivious folly.

Calming down, I realised Jerry and his team would have the answer to my next point. They'd be able to trace the mobile and I could understand the killer taking it.

I plodded and pondered on then, at twenty past twelve, I threw my notebook and pen in my bag, combed my hair and set off on the short walk to the Fox, my local pub. I bought an *Observer* and a Sunday redtop from the newsagents on the way, intending to read them over lunch. If I couldn't winkle any information out of the police then I'd just have to get it from the press.

The Fox Inn was a traditional English pub selling real ales, good food—including an excellent steak pie and a tasty beef stew with dumplings—and with a halfway decent wine list. It boasted no jukebox, piped music, widescreen TV, fruit machines, pool tables, karaoke nights, ridiculously named cocktails or children's play areas. Unpretentious, it refused to call itself The Fox at Sutton Harcourt— as if this made it sound classier or more up-market—and remained the plain Fox Inn. The staff were friendly and well trained to observe, as well as pass, the time of day. You'd get no, "Hiya" here but a warm "Good afternoon" or "Good evening", as the case may be.

I ordered a plate of thickly cut home-cured ham with chips and a glass of red wine.

"I've got some nice roast beef with Yorkshire pudding on today, Verity," the landlord offered.

"Thanks, Bob, but I've had a good breakfast. I'll stick with what I've ordered, I think."

I took my glass and the papers to an empty table, spreading the tabloid out in front of me. They reported no further news on the demise of Jaynee Johnson but a centre page spread by a features writer proclaimed, 'Stars Mourn Death of Showbiz Icon'. I read through the lurid prose with distaste and a growing sense of unease.

If this article by the, no doubt pseudonymous, Dolly Dawkins was anything to go by, the beatification of JayJay had already started. I learned nothing that I didn't know earlier and the piece concluded with the usual predictable quotes from her colleagues in the TV industry. They praised her character, her talent and, even, her work ethic yet nothing of the woman's personality, no insight into the real Jaynee Johnson came out in their words. To me, she remained as artificial in real life as she had appeared on the screen. I grabbed the paper off the table and threw it on the bench beside me in disgust.

I read the letters page in the *Observer* while I enjoyed my ham and chips then fetched another glass of wine from the bar. I returned to my seat and searched for an account of the JayJay case in the news section. It took up a mere two paragraphs on page 4. The staid nature of the writing came as a welcome relief from the hysterical style of the *Sunday Scream*, reporting only the facts.

The body of Jaynee Johnson, presenter of the popular Saturday night TV show, Star Steps, was found last Monday by an estate agent and his client viewing an empty property in Crofterton, home of Silverton Studios where the programme is recorded. The star, who had been missing for nearly a week prior to the discovery, had been stabbed with a thin-bladed dagger. Why and how Miss Johnson went to the neat Victorian villa in the centre of the town is currently unknown.

I read on but there was no mention of what she had been wearing or the missing handbag and phone. However, the next sentence held a surprise.

The police team, under the leadership of Chief Superintendent John Ward, head of Crofterton CID, are asking anyone who saw or heard anything in the area on the night of Sunday 6th or morning of Monday 7th June to come forward. The number for the incident room is …

Chief Superintendent John Ward, eh? Well, he was a new one on me. Presumably this was the guy cracking the whip over Jerry Farish and his sergeants' heads. Which could explain why my dinner date from yesterday had been like a cat on hot bricks on Thursday and needed to relax last night.

"Ah, there you are, Verity. I thought I'd find you here."

I looked up in surprise as Jim Hamilton slid into the chair opposite me and raised his glass.

"*Hobgoblin* on draught," he told me. "I'm impressed."

"Hello, Jim. What are you doing here? We don't often see you round these parts."

"I came to see you."

He smiled but then my heart sank as he reached across the table and put his hand on mine. This looked like a complication I could well do without. Still, maybe I could turn it to my advantage.

"Have you come to pump me about last Monday?" I asked as I folded up the paper and put it on top of its down-market companion.

"No, not at all but seeing you on Wednesday reminded me we hadn't been out for a drink together in ages. I called at your flat first and then came on here."

"I treated myself to Sunday lunch here," I told him.

"Any good?"

"Yes, it is. They buy all their fresh produce from a local farm, including the home cured ham I had with my chips, and it's first-rate quality."

"You're quite the gourmet, aren't you, Verity?"

"Hardly." I laughed. "I just enjoy my food. I shall probably pay for it in later life like my mother did. You know, spreading sideways like a ripe brie."

"I can't see that. You'll probably stay svelte until well into your seventies. So, have the police hauled you in for questioning, yet?"

"Me? No. Why should they?"

He gave a short laugh.

"You have to be their chief suspect. Statistically, the person who committed the murder is far more likely to supposedly 'discover' the body."

I stared at him in horror. Surely, he couldn't be serious?

"I'm surprised you don't know that. Working for a crime writer and all."

"I'm a researcher not a writer," I answered automatically, my mind churning.

"Well, I'm sure that wily beggar, Inspector Jeremy Farish, will be around soon. Knowing him, he'd probably dated JayJay at some point himself."

"Knowing him?" I asked with a dry mouth. I felt totally stunned.

"Oh, yes. He's quite a man for the ladies, is Fabulous Farish."

He smiled and I felt like smashing my glass into his face. My stupid daydreams of the morning lay shattered, their ruins more extensive than the hill of Troy. I said nothing because I couldn't trust myself to speak.

"Cheer up, Verity." Blithely unaware of the devastation he had caused, Jim rabbited inanely on. "We all know you didn't do it."

He grinned and I picked up my glass, fully intending to satisfy my inner rage by carrying out my unspoken threat. He took it from my hand.

"Get you another drink? What would you like?"

"I'll have a bottle of Merlot, please. No! Wait! Make that a case," I replied through gritted teeth.

He laughed again.

"Good idea. Drown your sorrows before they lock you up."

He strolled off towards the now busy bar. I sat with my head in my hands. God! What a fool I had been. Would I always fall for unsuitable men? Men who merely wanted to use me? Thank goodness I hadn't mentioned my dinner date with the Inspector to anybody. How they would laugh at me now. Not, I thought bitterly, that my relationship with Farish was ever going to be on a share-and-share-alike basis—not on the JayJay case, anyway. Well, I would deal with the Inspector when—if—I next saw him.

"You all right, Verity?"

My companion placed the refilled glasses on the table. Poor Jim, it was hardly his fault that Jerry Farish was a cad or that I'd been stupid enough to start falling for him, yet there I'd been mentally offering him physical violence. I must try and make it up to him.

"Yes, thanks. I was just thinking about Jaynee Johnson's murder and what happened to her handbag and phone."

"Umm?" Jim looked puzzled, his top lip covered with a foam of ale, as he sipped his pint and stared at me over the rim of the glass.

"They weren't in the house when I discovered the body," I went on, "so I wonder where they were. Did the police say anything about them in their press release?"

"No. It didn't mention them."

According to Jim, the statement had said nothing more than what I'd just read in the *Observer*. The police were playing this one very tight to their chests, I thought.

"But you say the handbag and phone are missing?"

"Well, they certainly weren't with her." I played with a strand of hair. "Which is odd, don't you think?"

Jim grinned.

"It's more than odd. It's a lead! Thanks, Ver."

"You're welcome. Are you going to ask your friend Inspector Farish about it?"

I made my voice sound as innocent as possible to hide the malicious intent behind the question. If I could make things hot for that two-faced Lothario, so much the better.

"He's not exactly my friend but, yes, I think I might. I'll also have a word with our Women's Editor. There could be a feature in it as well as a news item. Well! This has been a very profitable meeting."

I smiled, more at his eager tone that in agreement. Personally, I had the horrible feeling that I had lost far more than I'd gained.

"Why didn't you tell me?" I demanded, storming into the office the next morning.

"Hmm?" KD looked up from her keyboard.

"Why didn't you warn me?" I snapped.

"Do I detect a note of asperity in your tone this morning, Verity, dear?"

She peered at me over the top of the glasses perched on the end of her nose.

"No. Not at all."

I threw my bag onto the desk where it fell sideways, spilling the contents over the carpet. "Oh, bugger!"

"I see I do," I heard KD murmur as I scrabbled about on the floor.

"Well, good morning, Verity. About what, exactly, have I omitted to tell or warn you?"

Hell's teeth, but she could be very particular in her speech at times.

"You never told me that I would be the police's prime suspect for the murder of Jaynee Johnson." I sat back on my haunches, picking up a lipstick and comb and dropping them into my bag.

"Nonsense! Of course you're not."

"The person who finds the body is more likely to have killed them, statistically speaking, than …"

"Statistics, pfui!" KD put a hand in the air and snapped her fingers. "Statistically speaking, I could make a very good case for you becoming the next Archbishop of Canterbury. You are forgetting motive, means and opportunity. None of which you have."

"Oh."

"Yes. 'Oh', indeed. Who on earth has been filling your head with this rubbish?"

"Jim Hamilton. You remember, my friend the crime reporter."

"He's hardly a friend, Verity, to upset and worry you like this," KD pointed out, softly.

116

I shrugged. I had rather taken Jim's word for things. It had all sounded so very plausible yesterday morning. So, maybe no ulterior motive existed behind Jerry taking me out for dinner, after all. I would still be on my guard, though, when next I heard from Inspector Farish.

"Besides, it's nearly a week since the discovery of JayJay," KD added. "The police would have questioned you far more often and more closely than they have done in that time if you were their chief suspect."

"Really?" My voice was eager.

"Yes, really. So relax. In half an hour I have to leave for an appointment at Mariner Productions."

"Who?"

"They are a TV production company. I'm opening negotiations with them to bring Agnes Merryweather to the small screen and have a meeting scheduled with their CEO, Kenny Cameron, this afternoon. You might also learn something that helps your investigation into JayJay's murder. So, you're coming with me."

Mariner Productions occupied an imposing suite of modern, prestige offices in Middleton Street on the eastern side of Crofterton. By the time we arrived I had left several fingernails embedded in the roof of KD's large saloon car. Her driving, erratic at best and made worse by her nervousness of the forthcoming interview, had left me in dire need of a ladies' room.

I attended to this need while she announced her arrival to the receptionist.

The waiting area at the top of the dog-legged open tread stairs was deeply carpeted in soft shades of blue, the colour enhanced by the darker azure upholstery of the chairs. A huge painted mural on the facing wall depicted a lively, underwater scene where bright-hued fish darted and flittered through pale green fronds, while orange sea anemones clung to jagged coral fingers rising from the sea bed beneath. The potted ferns in gravel-filled tubs standing like sentinels either side of Kenny Cameron's door all added to the watery effect giving me the overwhelming sense of having stepped inside an aquarium. Even Cameron's PA had entered into the spirit of things. Dressed in diaphanous folds of aquamarine with a self-coloured scarf fluttering around her neck and shoulders, she looked for all the world like some modern day water nymph.

"I'm sorry to keep you, Mrs Davenport. Mr Cameron's got Mr Nafti with him at the moment. He arrived from Athens this morning."

"That's quite all right." KD graciously inclined her head.

"May I get you some coffee whilst you are waiting?"

We declined her offer and she drifted effortlessly away.

"Who's Mr Nafti?" I asked when she had gone.

"He owns the company. Greek. Has his own island somewhere in the Aegean."

I made the connection. Of course! Nafti is Greek for sailor—hence Mariner Productions and the watery theme of its rooms.

Kenneth Cameron's door opened.

"Mrs Davenport." He advanced, hand outstretched, as KD rose. "May I introduce Vasos Nafti?" He moved aside to reveal a swarthy-faced man with dark curly hair and a big nose.

"Yassou. Yassou." The man from Athens shook both our hands.

"Please, come in," Cameron indicated the open door.

"It's a real pleasure to meet you, Mrs Davenport. Mrs Nafti reads all your books."

Why was it always the wives, I wondered. I've never yet met a man who admitted that he read any detective stories, let alone KD's contribution to the genre. And what must it be like to read tales set in the supposedly quiet, leafy greenness of the English countryside from a dry, sun kissed island in the eastern Mediterranean? Maybe it seemed as exotic to them as their location was to us.

"We are very excited about our collaboration, is that not so, Kenny?"

Nafti turned to the younger man who smiled in response.

"Indeed. It will be a new horizon for us whilst still retaining the core values of Mariner Productions."

My heart sank. I loathe marketing speak with its abuse and distortion of the language. Verbose and platitudinous, in my opinion all practitioners of this art of stating the blindingly obvious should be lined up against a wall and shot. KD clearly felt the same; disappointment flickered in her eyes at his words.

"And what might those be?"

"A commitment to quality," he began.

Yes, well, he would hardly say the company was committed to producing shoddy work now, would he? Any minute now he would use the word synergy.

"Using viable opportunities for synergy with our collaborators, stakeholders and facilitators."

"Stop right there!" KD held up a hand. "I am not a marketing symposium for you to address, Mr Cameron. I would much prefer it if we continued this conversation in English. I am sure you will agree."

A smile flitted across Nafti's dark features, watching while his employee struggled for a moment—perhaps with the concept of English—before replying.

"As you wish, Mrs Davenport. I think your concept ...erm, idea of adapting the Agnes Merryweather books is an excellent one. We would envisa ..." He caught the look KD threw him and corrected himself. Changing tack, he went on. "How many books have you written? In the Merryweather series, that is?"

"Twelve," said KD. "Were you thinking of using them all?"

I could hear the sound of cash registers ringing in KD's head.

"Not initially, no. I thought six to start with, to whet the viewer's appetite as it were, and then, going forward, the er ..." He gave an apologetic smile, "the remainder after that."

KD nodded.

"I see. Well, you know your business best, I'm sure. The Agnes Merryweather books are massively popular—they sell in their millions, you know—we must hope that translates into viewing figures."

She smiled sweetly. Now I could see pound signs reflecting through Kenny Cameron's pale, almost colourless eyes.

"Who will you get to adapt them?"

He mentioned a name I'd never heard of though KD appeared to recognise it.

"Good. I must insist on seeing the scripts first though. Some of the more recent adaptions of the great AC's work have been appalling, an absolute travesty." She chopped the air with an emphatic hand. Cameron merely looked blank at this mention of the doyenne of crime writing.

"Agatha Christie," I supplied, speaking for the first time.

"Quite so," said KD.

She had been particularly incensed by two episodes in the last Miss Marple TV series where a pair of lovers had lost a gender and become lesbians and a troupe of players, that featured not at all in the original book, had been invented and shoe horned into the plot for the sole purpose of giving a so-called comedienne a leading role.

"What about casting?" demanded KD. "Will I get a say in that?"

"I'm sure our casting director would take your suggestions on board."

"Good." She ignored his momentary relapse. "Only, I quite fancy Barbara Flynn in the lead role."

"Hmm."

The sandy haired Cameron considered this for a moment. If he says I can see where you're coming from, she'll hit him, I thought, relishing the prospect. Unfortunately, my pugilistic hopes were not to be realised.

"Well, we shall certainly consider that."

"Do you have any idea of when the project is likely to start?"

"I was thinking of early in the new year. Obviously there are financial and legal aspects to be worked on first though. With your approval, I'll approach the screenwriter this week to make sure he is available. Once that is sorted to our mutual satisfaction, it will be full steam ahead."

He beamed, presumably on having uttered the entire sentence with only the merest of clichés and without recourse to a single instance of his habitual weasel words.

"I'll have my agent contact you to discuss finances and contracts," KD informed him, rising to leave.

"One other thing before you go."

She sat down again.

Cameron indicated Vasos, who had sat silently since his claim to be excited, watching his production director dig his own holes and attempt to climb out of them again. Now he leaned forward and said,

"We are planning a series of chat shows with a female host interviewing women of distinction. Would you consider being a guest on the show?"

If KD was disappointed that Nafti hadn't asked her to present it she gave no sign.

"Of course. Who will be hosting the programme?"

It was Cameron who answered, blinking his gingery eyelashes for a moment before chosing his words with care.

"Sadly, our hoped-for presenter is no longer available."

I made an intuitive leap.

"Jaynee Johnson?" I suggested.

His wariness remained but there was a flicker of some other emotion in his eyes. Fear, perhaps?

"Yes. Jaynee would have been perfect..."

A genuine sadness replaced the fear, if fear it had been. He looked about ready to burst into tears. His voice actually trembled as he added, "She will be sadly missed."

KD and I exchanged a glance.

"Do you have an alternative lined up?" she asked.

"We are working on that. For the moment it is enough to know that you are interested and we are glad to have you on board."

He had himself under control again and smiled broadly at my employer.

We left Mariner Productions shortly after. I knew KD well enough by now to realise that she had been boiling up throughout most of the interview but, fortunately, we were in the car park before she finally blew a head gasket.

"What a dreadful little man. I'll make sure Crispy Bacon-Sandwich screws him and his wretched company for every penny!"

I struggled to keep up with her furious stride towards the car. Frankly, I didn't much care for Kenny Cameron either but his reactions to the mention of JayJay intrigued me. There were a lot of questions I would like to ask Mr Cameron, though how to engineer this for the moment defeated me. And what of Jaynee? Had she been intending this as another string to her bow or had she been thinking of leaving *Star Steps* altogether? And was this sufficient motive to kill her?

"And I was really disappointed in Yassou Nafti. I'd hoped he'd look more like Tom Conti in *Shirley Valentine*. What on earth is the matter, Verity?"

Gripped by a sudden fit of the giggles and doubled over with laughter, I vainly tried to fasten my seat belt.

"Stop it!" She glared at me. "Control yourself."

I reached into my pocket for a tissue with which to wipe my streaming eyes.

"Please, KD. Don't call him Yassou Nafti to his face," I managed to gasp when my voice was back under control.

"Why not? It's his name!"

"No it isn't. His name is Vasos Nafti. Vasos. Don't call him

Yassou Nafti whatever you do. It's Greek for 'hello sailor'."

I was still laughing when KD stamped on the accelerator and we shot out of the car park.

Dinner over and done with, I was slumped on the settee, totally out of sorts with the world and everyone in it—especially me—when Jerry Farish called. Still trying to come to terms with Jim's revelations, KD's comments and my own feelings, I felt ill-prepared for his visit, nervous and fidgety, scared of losing my temper.

"These are for you."

I took the proffered roses from his outstretched hand—and put them straight in the bin.

"Oh! Don't you like flowers?"

"Not when they're used as a bribe I don't, no."

"A bribe?" he asked in measured tones, one brown eyebrow raised.

"Do you always treat your chief suspects to dinner and flowers? Or did you single me out for special attention?"

He looked at me suspiciously, then indicated the wine glass on the draining board.

"Have you been drinking, Verity?"

"Water," I snapped. "Just water."

Annoyingly, he picked up the glass then grunted on seeing the residue of colourless liquid at the bottom. The policeman in him still made him sniff the contents, though, which only stoked the fires of my anger.

"Verity," he began, his eyes pleading with me, "What is all this? What's the matter?"

I turned away. In truth it wasn't fair to blame him; my anger would be better directed at myself for I had broken my own guidelines, my own golden rule. I had allowed myself to hope, permitted myself to dream and ended up hurt, as so often in the past.

"Verity," he said again, softly, touching my shoulder. I shrugged him off and moved so that I put the table between us.

"Why do you think you are our chief suspect?" He tried again.

"Well aren't I? I found her."

I racked my brains for any figures Jim had quoted but his exact words were gone, washed away by the rising tide of anger that had swept over me since yesterday morning.

"Statistically, the person who claims to have discovered a body is most likely to have committed the crime. Isn't that what you policemen believe? "

He ran a hand across his forehead and through his brown locks.

"That is often the case, yes, but look, Verity …"

"And statistically …"

"Damn statistics." He brushed this aside with a gesture of his hand. "There are other factors to be taken into consideration."

"Well, Jim Hamilton …"

"What? That twerp from the Crofterton Gazette? I might have known he'd ferret you out. Is that who's been filling your head with this statistics nonsense?"

His voice was raised as he leaned towards me over the table, hands resting on his knuckles. I took exception to his description of Jim and wasted no time in telling him so.

"How dare you be so rude?" I flung at him. "Jim is a personal and long-standing friend. I trust him."

As though slapped, he took a step backwards but it wasn't my accusation of rudeness that had rocked him.

"And you don't trust me?" he asked quietly, looking me straight in the eye.

"Not when you use the pretext of a dinner date to grill me about the JayJay murder case, I don't."

"I did nothing of the sort," he protested. "It was you who raised that subject when we got back here."

This was so patently true it served only to incense me even more.

"And what of you? You knew Jaynee Johnson, didn't you?"

He looked baffled by this tangent but answered the question anyway.

"Yes, I knew her."

"And did you take her out? Did she get the 'Fabulous Farish' treatment, too?"

I saw his brow darken, the jaw clench in anger at the epithet but it was too late; my temper bubbled over.

"Were you screwing her?"

Conscious of my coarseness I stopped, my lips clamped, the shame of my words colouring my cheeks.

"I wasn't, as it happens. I never had the pleasure. Not that my sex life is any of your business. This case is not your business."

"What do you mean, 'not my business'? I found her wretched body."

"Which gives you no right to interfere with my investigation. Look, I've told you before, stay out of this. And stay out of my life."

"I'm not in your life," I retorted.

"No, you're not but I had thought … even hoped, that you might be."

He wrenched open the door and strode through it, slamming it behind him.

That night, for the first time in fourteen years, I cried myself to sleep.

Chapter 9

AS I'D EXPECTED, I ENCOUNTERED no difficulty getting past reception when I announced my presence at Silverton Studios that Tuesday afternoon. After all, I did have an appointment. I'd made it that morning before I left KD's, though not for another half hour yet, leaving me plenty of time to visit the Penthouse suite. Once out of the lift on the top floor I walked up the remaining two flights of stairs, pulling on a pair of thin cotton gloves as I did so—no point in leaving evidence of my visit. I tapped quietly at John Brackett's door. I'd already checked that he was away from the studios that afternoon, but I wasn't taking any chances. I'd expected to see an enormous room covering the whole of the top floor but found the CEO's office appeared built to more modest proportions, a fact explained by the wooden partitions of the folding wall to my left. The floor to ceiling window that faced me offered a wide view of the surrounding countryside and the studio car park directly below, thus allowing the head of Silverton to observe the comings and goings of his staff and the arrival of visitors from the comfort of his executive chair behind the desk. Only an old fashioned, leather edged blotter and a gilt framed photo of JB's wife (at least I assumed it was his wife—the one KD said he never slept with) cluttered the top. I worked my way quickly and methodically through the drawers on the left hand side finding nothing more interesting than a few executive toys and a printout of Health and Safety regulations. A folder in the top drawer on the other side offered greater food for thought containing, as it did, a list of all the Studio's employees, including contract staff like JayJay and Ferrari, and their current salaries. I gave a silent whistle, quickly scanning the sheets. How much? This lot of talentless dross made more money in a 'season' than I was likely to earn in a lifetime. I put the file back where it came from then hit pay dirt in the drawer below. Written on a single sheet of paper in the neat round lettered hand that I instantly recognised as JayJay's, I read this curious billet–doux, dated Monday 17th May.

'My dear John,

Further to our recent meetings, you are aware of my current dissatisfaction with Star Steps and my desire to quit the show. After considerable reflection, I have decided that a financial incentive, no matter how generous, is an inadequate reason for me to stay, and only the removal of the problem we discussed will suffice for me to remain.

I will leave this in your capable hands, you have always satisfied my needs until now, and await your reply before making further decisions about my future.

Yours, etc

Jaynee Johnson.'

Well! This was a turn up for the books.

I put the letter back and pushed the drawer closed on its silent, easy glide runners when suddenly I caught the sound of voices in the corridor outside. In a panic I ran for the nearest door, barely pushing it to, but not closed, before Candida Clark entered with Greg Ferrari a step behind her.

"Really, Greg. What do you want?"

"You know what I want. It's the price you're asking that's the question."

This sounded like manna to a curious woman like myself and any thoughts I might have had about silently closing the door and leaving them to it vanished like an ice-cube in a heatwave. I bent my ear to the door.

"Did you like my idea?" asked the dancer.

"Loved it! Absolutely loved it." The producer oozed insincerity. "But I can't give you your own show, Greg. The Studios haven't got the money and, besides, you haven't got the ..." she paused. I thought she was going to add 'the talent' but she went on, "... the presentation skills."

"I'm hardly likely to learn them then, am I, if that's the case?"

Greg's reply was the whine of a petulant child.

"Maybe, if you took that show I mentioned ..."

Her voice was soft, caressing, tempting.

"And if I did?" The reply came huskily.

I risked a glance. The pair stood very close together, his hands on her hips, head buried in her neck, mouth close to her ear. She was backed up against the desk with her arms around his neck. With mounting horror, I watched his hands slide upwards, pushing the sheath of her dress almost to her waist—she wore nothing underneath—while she fumbled at the front of his trousers.

Hell's teeth! They weren't going to ...? Were they? They were!

She spread her legs and with a soft moan let him enter her. I had one quick view of Greg Ferrari's rather nice, tight, little butt before silently closing the door and moving away from it.

Oh, great, I thought, as I looked around me. My refuge was John Brackett's personal bathroom. I took the only seat. And waited. Unfortunately the partition walls weren't sound proofed. I consoled myself with the thought that at least this meant I would know when they had finished and ran over their conversation again in my mind. If JayJay's letter and Greg and Candy's conversation was anything to go by, neither of the presenters of *Star Steps* had been particularly happy bunnies of late. Would that be enough for either of the current occupants of the room next door to bump her off, though? And what of the problem she had mentioned in her letter to JB? Had she been asking for someone to be sacked and if so, who? That might be reason enough to kill her but wouldn't the threat of a quick trip to the *Daily Scream* with some salacious gossip about her have been just as effective? Whilst the comment regarding JB always satisfying her needs intrigued me, I decided this was merely a veiled reference to an affair between them. Maybe Holly might know. I would certainly add it to the list of questions I intended to ask when, if, I saw her. I looked at my watch, it said twenty five to three, so I was already late for my appointment. Come on, come on, I thought impatiently, a poor choice of words under the circumstances. Didn't this pair know the meaning of the term 'a quickie'? A final groan announced the finale of their performance and I breathed a sigh of relief. Too soon, as usual, for I heard Candida say, "I'll just use the bathroom."

I cringed, my mouth dry, heart racing, palms wet. A bead of sweat trickled slowly down into the small of my back. I shivered, my throat constricting at the thought of my imminent discovery. Her footsteps approached the door. The handle turned.

"No, wait, Candy."

Just in time Greg's voice stopped her.

"JB's back. He's just pulled in to the car park."

"Shit! Come on, let's get out of here."

I offered up a silent prayer of thanks to a deity I didn't believe in for my deliverance then, when I heard the outer door close, was off the executive porcelain faster than a heat seeking missile. There was no sign of the lovers when I inched open the door and glanced into the corridor. With the penthouse lift fast approaching, I ran for the stairs.

It took me the better part of ten minutes to calm down and regain a measure of composure after my narrow escape. I spent most of that time locked in a cubicle in the ladies where, thankfully, I did not encounter Ms Clark, before I felt ready to face Holly Danvers.

"I'm sorry I'm late, Holly," I said when I finally sat facing her across the desk.

"Oh, don't worry about it." She waved a hand. "Are you all right? Only, you look a bit flushed."

She, on the other hand, looked cool, calm and neat in dark blue trousers and a crisp, white blouse. The string of chunky wooden beads she'd worn on my previous visit had been replaced by a slim gold chain half hidden by the auburn curls.

"Yes, I'm OK thanks. It's this heat. It doesn't suit me."

I was referring to the weather though my comment could have applied just as easily to the passion I'd just witnessed upstairs.

"So, what did you want to see me about? How have you got on with the diary?"

"Not bad. I'm halfway there with the list of names I made before I gave it to the police."

"Did I help on Saturday?"

"Yes, you did. It meant I could cross you of the list."

"Me?" Her voice came out as an indignant squeak. "I can't think why on earth I'd be in there. I mean, it's not as if I saw her anywhere else but here."

"Oh, you were only in there once," I reassured her. "That interview I asked you about."

Mollified, she nodded.

"There's just three now. Three names or entries I can't account for. Dawn, Mr Smith and Spaniel. I don't suppose they mean anything to you?"

She thought about this for a moment, looking gravely at me, forehead creased.

"No, I don't think so. Sorry."

"Well, never mind." I remembered the letter I'd found in the drawer upstairs. "Holly, do you think JayJay could have been having an affair with John Brackett?"

Her eyebrows nearly reached her hairline.

"Golly, no. He's the head of the Studios and he's married."

I wanted to say, "so what?" but in Holly's world view these things were obviously considered to be mutually exclusive.

"What about JayJay and Greg?"

"No. He's already spoken for."

I was so surprised at the sureness of her tone and the flash of cunning behind her eyes as she leant towards me over the desk that I nearly missed the glimpse of a small, golden crucifix that her movement revealed on the chain round her neck.

"Spoken for? In what way?"

"You know, he's engaged."

"Is he? Who to?"

She gave this some thought for a moment before replying.

"I don't know. But it's fairly common knowledge, I think."

Not to me it wasn't, but then I didn't work here and hear all the canteen gossip. Could she be making this up, I wondered. And if so, why? I jotted away on my notebook for a moment, the silence between us growing.

Holly was a definite enigma, I decided, as much an anachronism in her own age as I was in mine. I glanced up at her sharply. There she sat, on the other side of the desk waiting patiently and calmly for me to finish my notes. Then, as if to distract me, she suddenly announced, "I have remembered something that might interest you, though."

"You have?"

"Yes. JayJay was writing a book. An autobiography."

Was she indeed? Now that might well make interesting reading, especially if it was the usual kiss and tell revelations about her celebrity friends.

"That could be very important. Well done."

I smiled across at her pleased face before making a note of this on my pad.

"She also said it was going to be an exposé," Holly pronounced this ex posy, "and would include the struggle of her rise to the top."

I groaned inwardly. Spare me the sob stories of talentless tarts. I reckoned any struggle in JayJay's getting on top merely involved a change in her sexual position.

"Had she finished it?" I asked. "Is it with an agent or publisher?"

"I don't know. She hadn't said anything about that. Not to me, anyway."

"So what had she told you?"

Once again that delicate crease appeared on Holly's brow. After a moment she said, "Well, she said she was writing this book about her life and that it was going to be called 'The Wash'?"

"The Wash?"

"Yes. I said it was a strange title and she said I'd understand when I read it. She promised to give me a signed copy."

Her face drooped with sadness. I thought she might burst in to tears. To change the subject I asked her another question,

"JayJay had a mobile phone, I take it?"

"Of course!"

Her tone suggested I'd asked if the Pope was Catholic.

"She had one of the latest 'iPhones'. I occasionally had to call her on it."

"Recently?"

"Oh, no. Not since April or early May, I shouldn't think."

So it couldn't have been Holly who'd been the last one to call JayJay. Unless she'd called after the killer. So why not admit it? My brain was reeling with too many questions.

"Well thanks, Holly. That's been really helpful. You'll let me know if you remember anything else, won't you?"

She followed me to the door.

"I hope you and the police find who killed her soon, Miss. I miss her," she said simply.

I nodded and softly pulled the door to behind me.

God, but he was beautiful! Beautiful in the classical sense. Standing in front of him outside the restaurant was like being in Florence looking up at Michelangelo's David. Well, all right, not exactly, of course. David hasn't got any clothes on and Greg Ferrari came dressed in Armani.

"Verity! You look wonderful."

He kissed me on the cheek.

"Thank you," I replied as he put a hand beneath my elbow and ushered me into the restaurant.

If Jacques was surprised to see me twice in four days and with two different escorts, he was far too dignified to show it as he led us to our table.

I slid onto the chair Greg held out for me, shivering nervously as his hands brushed my bare shoulders. His presence had made us the centre of attention, heads had turned when we walked in, 'oohs' and 'ahs' of recognition had accompanied our progress through the restaurant. Jacques whisked my napkin off the table, flicking it out before laying it across my lap. There was the merest hint of a raised eyebrow when he handed me the menu before moving smoothly away.

"So, Verity. What do you like to eat? I hope you're not watching your weight."

"No. Do you think I need to?"

Greg laughed, a harsh bark.

"Not at all. It's just that so many women are."

I wondered how many women he went out with.

"What about you?" I asked. "As a dancer you can hardly pile on the pounds."

"Oh, I go to my gym and work out everyday. Dancing does help to keep the weight down and as long as I don't overdo it on the pasta or potatoes my weight is fairly constant."

"Chocolate is my downfall," I said, scanning the menu quickly to make sure Jacques' famous chocolate mousse still featured. It did. I decided to skip a starter. Unfortunately, Greg went for oysters which meant that, when they arrived a short time later, I had to either watch him lasciviously pouring them down his throat or stare at the occupants of the other tables. I chose the latter option.

"I love seafood." He wiped his lips and chin on his napkin. "It reminds me of my childhood in Naples."

"You were born in Naples?"

"Close to. A small town near there, Pozzuoli. We moved to Naples when I was three. I helped my father with his lobster pots and shellfish." His eyes took on a wistful, far-away look, very likely intended to make me think he was remembering the halcyon days of his Italian youth.

In a pig's ear, you did, I thought. For a start it's pronounced Pots - woe - lea, not Pass-you-oli as he'd said it, and if there were any shellfish still in existence in the pollution-rich waters of the Bay of Naples, it wouldn't be long before his father had no customers left alive to eat them.

What an interesting evening this was turning out to be. Twenty minutes in and I'd already caught him out in his first lie. Let's see what else we could unearth of the (literally) fabulous back story of Greg Ferrari.

"So when did you move to England?"

I made my voice casual while turning what I hoped was a suitably rapt gaze upon him.

"I was nineteen. My father had died and my mother decided to start a new life here." He finished the last of Whitby's finest, for which I was inordinately grateful, and signalled to Jacques that he could take the plates away.

"That must have been hard for her."

And totally un-Italian, where families are important and stick together. Still, it tallied with the fact that I had been unable to find out anything about him before the age of twenty. The man seemed to have sprung into life fully formed—like Aphrodite out of Zeus's head, and just as beautiful.

"Yes, but we Ferraris are nothing if not adventurous."

He smiled at that, wrapped up in the fairy tale he had created for himself.

"What other adventurous things have you done?"

I'd thought it an innocent enough question but, for a moment, a look of sheer panic had flitted across the chiselled features.

"Oh, this and that." He waved a dismissive hand, nearly knocking the empty plates that Jacques was carrying from the table behind us onto the floor. The maître d' executed a swerving sidestep manoeuvre equal to any that Ferrari had ever performed with his deceased co-star and sailed smoothly past.

"Do you ever get home to Italy, Greg?"

"Not as much as I would like. My place now is here. I must tell you, Verity,"—he leaned confidentially towards me—"I have great hopes for my future."

"I'm not surprised. A man of your talents."

Even to my own ears it sounded the worst kind of oily, insincere flattery but the man lapped it up as if it was no more than his due. Now was the time to use that self-absorption to my own advantage.

"Will you carry on with *Star Steps?*"

"Perhaps. If they find me a suitable replacement for the divine JayJay."

"I would imagine female presenters are queuing up to star with you, Greg, and there can't be a woman at Silverton unaffected by your looks and charm. You probably have to fight them off."

He appeared to give this outrageous fawning serious consideration for a moment, chin raised, fingers tapping one immaculate cheek bone, before bestowing on me the sort of 'come hither' look that had me crossing my legs and reminding myself that he was my chief suspect for JayJay's murder. Fortunately he shattered the moment with his next words.

"Let's just say I've been able to take my pick of bed-warmers since my arrival at the studios."

Stunned by this monumental piece of arrogance, I missed the moment to ask if this included his co-star when Jacques placed a plate of noisettes of lamb before me and a rare and bloody fillet steak in front of Ferrari and drifted off to fetch the accompaniments—a side salad for me and a plate of chips for my companion.

I ate in peace for a while, enjoying the perfectly cooked meat, so tender that my knife slid through it like butter. I sipped at my wine, Greg's choice—an Italian red too lightweight to properly complement the meat. Still, it was pleasant enough and its low strength meant I stood a better chance of keeping a clear head.

"This is good." Ferrari lifted a slab of steak on his fork.

"So's mine. Well up to the *Chez Jacques* standard."

He nodded but appeared totally uninterested in my culinary opinion.

"I've signed up to do Panto this year, at the Royal Theatre," he suddenly announced, apropos of nothing.

"Oh really? Which one are they doing?"

"Cinderella. I'm playing Buttons." He gulped his wine.

"Have you considered hosting a chat show? You'd be so good at that."

I smiled at him, picking up my glass.

He winked at me. "Well, 's on the cards, Verity."

He slurred the words ever so slightly. Hell's teeth! Was the man pissed, already? On this stuff? I took another sip. Look on the bright side, Verity, I told myself. He might be too drunk to try his luck with me later and my mind was already working on the problem of how to beat a strategic exit. Of course, I might not need to if the man was exhausted after his efforts with Candida that afternoon, but I was taking no chances.

"So really then, you could say that poor JayJay's death hasn't harmed your career at all."

"Well, I don't think I'd go so far as to say that."

Would you go so far as to kill her, though, I wondered, as he looked at me mournfully.

"I shall miss her. She was a great artiste."

"I wonder who killed her?"

He shrugged. "Not me," he said and sounded sincere, "though the police seemed to think so. They gave me a right old grilling, I can tell you."

Jacques removed the plates and handed out the dessert menu. I didn't bother looking. I knew what I'd have.

"I suppose they've interviewed everyone at the Studios?" I said.

"Several times. Our producer went and complained to the studio head, as if there was anything he could do about it. For all I know he was on the receiving end of the third degree from Crofterton's finest himself."

I bridled at this disparaging reference to Jerry Farish and his team notwithstanding our quarrel last night but the news that Candida Clark had complained (about what exactly?) was interesting. I wondered if I could make use of it. Probably not.

"What would you like now, Verity?" Ferrari asked on Jacques' return.

I asked for the chocolate mousse, to which the Frenchman gave a brief, knowing, smile. My companion settled on coffee and an Armagnac. Only once these items had been placed in front of us did Greg consider an infinitely less fascinating topic of conversation than his own life and career - his date for the evening.

"So, Verity, what's it like working for a writer?"

"Very interesting." I kept my reply brief. My mouth was better occupied in enjoying the pure sensual indulgence of Jacques' chocolate creation.

"What are you working on at the moment?"

I think my companion leant towards me but I neither saw nor heard him. For an all too brief moment the world around me faded to insignificance as I gazed at the rich, airy, luscious morsel on the tip of my spoon. Anticipation can be as pleasurable as the fulfilment—but I didn't keep myself waiting long. I almost moaned with delight as the chocolate hit my tongue before filling my mouth and sliding, silkily, luxuriously down my throat. I took another spoonful. And another.

"Mmm?" Had Greg said something?

I placed the last teaspoonful of unalloyed velvety pleasure on my tongue.

"I asked what you were working on just at the moment?"

I licked every last trace of chocolate from the spoon before replacing it, regretfully, on the saucer. That's the problem with Jacques's dessert—it never lasts long enough. With a replete sigh, I finally answered Greg's question.

"Oh, a twenty year old case involving a schoolgirl called Charlotte Neal."

He coughed, spluttering slightly, as if his brandy had gone down the wrong way and the fiery spirit hurt his throat.

"Really?" he managed at last, sounding and looking totally bored by the subject. Discreetly he wiped his eyes and mouth then, with an abrupt change of subject that totally threw me, he said, "I shan't be able to see you home tonight, er, Verity, but I'll get the maître d' to order us two taxis, OK?"

I tried to sound disappointed when I answered but actually felt mightily relieved. Being pawed over by the sexually athletic Greg Ferrari would have ruined the memory of an excellent meal. Given the choice, I'd rather remember the chocolate.

Chapter 10

I AWOKE THE NEXT MORNING aware that I had made what could be a vital connection. While I had slept—my conscious mind and its obsession with the Jaynee Johnson murder put on hold—my subconscious had retrieved the missing fragment, the link that I'd forgotten; the other Charlotte Neal. Over breakfast of coffee, a bowl of Greek yoghurt and a slice of toast, I read through my interview with Chief Superintendent Plover again. Towards the end I had written, 'two Charlotte Neals, hit and run, up north somewhere', and the word 'coincidence' followed by two question marks. In the case of the two girls it was certainly nothing more than a chance similarity in their names but if KD was right and the attack on me had nothing to do with my sudden curiosity about a dead celebrity, then my interest in a twenty year old case, spoken aloud in what I had assumed was an empty wine bar immediately followed by a near nose dive into traffic... well, that might well be no coincidence at all.

"I've got a hair appointment in half an hour," said KD as I walked into the office. "So I'll catch up with you and any reports later, if that's OK?"

"Yes, fine."

"I really must find a new hairdresser. This one cuts beautifully but I can't stand her. She's such a dreadful topper."

"A topper?" Was this a new term for a hairdresser that I'd not come across before?

"Yes, you know the sort. Whatever you've done she can top it. You've had a ten pound win on the lottery but she won thousands. Spent your holiday in Fuengirola? She went to Fiji and, of course, your minor op was nothing compared to her surviving terminal cancer."

"She did?"

"Did what?"

"Survive terminal cancer?" I asked stupidly.

"Don't be ridiculous, Verity. You can't survive something that's terminal."

She looked at me crossly.

"Oh, of course not, sorry."

"Are you all right? Only you don't seem quite 'with it', this morning?"

"I'm sorry, my mind's elsewhere. I was thinking about two Charlotte Neals."

"Two of them? Isn't one enough?"

"Well, if you remember, Superintendent Plover said that another girl had died at the same time."

"Ah, yes. I do remember you saying something about that. My mind had latched on to the local one and forgotten the other. What about her?"

"Well, I think I'd like to look into that case a bit more. It might come in useful, if not now, then sometime in the future."

"Yes, why not? I quite like the idea of having a stockpile of cases to choose from. Right, I must dash. See you when I get back."

I waved a hand as she passed and then reached for the phone.

"Miss Long? Yes of course I remember you." said George Plover in answer to my question. "I've been meaning to call you."

"Have you remembered something about the Charlotte Neal case?"

"Not exactly. It was something that happened later."

"Oh?"

"Her parents had moved away to the coast by then and her father came to the attention of the local force when he was reported for following and harassing a young girl down there. He claimed he'd only been walking behind her. Nothing could be proved and no further action was taken. I thought it might interest you, for your story, I mean."

I laughed.

"It's Kathleen Davenport's story, not mine. I'm just the leg man but thank you. I've made a note and will pass it on. I actually called about the other case. The Charlotte Neal that was killed in a hit and run accident."

"Oh, yes?"

"You said it happened up north somewhere. Can you remember where?"

"Well now, let me think."

The line went quiet for a moment before I heard him muttering to himself.

"Up north or north somewhere? North, north … oh! Of course! You still there, Miss Long?"

"Yes."

"It was Northworthy. Can't remember who was in charge, though he might still be on the force if he was young enough at the time. Is that any help to you?"

"Loads! Thanks, Mr Plover."

"You're welcome."

Northworthy. I did KD's trick of swivelling on my chair while I thought about things. Coming to a decision, I fetched the road atlas from the bookshelf. Northworthy, nestling on the edges of the Peak

District, appeared to be a sizeable town about a hundred miles from Crofterton. I put the atlas away and Googled it. The search engine reckoned it was 102.4 miles from centre to centre and the route looked fairly simple; drive across country to the M1 motorway and then turn left. I could get there in a couple of hours, but what I really needed was a contact in the local police force and I could think of only one way to get it. With a trembling hand I dialled the number of Crofterton police station.

"May I speak to Detective Sergeant Stott, please?"

I gave my name as requested then waited while the connection was made, praying that the sergeant would answer.

"Verity! What a lovely surprise."

Damn! And damn my heart for leaping so when I heard the sound of his voice. Get a grip Verity, I told myself, and stop acting like a fool.

"Good morning, Inspector Farish. I was hoping to speak to your sergeant."

"Won't I do? And why so formal?"

I ignored the second question.

"Very well. I wonder if I might ask a favour, please?"

"Yes, of course I'll take you to dinner again. Unless you'd prefer the cinema, only these days they don't turn the lights down low enough for me to snuggle up and kiss you. I could book seats on the back row, though."

What was the man wittering on about? After my words on Monday, I'd expected him never to want to speak to me again. Now he was burbling away, sounding a bigger fool than I felt.

"I'm thinking of going away."

"Oh."

Suddenly, he was serious.

"Yes, I'm going to Northworthy."

There was no need to tell him it was only for one night.

"And what delights does Northworthy hold that I can't provide

142

you with here?"

He was definitely in a silly mood this morning. Maybe they were making progress or had a breakthrough on the case.

"It's work. I'm researching a case for KD."

"So you will be coming back?"

Did he sound eager or was I just hearing what I wanted to hear in his voice?

"Yes."

"And this is where you need the favour, is it?"

"Yes, I need the name of an Inspector or even a Superintendent at the police station there."

"Do you, indeed? Well, give me a moment."

I waited impatiently, tapping my fingers on the desk while he found the information I'd requested.

"Right, I've got your names. Chief Inspector John Rock and Chief Superintendent Darryl Andrews. I met John Rock on a residential training weekend a few years back. I'll give him a ring and let him know to expect you."

"That is very kind. I hope to call in some time on Friday."

"I'll let him know. Take care of yourself, Verity, and stay out of trouble."

"I will do my best, Inspector," I promised.

He gave a sigh.

"Well, make sure you do. Bye."

I made several more phone calls and wrote a whole pile of notes, both for myself and my employer, before KD got back to the office.

"Hi. How are you getting on?"

"Fine," I said. "I've put all the notes I've made and all the information I have on the other Charlotte Neal on your desk."

She nodded as she helped herself to coffee. With her newly dyed, feather cut hair and black Chanel-style suit she looked like a giant crow.

"And I've spoken to that nice retired policeman, who remembered that the hit and run happened in Northworthy."

"Ah ha."

KD sat at her desk.

"So, if it's all right with you, I thought I'd drive up there tomorrow night and spend Friday researching.

"I did a book signing in Northworthy once."

She wrinkled her nose. KD hates book signings.

"Stayed at a lovely hotel not far from the centre. The Georgian. Friendly and comfortable and reasonably priced. Save your receipts and put it on expenses."

"Thanks, KD."

"When will you be back?"

"Oh, Friday night, all being well. I'll be in for work as usual Monday morning."

I didn't want her thinking I was spending the whole weekend on her expense account.

"Have you told the police yet about that attack on you?"

Her abrupt change of subject threw me.

"Nnn … no," I stammered. "I haven't had the time."

Or the right opening. It is difficult to say 'By the way, I think someone's trying to kill me' when your mouth is covered by a kiss or you're having a flaming row.

"Nonsense. You seem to be spending enough time with that Inspector. Is he sweet on you?"

I blushed.

"I very much doubt it. I'm just his chief suspect for the JayJay murder."

I turned away, pounding at my keyboard, entering 'Georgian Hotel, Northworthy,' into Google.

"Are you sweet on him?"

I have to admit she was nothing if not persistent.

"You could do worse. He's in a good job and it's about time you settled down."

I ignored her, refusing to look away from my computer screen.

"And you're still young enough to have kids. I quite fancy being a surrogate grandmother."

"Stop it, KD. You're about as subtle as a train crash. And you're beginning to sound like my mother."

I swung round ready to lay into her and stopped at sight of her grin. She'd been winding me up. Well, two could play at that game.

"Anyway, I've got more than one string to my bow. You forget I had dinner with Greg Ferrari last night."

Her grin disappeared quicker than a ferret up a drainpipe.

"I don't like that man. Be careful, Verity. It could be him who's trying to kill you."

If I was right about the Charlotte Neal connection, then yes, he probably was. I didn't let on to KD that this was one of my reasons for journeying north. Knowing her, she would only try to stop me and I was determined to get at the truth of Mr Ferrari's background.

"Oh, I don't think Ferrari is any more serious about me than I am about him." I said, casually. "But it was a useful evening, none the less, and the food is always good at *Chez Jacques*."

She made a noise suspiciously like 'harrumph' and reached for the pages I'd placed on her desk.

I made my booking at the Georgian Hotel before leaving for a late lunch.

My lunch had consisted of a cheese and tomato sandwich and a cup of coffee. The sandwich had been soggy, the bland, white bread holding together such a meagre amount of grated cheese and tasteless tomato it had been both unappetising and unfilling. The coffee was a turgid brown sludge, served lukewarm, with all the fresh aroma of used washing up water. I hadn't enjoyed it. In fact, I'd spent the time it took to consume it longing for the contents of KD's marble and chrome kitchen or dreaming of a mouth watering brie-filled baguette at the ABC. Nor were the surroundings any better; drab and dirty beige walls hung with obscure prints in dark and dingy frames by equally obscure and long forgotten artists. I wouldn't be visiting Jenny's Café—'freshly prepared, home cooked food daily'—again any time soon. If I lingered now it was only because I lacked the energy to move—inert of brain and body I ran through my notes again, doodling on a separate pad as I did so.

Trying to get into a dead woman's brain is hardly the easiest task to set yourself, yet I felt driven to understand the woman whose body I had discovered just over a week ago and to play some part in bringing her killer to justice. Maybe I was still suffering from shock, the shock of finding a corpse, close encounters with moving traffic and the dreadful thought that someone had tried to kill me. My bust-up with Jerry hadn't helped my mood either. I sighed, mentally trying to shake the fog from my brain. Thinking of brains brought me round to Holly Danvers. She had been right. Jaynee Johnson had certainly had more intelligence than I had given her credit for. At the moment she was certainly beating me in the 'how to be cryptic' stakes. As for Holly herself, whilst she came across like an ingénue, could I take such innocence seriously?

A couple of girls in their late teens asked if they could join me. The coffee shop was still full with lunchtime shoppers—why did people come here?—and so far I'd had the table to myself. I nodded absently, listlessly, my mind elsewhere.

"Of course."

The two girls, one blonde with a bright purple streak down the side of her hair and enough piercings to stock an ironmongers, placed their cups on the table and noisily pulled back chairs. The other youngster, dressed all in black—and that was just her hair, eyes, lips and fingernails—smiled across at me as she sat down.

"Thank you. Anyway. You'll never guess! I've just seen Greg Ferrari going into House of Fraser."

"Really? Oh, I like him. He's gorgeous, in't he?"

Mention of my chief suspect perked me up. I kept my head averted, eyes on my pad but tuned in my ears to their conversation.

"Yeah, I wouldn't mind a bit of that."

"Oh, he's way out of our league, Rache. He's way too flash for the likes of us."

"Oh, I dunno, Keeley. Stranger fings 'ave 'appened and a girl's got to dream. Still," she sighed sadly, "you're probably right. Shame, innit?"

"Yeah. Anyway," The oddly named Rache—I assumed it was short for Rachel—strove to get back on track. "The thing is, my friend Donna reckons that Ferrari in't his real name. You'll never guess what is?"

"Donna? How would she know?"

How would she indeed? I'd spent more than an hour searching the Internet for Ferrari's background, fruitlessly, as it turned out. I'd been unable to find anything about him before the age of twenty. Even his own website was remarkably reticent about his past and I could dismiss as fantasy the story the man himself had spun the night before. It bore as much resemblance to the truth as the phrase, 'I did not have sexual relations with that woman'. I wrote the words 'GF not his real name' next to the abstract doodle I'd just made on my pad and carried on eavesdropping.

"Well, Donna's mum's Italian, right?"

"Yeah, that's right, she is."

"And she told Donna that Ferrari's Italian for Smith, you know, like in blacksmith."

"Blacksmith?"

Keeley had obviously never heard the word but, thankfully, Rache laboured her point.

"Yeah. So Greg Ferrari is really Greg Smith, then, in't he, if that's right?"

I wanted to jump across the table and kiss her. I wanted to stand up and pump my arms in the air yelling, 'Yes! Yes! Yes!' I wanted to cheer wildly. Instead I kept my face averted to hide my grin, while flicking rapidly back through my book. I made a heavily underlined entry next to JayJay's list, wrote 'GF' next to it and then gave it a tick. The presenter's Mr Smith referred to Greg Ferrari. Four down, two to go. At this point it occurred to me that I should call Jerry Farish and his team to pass on what I'd learned, but told myself they'd probably worked all this out for themselves by now and besides I didn't want to speak to him. Instead I decided to get out of the hot and steamy atmosphere of the café and take a walk to Victoria Park where I could find a shady tree and sit in the open air to mull over this new piece of information. I put my book and pen in my bag, smiled at the two girls and left.

Outside the sun beat down, hitting my skin with all the intensity of a chef's blowtorch on crème brulée. Glad that I had at least applied suncream that morning—the rest of the tube lay in my bag ready for use when I got to the park—I now regretted not bringing a hat or even a scarf with me to shade my head and neck. Accompanying the heat came a sultry, almost damp, feeling to the air. Maybe the good weather of the last few days was finally about to break and that would be summer over for another year. I strolled along, anxious to reach the quiet coolness of the trees, my mind occupied by the conundrum of Jaynee's diary but not that distracted that I forgot to pay extra attention at road junctions. I appreciated the element of shutting the stable door after the horse had bolted in this belated sense of caution, but wasn't prepared to help out any would-be killer by making the same mistake twice.

The squeals of happy toddlers excavating the sand pit greeted my entrance to the park, while their older siblings swung and whooped on the children's playground watched over by gossiping mothers. I passed the public toilets—sadly now closed—the floral clock and the wrought iron bandstand before I found a suitable seat under a horse chestnut. The walk had done me good and stimulated my brain for I reached into my bag for book and pen and started writing almost as soon as I'd sat down.

Assuming that Mr Smith *was* Greg Ferrari, then JayJay had seen him on five occasions between February and April. Both the April dates had been on a Friday, a day when, according to Holly, they were not rehearsing or even at the studios. Annoyingly, JayJay had rarely bothered to write down the times of her appointments in the diary—maybe she had a good memory for those—thus making it impossible to tell when exactly she had met her co-star or the nature of their get-togethers. Were they business meetings, committee meetings or political meetings? All of which I thought as unlikely, quite frankly, as the two of them having joined the Golden View Cribbage and Canasta Circle. Which left only lovers' trysts but, if this were so, then their affair had been over before the end of April. Why wait until June to kill her? I heaved a sigh, rubbing the strain from my neck.

A blackbird landed in the border next to my bench. Diligently, it began sorting the leaf litter into separate piles, turning its head first this way then that, until the moist soil below lay revealed, and into which it now drilled its yellow beak. I smiled to myself, amused at the similarities between us. In a way we were both sifting through our respective middens, searching for the prize beneath. The bird cocked a bright eye in my direction before swallowing what it had unearthed. If only finding JayJay's killer were that easy. I fanned myself with my notebook and mopped at the beads of perspiration on my brow. Disturbed by the movement, my companion gave a disapproving chirp and flew away.

Returning to my notes, I wondered again about the link between Smith and Ferrari. Had JayJay simply translated the word or had she used it because she knew that Smith was Greg's real name? And how had she found that out? I scratched at my temple with the end of my pencil. This was all well and good but I still had no motive. Neither the end of their relationship nor the knowledge of any name change would be sufficient cause to kill her, surely?

Betting that Agnes Merryweather never faced these sorts of problems, I decided to give it up for now. I would go home and throw some things in a case for my trip tomorrow and drop in on the ABC wine bar later.

I strolled into Valentino's place about nine o'clock, delighted to find it so busy that I had to fight my way to the bar. The fact that my favourite stool was occupied was a small price to pay for the good business Val was doing and besides, he passed me a glass of wine as soon as I came within reach of the counter. He even waved aside my offer of payment—now that's my idea of a good barman!

I wasn't drunk by the time I left nearly two hours later but I'd had enough to make me glad I'd decided to come into town on the bus and take a taxi home. Black Cat Cars had an office about half a mile away on the other side of the canal; it was a fine night, warm and still, and I didn't mind the walk. It would clear the last vestiges of Merlot from my brain, or so I hoped, and give me time to think. I was still wrestling with the motive for Jaynee Johnson's murder and moving out of my flat in Sutton Harcourt and I needed to make decisions.

Instead, my thoughts kept coming back to little Charlotte Neal and what had happened to her all those years ago. Something was nagging at the back of my brain. Someone, somewhere had said something that might be important, something that had passed me by at the time. But who, where, when and what escaped me. I wasn't even sure it had to do with that case. Maybe it was a snatch of conversation I'd heard at Silverton Studios, from Candida perhaps. I could always check on that when I got home, I had written plenty of notes in my book during the interview and Ms Clark had been nothing if not forthcoming. I dodged a young couple saying a passionate goodnight outside a Chinese takeaway—really! The places they choose—trying to scratch at the itch in my memory. It remained elusive. Maybe I needed to sleep on it and would wake up tomorrow morning with the answer fresh in my mind, though I considered it far more likely I'd wake with a hangover.

I had reached the end of the shops along the high street and with it the comforting yellow glow of their neon lights. Ahead of me now lay a dark patch leading up to and over the canal bridge with the taxi office a hundred yards or so beyond that. I walked into the blackness and onto the bridge feeling the rough stone of the centuries-old parapet under my hand, hearing the lapping of water. When I reached the top I stopped, taking a moment to let my eyes adjust to the lower light levels. Above me the bright stars of the summer triangle sailed through the June night. I brought my gaze downwards, leaning on the top of the stone. It was very quiet and still. Below me a narrow boat lay moored, its ropes taut to the tow-path, cabin lights barely masked by floral curtains. I stood on tiptoe and peered over.

Suddenly, everything was happening at once. I heard a pattering noise, strong hands gripped my legs, I was pitched forward and barely had time to scream out, "What the ...", before being catapulted into the inky blackness below.

It wasn't a graceful dive, no forward somersault, half-pike and twist, but there was definitely a degree of difficulty in it as, arms and legs flailing wildly, I cleaved the ice-cold, filthy water with all the elegance of a pregnant buffalo and went under.

Fortunately, canals aren't deep and I came to the surface quickly, coughing and spluttering, hair and weed plastered over my face. I felt a thump in my back and thrashed about madly, convinced whoever had thrown me from the bridge was hanging around to finish me off.

"Keep still, gal," came a man's deep voice. "I've got the boat hook on yer."

I relaxed as someone skilfully drew me in to the side of the narrow boat.

Then a woman's voice said, "I told you I'd heard a splash. Get her up, Ned, and bring her in. I'll put the kettle on."

Well-muscled arms reached down to grasp mine and hauled me

over the side of the boat where I lay for a moment doing my best impression of a freshly caught trout.

"Thank you," I managed, as I staggered to my feet feeling like a drowned rat. I probably looked like one, too. I shivered with shock as much as with cold as the man led me down the steps and inside.

"Welcome to *The Mermaid's Lair*. I'm Ned, Ned Oldfield, and this good lady is my wife, Alice."

"Verity Long," I replied in a shaky voice as Ned wrapped a blanket round my shoulders and settled me on a chair.

His wife put a mug of hot, sweet tea in my hands and I hunched over it, sipping the dark brown liquid, warming my hands as well as my insides.

"How on earth did you come to end up in the canal, gal?" Ned asked, having brushed aside my thanks.

"I was pushed in, I think. Well, thrown in, really," I amended, remembering the arms around my legs.

"Thrown in?"

"Yes. It was probably somebody's idea of a prank." I tried to make light of it.

"Harrumph. Not much of a prank in my estimation," said Ned.

Nor in mine either but I didn't want to admit to this kind stranger that someone was trying to kill me. I hadn't truly acknowledged it to myself, yet. I shrugged my shoulders, ignoring the look of concern on the boatman's face.

Alice, who having supplied both the blanket and the drink had left us and gone further down the boat, now returned with a pile of clothing and a large towel.

"I've looked you out some clothes. They're only old ones, I'm afraid," she added apologetically, "but they are dry."

I opened my mouth.

"No, no." She stopped what would have been a churlish attempt to refuse this kindness and I took them from her gratefully.

"Now I think you'd better have a shower, there's plenty of hot water and sitting around in wet clothes after a dip in a stinking canal is not a good idea."

"You have a shower?" I asked, overlooking the implication that I was starting to smell.

Both of them laughed.

"Oh, we've got just about everything in here," said Ned, proudly. "She may be narrow but she's perfectly formed."

Realising he was talking about the boat and not his wife—no one could honestly describe her as narrow—I followed Alice along the companionway.

"You'll find everything you need in there."

She pointed to a door on my right and left me to it.

Showering in a narrowboat is obviously an art form all of itself and one I didn't have time to master. I managed to bang my leg, my bottom and both elbows before emerging clean, sweet smelling and fully dressed, into the corridor.

"Pass me your wet clothes, I'll rinse them though before you go."

I demurred at this kindness but Alice insisted. While she did my laundry Ned showed me the boat, his obvious pride in it well merited.

"Do you live on the canals permanently?" I asked when we returned to the cabin.

"Yes, we do, and travel the length and breadth of the country. At the moment we're heading to the festival at Stoke Bruerne."

"Oh, yes."

I knew it; a pretty little village on the Grand Union Canal with a waterways museum, some twee and expensive shops, and a couple of decent canal-side pubs.

"How are you getting home, lass?" Ned asked, as Alice handed me a bag containing my damp clothes. I explained about the taxi.

"Come on then, I'll walk you round there."

"Thank you. You've both been very kind."

"That's all right, love. Drop in again, soon," said Alice with a wicked grin and a wink.

I relaxed in the back of the taxi, waving goodbye to Ned who'd insisted on seeing me safely on my way, trying in vain to forget the whole incident. But I had to face it. Somebody wanted me dead.

Chapter 11

*Y*OU COULD HAVE BEEN KILLED!"

"Yes. I rather think that was the intention," I pointed out.

"You mark my words," KD carried on as if I hadn't spoken. "Someone is definitely trying to kill you."

It was the morning after my late-night swim in the canal and I'd just filled her in on what had happened. Now we sat in the office drinking freshly brewed coffee. I needed the caffeine, having arrived for work after a poor night's sleep but without any time for breakfast.

"Face it, Verity, it can't be coincidence. Two attempts in a matter of days? You should have gone to the police."

I shrugged.

"It was nearly midnight when I got home. I just wanted to crawl into bed and sleep."

"Even so, you should have told them. Someone is trying to kill you."

"Yes. I know they are! Or it's certainly beginning to look that way," I admitted. "The question is, why?"

She swivelled from side to side on her chair, balancing a pencil between her fingertips, as she considered this.

"Well, I can think of quite a few reasons."

"You can?" I was aghast. I prided myself on being friendly to everyone, though I'll admit I don't suffer fools gladly and have a waspish tongue at times but that was no reason to kill me. Was it?

"Maybe you're getting too close on the Jaynee Johnson case."

"Close, Pfuii!" I dismissed this with a wave of my hand. "KD, I'm not close. I'm miles away from the truth. I've no idea who killed the wretched woman."

"No, but you'd like to find out," she responded sharply, "and you've been asking an awful lot of questions."

I shook my head at this.

"Come on, Verity, whoever murdered JayJay is a pretty dangerous person. They're not going to take kindly to you waltzing in, in your size nines, poking your big nose in where it's not wanted."

"Seven," I muttered.

"What?"

"I only take size seven," I snapped, resenting the suggestion that I had big feet. Or a big nose, for that matter. I ran a thumb and forefinger down the front of my face, just to confirm my mirror wasn't lying to me.

"Whatever. The point is, you should leave it to the police."

I shrugged again.

"That's not going to be easy. I feel involved now. I especially feel involved since some bastard tipped me into the Crofterton arm of the Grand Union Canal."

"And you've no idea who it was?" KD stopped swivelling and leaned forward over the desk.

"No." I shook my head again, trying to remember if I'd seen anyone around as I'd walked towards the bridge and the taxi office.

KD pushed back her chair and started to pace up and down behind the desk. I recognised the signs. She was in what she referred to as 'noveling mode'. Any minute she would say, "What would Agnes Merryweather do?"

She steepled the well manicured fingers, nails painted orange this morning, under her chin.

"What would Agnes Merryweather do?"

I smiled to myself at this demonstration of my psychic powers.

"OK, so let's go back."

She continued to pace and to ponder and I knew better than to interrupt. Her books were always plotted out this way, for her it was a necessary part of the process, but I wasn't best pleased to be considered as merely a character in one of her stories. What had happened to me was real. Somebody had intended me to take a dive—whether headlong into traffic or head first into the canal was immaterial. Somebody wanted me dead.

KD nodded to herself a couple of times and turned to face me.

Before she could say anything, I burst out, "This is for real, you know. I'm not sure I like you turning it into a story with me as the victim."

She gave a grin.

"*Agnes Merryweather and the PA in the Canal?* Sorry, Verity." For a moment she looked shamefaced. "You're right, of course, but fiction can be a useful tool in helping us find the truth, you know."

Great! Kathleen Davenport as philosopher I could well do without. I held my tongue. All I said was, "And what has Agnes told you?"

"Well, as I said, let's go back." She sat down again at the desk. "When did these attacks on you start?"

"Saturday. No, it can't have been. It must have been Friday. I was heading for the car to come back here after my trip to Darrington."

"So you were in Darrington immediately before?"

"No, I was at Val's place. I'd popped into the ABC for a late lunch."

"OK. Who did you see in Val's? What did you talk about?"

I could see where she was heading and I gave the questions some thought before I answered.

"I got to the ABC at about half past one. There were still plenty of customers finishing lunch in the front section but the only one I recognised was that bloke from Knight's. The oily manager chappie, I mean, not Tom Powell. Tom Powell probably can't afford Val's."

"Did you speak to him?"

"No. He didn't even notice me and if he had he wouldn't have remembered me. The only person I spoke to was Val."

She raised an eyebrow and then shook her head.

"I can't see Val involved. Can you?"

"No. Val's my friend and besides he was on the phone when I left. Although …"

"Yes?"

"Well, it's only just occurred to me that both attacks happened after leaving the ABC. The first on Friday lunchtime and the second one last night."

"Hmm. Well, leaving aside the fact that you seem to spend an awful lot of time in that wine bar, let's concentrate on the first attempt. What did you talk about with Val?"

"Whether I should go for the rillettes or the ham. Whether I could risk a glass of wine before I drove here." I could sense KD's growing impatience as I counted these riveting conversational points off on my fingers. "How the job was going."

"Ah," she pounced, "what did you tell him?"

"I was getting to that," I rebuked her as I tried to recall what I'd actually said to Val. It wasn't easy—I'd had several drinks and a couple of sleeps since then.

"Sorry. Go on."

"Well, after I'd eaten my baguette—I chose the rillettes by the way and had a glass of mineral water …"

"Verity!"

I ignored the interruption—I was deliberately winding her up after that jibe about me spending too long at Val's.

"… I told him that I was enjoying the job and that it involved a lot of research. Then I said I'd just been out to Darrington …"

"Did anyone overhear this?"

"I don't think so. The place was just about empty by then. I was on a bar stool, chatting to Valentino at the counter. I said we were looking at using a case from twenty years ago."

"How much detail did you give Val?"

"Not a lot. We don't have much information ourselves on this one, do we? I said it was about a missing schoolgirl and that the police had never found out what happened to her or where she went."

"Did you mention her name?"

"I think I might have done. So what? It would mean nothing to Val. He and Jacques have only been in this country for ten years."

"Hmm…" She pulled at her lower lip, then reached for a tissue to wipe lipstick off her fingers. "Well now, I don't spend as much time in the ABC wine bar as you obviously do. Didn't you tell me there were booths at the back?"

Really! She was beginning to sound like my mother. I glowered at her.

"Yes, there are four. Two on each side."

"So somebody could have been in there and overheard you."

"It's possible," I admitted, "But they must have been in there for a long time. Since before I got there anyway and I didn't hear anyone moving about."

"And you didn't mention anything about JayJay or finding the body when you and Val were talking?"

No, we hadn't. Val had sensed that it wasn't something I was keen to discuss. I wanted to find the woman's killer, yes, but I would sooner forget the memory of that slim, young figure on the bed. I shook my head.

"I'm probably barking up the wrong tree anyway," KD went on. "It's far more likely that the attacks on you are connected with the killing of JayJay, not Charlotte Neal's disappearance all that time ago."

"Agreed." Although I quite liked the idea of Roger Hughes lurking unseen in a wine bar. When I suggested this, though, KD didn't seem convinced.

"You're really sold on the idea that he had something to do with it, aren't you?"

"I don't know, it just seems likely to me but I do think he's the ideal villain for your story."

"We'll see. I'm thinking of calling her Emily Howard, by the way."

I nodded, glad to have got off the subject of real-life crime but KD wasn't finished yet.

"Do me a favour, Verity. Go back and ask Val if anyone followed you out of the wine bar on Friday afternoon or last night, for that matter. No, please," she continued, seeing the sceptical look on my face, "I'm concerned for your safety. Why should the attempts stop at two? Whoever it is could, possibly, try again."

"Thanks, KD. That's a comforting thought."

"I'm serious."

She looked it.

"OK, I'll ask Val."

"Good."

The further north I drove the darker it became, as the weather rapidly deteriorated. Storm clouds boiling up in the west rampaged towards a similar dark mass coming from the east. They met over my head, with all the fury they could muster, like some celestial clash of titans. The wind howled in frustration as it proved incapable of deflecting the torrential rain which fell straight down, a string of shining drops in the car's headlights. The windscreen wipers were set to overdrive but it was still almost impossible to see. I cursed myself for a fool for coming off the motorway when I did. It was madness to try and find the short cut through to Northworthy in this weather. Had I missed the turning? I strained my eyes through the sodden gloom, convinced

I was driving towards the middle of nowhere. I slowed down and dipped my headlights as another car came towards me and, as I did so, saw the turning to the left. A drunken, wooden signpost, pointing more towards the ground than the road, said Upton and Northworthy. I breathed a sigh of relief. Not far now, a mere five miles if the distance could be trusted.

The rain had passed and the skies held the promise of a clear evening by the time I pulled into the hotel car park. The storm had taken with it the excessive heat of the last few days and I felt glad of my jacket as I approached the front door. The Georgian had once been an elegant town house, its smooth, cream-coloured face to the street, proudly announcing its owner to be a man of taste and wealth. Instead of ripping the building's heart out in a frenzy of glass and chrome, whoever had modernised it had done so with style and sympathy. Polished wood, plain walls and soft-hued patterned carpets greeted the guest with the offer of warmth and comfort. The welcome from the receptionist was equally cordial as I checked in, without any "Howdy, my name is Lisa and I'm your receptionist this evening. How may I serve you at this time?" The Georgian approach was far more discreet.

"Good evening, madam, do you have a reservation?"

I gave my name and credit card details then, the niceties sorted to our mutual satisfaction, she pushed a key across the desk to me.

"Can you recommend a restaurant for this evening, please?" I asked, glancing at my watch which showed seven o'clock.

"Do you know the town, madam?"

When I admitted I didn't and that I would be on foot, she reached for a pocket-sized map spreading it out across the counter between us.

"There's a very nice French restaurant on Monk's Gate and a Thai restaurant a little further along on the opposite side."

She marked the locations on the map with neat crosses.

"After that the road becomes the Wardrow which is almost in the centre. You'll find plenty to choose from there: Mexican, Chinese, whatever you fancy."

I smiled my thanks taking the carefully refolded map from her outstretched hand.

"The front door is locked at 11 o'clock. If you are likely to be late back I can give you the key."

How very trusting, I thought, as she reached into a drawer beneath the desk.

"No, that's all right. I promise to be home by half past ten."

She smiled at that, closing the drawer. "Well, if you change your mind, you can pick one up on your way out. Room 12 is on the first floor. Turn left at the top of the stairs."

It was easy to find and just as easy to feel at home as soon as I opened the door. It had the usual items to remind you that you were in a hotel and not the home of a rich friend—the mini bar, the tea and coffee making equipment, the chocolate on the pillow—but the furniture, mainly rosewood and mahogany, reflected the period when the place was built. The mattress was firm as I sat on the bed and slipped off my shoes. Impressed by the facilities that it did provide, I was equally pleased by those it didn't. There were no tent-cards written in text-speak, exhorting the guest to 'try our two-4-one deals'—what's wrong with writing the word **for**, for heaven's sake?

Not bad for eighty pounds a night, I reflected. I could have done a lot worse. I switched on the kettle before I headed into the bathroom. Wow! Here was the gleaming chrome and glass, the arctic white tiles, the mixer taps, the press-flush loo. It was like stepping forward in time. Soft white towels lay draped over heated rails and colourful toiletries spilled out of a steel wire basket.

I drank my tea then stripped and showered. The hot water sloughed off my tiredness from the drive though the shower gel— apple and camomile—left me smelling like a herb garden. Invigorated, I slipped into a royal blue skirt and jacket that brought out the auburn colour of my hair, a lighter blue roll neck jumper completing the ensemble. Thus prepared I sallied forth, map in hand, to find some dinner amidst the culinary delights of Northworthy.

I studied the menu with some care in the *French Revolution* restaurant then, having made my choices, I studied the other diners, of which there were few. Out of a possible forty covers only about a quarter of that number were taken. Framed caricatures of Napoleon dotted the plain white walls, the only reference I could see to the Bistro's name. Hopefully that meant the emphasis was on the food not the surroundings or, dreaded word, the ambiance. The smiling waitress who had shown me to my seat at a table against the right hand wall returned to take my order. I asked for a plate of charcuterie followed by a medium rare *steak frites*. As KD was paying, I also ordered a half bottle of house red.

"It's Cabernet Sauvignon, miss. Is that all right?"

I assured her that it was and returned to my perusal of my fellow customers. A table of four twenty-somethings got up to leave, off on a night's clubbing or so I gathered from their conversation, which left a middle aged couple, an older man on his own, and love's young dream. This pair, close to the door, had gazed rapturously into each other's eyes, fingers entwined, for the entire time I'd been in there. Every now and again one or the other of them would heave a sigh. Two cups of coffee in front of them remained untouched. They were either empty or the contents stone cold by now. Aware, suddenly, that I too was being stared at, I looked away. The single man, a fork full of mushrooms close to his mouth gave me a conspiratorial smile. I nodded in reply and took my notebook from my bag.

The memory of Greg Ferrari and the fabrication and lies he had concocted to conceal his past, occupied me for most of the first course, while still allowing me to enjoy the selection of sausage and salami on the plate in front of me. I ate with satisfaction and pleasure, helping myself frequently to slices of soft white loaf on which I spread generous amounts of creamy pale yellow butter. The simplicity of the meal and the wine made a fine counterpoint to my dinner the previous night. Not that the food at *Chez Jacques* is elaborate but the history invented by my companion certainly had been. That he was a liar and a fantasist I did not doubt. Whether he was a murderer as well, I would leave until tomorrow. 'Sufficient unto the day' and all that.

The waitress cleared my plate and came back promptly with the main course. I topped up my wine glass and poured a half glass of water from the carafe she had placed on the table earlier. The lovers, arms entwined, had left and, apart from the gentleman sitting on his own across the narrow room and to whom the waitress paid particular attention, I was alone in the place. They must, I thought, eat early in Northworthy and the restaurant probably did not attract much custom mid week - which was a shame for the food was very good. My steak, cooked just as I like it, melted in the mouth and the frites were crisp and golden, still soft on the inside. The house wine proved perfectly drinkable although its label provided me with the usual laugh going on, as it did, about 'sun-ripened fruit'—what other way is there to ripen fruit?—and 'luscious hints of vanilla and pomegranate', neither of which I detected.

I declined the waitress's offer of dessert and asked for a white coffee.

"You permit, ma'm'selle?"

The old man stood at my table indicating one of the empty chairs.

Surprised, I nodded.

"Of course."

"If you do not mind, I should like to join you for coffee and, perhaps, a liqueur, a *digestif*?"

He smiled, seating himself with precision, pulling at his trouser legs so that they did not crease at the knees. He carried a pair of leather gloves and rested his hands on the top of a cane. He reminded me so much of Maurice Chevalier I expected him to break into 'Thank 'Eavens for Leetle Girls' at any moment. Instead he offered an aged hand.

"Henri Broissard."

"Verity Long. You are the owner?"

I indicated the restaurant with a sweep of my hand. It was, I felt, a reasonable assumption after the deference paid him by the waitress.

He bowed his head in acknowledgement.

"Once I was chef patron, now I am only patron."

A regretful tone sounded in his voice to match the sad grey eyes.

"Time passes," I agreed.

The waitress, he called her Jenny, brought my coffee and an espresso for M. Broissard, then scurried behind the small bar to pour a cognac and a Benedictine for me.

"I have not seen you in here before, Ma'm'selle Long."

Did he come in every night, I wondered, with nothing better to do than recognise and observe his customers. Maybe. There had been few enough of them that evening, certainly.

"I am a visitor," I told him. "I've not been to the town before."

"Ah," he nodded, as if this explained everything. "What brings you, may I ask, to Northworthy?"

"My research. I work for a writer and help her find the background to her novels."

"Ah, *bon*. That is interesting."

He swirled the brandy in his glass. I wondered how long he had lived in England. The Gallic accent was still pronounced and he retained the speech patterns of his mother tongue—far more so than Val or Jacques. Being the inquisitive sort, I asked him.

"A long time. Thirty years or more. I still miss Paree."

"Me too."

The long buried memory of Laurent, my flamboyant Parisian lover, resurfaced from the silt-covered depths where I had left it, along with that of the bastard's undisclosed wife. I hate Paris in the Springtime.

"You worked in Paree?"

I dragged my mind back to my current companion and his question.

"No. Just a holiday."

It hadn't been—I'd had a job of sorts—but it was too involved and too complicated to talk about, so I left it at that. It was still, I discovered, a painful subject.

We sat in silence for a while, both wrapped in our own reminiscences, sipping the drinks.

"Where is it that you stay?"

M. Broissard finally broke the hiatus in in our conversation. I couldn't see any harm in telling him.

"I'm at the Georgian Hotel, just up the road."

"Ah, yes. I know it. It is a very comfortable, very friendly place, *n'est-ce pas?*"

"Yes, As long as they don't lock me out."

I looked at my watch—nearly an hour yet before that happened.

"I remember. It is like *Cendrillon*, yes?" He used the French name for Cinderella. "If you do not return from the ball before midnight …"

"I turn into a pumpkin."

He laughed.

"But no, ma'm'selle. You are the wrong shape for a *citrouille*."

I joined in his laughter.

"For the moment."

Give me twenty years of good food like tonight's and I might well come to resemble a pumpkin.

The mention of Cinderella brought to mind my conversation with Greg Ferrari on Tuesday evening. Mentally I shook my head, trying to clear away the vision of a red suited Buttons dancing about the stage of the Royal Theatre in Crofterton around some necessarily static and wooden C-list celebrity with big boobs.

Jenny flitted to the table to ask if we wanted more coffee or brandies.

"No, thank you. It's about time I was going. I'd like the bill, please."

I paid the modest amount—KD would be pleased—with my card and then pushed back my chair.

"Jenny, my coat, *s'il vous plaît.*" The old man rose. "You permit that I walk you to your hotel, ma'm'selle?"

I paused. The waitress, returning with a camel coloured coat, gave me a reassuring nod as she helped him into it to let me know that my companion was unlikely to attack me on the way. Well, why not, I thought. It wasn't far.

Wrapping a white woollen scarf around his neck, M. Broissard looked remarkably dapper with his gloves and cane. He opened the door for me and muttered his goodbyes to the waitress before offering me his arm. I felt as if I'd been transported back to the turn of the century as we ambled along the Old Upchester road.

"I am pleased to have met you, Ma'm'selle Long and I have enjoyed your company this evening. Will your stay in Northworthy be a long one?"

"No. All being well, if I can find what I need, I shall go home tomorrow night."

"Tchah! *C'est dommage.*"

A pity? Well, perhaps. I really hadn't seen enough of the town to be able to agree, or disagree, with that.

"Who knows," I said, smiling at him in the glow of the street lights, "I may come back another time."

"And if you do, you will return to my restaurant, yes?"

"Yes, of course. I enjoyed my meal very much."

I had too. The price hadn't been bad either, at under twenty five quid for two courses, a half bottle of wine, coffee and a Benedictine.

"Good. I am glad."

He watched me go in, standing at the bottom of the stairs leading up to the front door, before raising his hand in an elegant *adieu.* I said goodnight and closed the door.

Once again, I found myself in the house on Willow Drive. Inexorably, my footsteps led down the landing towards the bedroom door.

"It's behind that door," I said to some unseen companion. I faltered, afraid of what lay ahead.

"You must go on. You must open it and enter." A voice urged me onwards.

I reached out with a white, lifeless hand.

"Push it. Push it. Don't be scared. Discover the truth," came the insistent voice. I looked around trying to find the speaker, but I was alone in the dark and dingy corridor. A heavy, cloying fragrance filled the air as the door in front of me shimmered and shook. A face appeared through the panelling and I opened my mouth to scream.

The shrill ring of the telephone on my bedside table roused me from the nightmare. Covered in perspiration I shook myself awake. I hadn't been asleep long—my alarm clock showed 12.10 as I picked up the phone.

"Hello?" I mumbled. "Verity Long."

"Good evening, Verity. Sorry to call so late."

Jerry Farish? For a moment I thought I must still be dreaming. Struggling to wipe the last whispers of sleep from my brain, I eased myself into a more comfortable position in the unfamiliar bed.

"Verity? Are you still there? I'm sorry, did I wake you?"

"Hmm? Yes, sorry. How did you find me?"

"Don't sound so suspicious." His voice seemed relaxed, friendly even. "Mrs Davenport told me where you were."

"Oh? And why did you call my employer?" I was fully awake now and prepared to be difficult. "To check up on me?"

I heard an exasperated sigh from the other end of the phone.

"Actually, she phoned me."

"Oh."

"Yes. She's concerned about you, Verity. So am I since she's spoken to me. Why didn't you tell me about the attacks on you?"

"Oh," I said again.

"Is that all you have to say? 'Oh'? If someone is trying to kill you, don't you think the police ought to know about it?"

"I can take care of myself." It was all I could think of to say. I was still busy wondering why he'd called and what else KD might have told him.

"What, by learning to swim, perhaps? Taking diving lessons, are we?"

I laughed, despite myself, then wished I hadn't. I could love a man who makes me laugh.

"It's no laughing matter, Verity."

"I know. Jerry, I'm sorry."

"That's all well and good …"

"No. I meant, I'm sorry about what I said on Monday. The way I spoke to you. It was unforgivable."

I gulped, though it came out more like a sob, after offering this olive branch. The line went very quiet and for a dreadful moment I thought I'd lost him again. After what seemed like an age I heard him say, "Well, you're forgiven on the condition that you let me take you out to dinner again."

And breathe, I told myself, exhaling the air I'd been holding as I'd waited for his reply.

"I'd like that very much. Thank you," I said, relieved at this second chance.

"Good, then that's settled. Now, tell me about these attacks."

I kept my account of the assaults as brief and undramatic as I could, trying not to make more of them than they warranted.

"So, both attacks happened after leaving the ABC?"

Jerry's voice was matter-of-fact but I hurried to Valentino's defence.

"No, no. I don't think your friend Val is involved but we can't honestly say the same for his clientele, can we?"

"No…o, I suppose not," I agreed.

"Well, I'll have a word with him. Just to see if he can remember who was in the bar on those days. He might recall something useful."

"OK. Jerry, I haven't told Val about what happened. I've hardly had the chance."

"No, understood. Hopefully, you'll be safe enough in Northworthy … as long as you behave yourself."

I played with the telephone wire, running it through my fingers, watching the glimmer of light that filtered under my bedroom door from the hotel corridor. Outside, a lorry rumbled past along the Upchester Road.

"Oh, but Jerry, I don't 'do' behaving." I laughed. "Behaving's boring."

"Wretched girl." He sounded light hearted. "Do I have to come up there and look after you myself?"

"Yes, please," I whispered, low enough for him not to hear.

"Seriously, Verity, just be careful."

"I will be," I promised. "Have you made any headway on the JayJay case? Do you know how she died?"

I held my breath, waiting for his reply. The subject could well be off-limits.

"Yes, we've had the report on the PM. She was drugged with Midazolam before she was stabbed."

"Midazolam?"

"Yes, it's a sedative and one of its side-effects can be lowered blood pressure. Jaynee already suffered from a low BP."

"Does that explain the lack of blood?"

"Yes, partly. The weapon, a fruit-paring knife, wasn't very long— it punctured the heart but didn't skewer her to the bed."

I shuddered silently in the darkness.

"When are you coming home?" He changed the subject quickly.

"Tomorrow evening sometime, all being well. I'm researching for KD in the morning and seeing your contact at the police station tomorrow afternoon."

"OK. Drive safely. I'll call you when you're back. Good night."

"Good night, Jerry."

"Sleep well." He put the phone down.

I lay in the dark for quite a while after the call ended, making no attempt to sleep. Knowing that JayJay had been drugged only raised a lot more questions. How had it been administered? Was she lying down when she was stabbed? And I still didn't know who. I dismissed the problem of JayJay's death and thought instead of my roller-coaster relationship with Jerry. I pulled the light quilt around my shoulders and drifted into sleep.

Chapter 12

L IKE SO MANY GREAT NORTHERN cities that had first fuelled
and then fed upon the Industrial Revolution, Northworthy
appeared unsure of its role, or even if it had one any longer,
in the modern age. The Victorian buildings at its heart might have
been scrubbed and scoured to present a cleaner, more youthful face
to the 21st century but far greater damage had been inflicted upon
the area immediately outside the centre. Gone were the old terraced
houses and the football ground where once on a Saturday workmen
trudged through the streets—freed for a while of the daily grind and
the need to earn a living—to stand and shout on freezing terraces,
roaring on their pride and joy to victory or defeat. All that had been
replaced by a modern all-seater stadium that was as likely to host
bankers, businessmen and sponsors with fat wallets as it was men in
cloth caps. Gone too were the old railway sidings and marshalling
yards, swept away to make room for the new inner ring-road and a
one-way system designed by some sadistic town planner with a
cunning equal to that of Machiavelli. I had driven four times around
the same industrial estate before I found my objective.

The offices of the Northworthy Evening Telegraph had once
occupied Bycliffe House situated on a bustling corner right in the

heart, and therefore the action, of the town centre and not stuck out in the middle of nowhere as it was now.

This information, supplied by the friendly chap on the front desk, was small consolation for the time, and petrol, I had wasted trying to find it.

"Ah. It's a bugger of a one-way system," was his laconic comment when I voiced my opinion of the current location of the building he worked in and the ease, or otherwise, of getting there.

When I explained what I needed he eagerly handed me over to 'our Miss Cunningham from the archive department', a prim looking individual who could have passed for the twin sister of the librarian in Crofterton. However, for all the rigidity of her posture and the tightness of the grey bun on the back of her head, she was knowledgeable and efficient, taking me swiftly downstairs—archives are always in some concrete bunker of a basement as if fearing destruction of their precious historical contents by an alien invasion fleet— and placing the relevant enormous ledger in front of me.

"We've only managed to get the last ten years on computer. These are the original editions for 1990."

"That's fine, thank you. Does it include all the pages?"

"Yes, but not any inserts."

"Inserts?"

"Yes, special advertising features, or editions to mark particular events. Like a Royal Visit or a major sporting event, the World Cup or the Olympics, for example."

"Oh, I see. Fortunately, it's not that I want, just the news."

She pointed to the heavy tome she'd placed in front of me.

"Then it's in there."

I thanked her again.

"I'll be at the computer terminal when you're done," she said, and wandered off.

I turned my attention to the pile of papers. They were new, probably unread, slipped into the bindings on the day of printing and never looked at since. The smell of newsprint lifted from the page when I turned it. The paper crackled and felt crisp and fresh. I turned each complete edition from the start of the year until the first of May over and out of the way, then began my search of each individual page.

I found what I wanted right at the end of June, the thirtieth to be precise. It was a small paragraph of no more than two hundred and fifty words under the heading 'Girl Dies in Hit and Run'. The reporter had listed the bare facts, that Charlotte Neill aged 14, of Cotdene Park Road, Cotdene, had been knocked down and killed the previous evening by a driver who did not stop. If anyone was in the vicinity at the time—though the report did not spell out exactly when it had happened—and had witnessed the accident, then they were asked to contact the police, either at Northworthy Central Police Office or their local police station.

This had to be it, despite the discrepancy in the spelling. After all, Neal and Neill sound alike and Chief Inspector Plover might never have seen the name of the girl in Northworthy written down. I made a note of the details to give to Inspector Rock later that afternoon and carried on with my trawl. I went through another month's worth of editions without finding anything more substantial than the original report except for a slim column under the heading 'Police Updates', dated the 14th July. This repeated the request for information on various outstanding crimes including the case that interested me but, other than that, Charlotte Neill's name made no further appearance in the pages of the 'Evening Telegraph'.

Sadly I closed the ledger, suddenly aware of how the time had flown past and that Miss Cunningham now sat eating her lunch. I thanked her for her help, made my way up to ground level and prepared myself to battle once more with the monstrous entity that rejoiced in the name of the Northworthy Inner Ring Road.

The brick built police station hovered on the western side of the town market place. What had once been an elegant, open space with a Victorian Guildhall on the south aspect facing a central fountain and cenotaph had been developed into an eyesore by the addition of a hideous modernistic arts centre, made from black glass and steel, on the northern side.

I gave my name to the desk sergeant and took a seat while I waited to see Detective Chief Inspector John Rock—who had obviously been promoted since Jerry Farish had met him. A young constable escorted me through a labyrinth of corridors before opening a door on the top floor and ushering me inside.

"Come in, Miss Long. Take a seat. My colleague, Detective Inspector Farish has asked me to give you every assistance on an old case you are writing about."

Taking the offered seat, I judged this example of Northworthy's finest to be in his late fifties though his hair and the military moustache on his upper lip were still startlingly black. I suspected Grecian 2000.

Notepad and pen ready on my knee, I once again went through the rigmarole of what I did, who I worked for and the method we used. Chief Inspector Rock listened, hands steepled in front of his face, index fingers pushing at his lower lip. He made a note on the jotter in front of him when I mentioned the case that interested KD, then picked up the phone and gave these particulars to a minion.

"It will take a while to locate the relevant file, Miss Long. It wasn't a case I was personally involved in so I can't give you any first hand information."

His face assumed a sorrowful look, as though he'd admitted to some failing on his part.

"Are you enjoying your visit to Northworthy, Miss Long?"

I assured him that I was—what else could I say?—whilst regretting that my visit would be a brief one. I've never had any talent for small talk but, fortunately, the pretty policewoman who had shown me to the Inspector's office reappeared within a few minutes with a slim brown folder clutched to her chest. She laid it on his desk.

"The case file you requested, sir."

She gave me a friendly smile as she left.

"Now then, let's have a look."

Rock's short, stubby fingers opened the folder, sliding the papers around inside.

"Hmm. Your Inspector Farish has a good memory."

My Inspector Farish? I liked that!

"Oh, Inspector Farish wasn't involved in this. It was Chief Superintendent George Plover who was in charge of the local case, a disappearing schoolgirl called Charlotte Neal. He remembered the coincidence of the girls' names."

He nodded.

"Well, Charlotte Neill, N, E, I, double L," he spelled it out, "was knocked down and killed by a hit and run driver on the 29th of June 1990. We never found who did it."

He shook his head. Once again that sense of personal failure pervaded his words.

"What else can you tell me?" I didn't like to tell him that I'd already gleaned all this from the report in the local paper.

"The car, a Ford Mondeo, had been abandoned about five miles from the scene of the accident. We traced it back to a Mrs Francesca Smith in Cotdene."

My heart gave a lurch at the name. This was it. I was sure of it.

"She claimed it had been stolen earlier in the day—the hit and run happened at about nine thirty at night," he slid a paper aside and read the one beneath, "and it wasn't completely dark."

"Close to the longest day," I said, writing furiously.

"Of course. That would explain it."

"Did Mrs Smith know who had stolen the car?"

He shook his head. "Apparently not. According to the statement taken by Sergeant Peat—he's still here by the way if you want a word

176

with him—she'd been watching the television and heard nothing until she came out about eight o'clock to drive to work."

I sat back in my chair.

"I see. Well, thank you Chief Inspector, you've been most helpful. If I might just have a word with Sergeant Peat?"

He reached for the phone and made arrangements.

The same policewoman reappeared a few minutes later—I wondered if this was her only job, showing people around the station—and placed another folder on Chief Inspector Rock's desk.

"Update on the Mwengo murder, sir."

"Thank you, Liz. Take that down to Al, will you?"

He handed her the folder before standing up.

I rose from my seat, leaning across the desk to shake Rock's outstretched hand.

"Thanks again, Chief Inspector."

"You're most welcome, Miss Long. All part of our Duty to the Public."

His voice reflected the capital letters. Here was a man who probably read all the handouts on the Police Policy Directive and Amendments Thereto over breakfast. For a moment I wondered if Jerry Farish did the same.

I smiled and followed Liz through the door.

I liked Sergeant Al Peat on sight. Short and round with wispy, grey hair over a balding pate, he was a friendly jolly soul who, with the minimum of padding, would have made an excellent Santa Claus at some kid's Christmas party.

He picked up the folder Liz had put on his desk and invited me to take the chair next to his.

"Takes me back, this does." He leafed through the folder, then sat with the sheets in his hand, smiling expectantly at me.

"Mrs Francesca Smith. What do you remember of her or her

family?"

He closed his eyes briefly, trying to picture the scene from twenty years ago.

"She was a widow. Husband had been killed a year or so before in an industrial accident. They both worked at the big Reeson's factory on the edge of town, she had a job on the night shift. He was English, she was Italian. Got very voluble and excited and waved her hands about a lot when we questioned her, as I recall."

He grinned at me, though whether at the memory of Mrs Smith or this depiction of Italians, I couldn't guess. Still, definitely no lobster pots in the Bay of Naples for Mr Smith, then.

"Any children?" I asked, eager to connect Greg Ferrari to this case.

Sergeant Peat looked down at the yellowing pile of paper in his hand.

"One. A son, Graham, aged about 15. He'd been out with his mates playing football on the rec. when the car had been stolen."

"Did either of them have a record?"

"Nope. Clean as a whistle." His faded blue eyes twinkled at me. "You might have expected the lad to have had one, I'll admit. It's a bit of a rough area is Cotdene, got a bad reputation in some parts, but he seemed a good enough kid, only average at school but mad keen on sport."

"What about dancing?"

"Dancing?"

A frown appeared on the lined forehead, taking his wrinkles even deeper.

"I don't think so. Bit unlikely for the residents of that area, I'd say."

"How far away from where the car was stolen did the accident happen?"

"A couple of miles. Greentrees Avenue is on the edge of the estate, you're not far there from open countryside and the main road through to Upton."

I made a note on my pad.

"I don't know this area," I began.

"Here lass, I'll show you."

He got up and pattered on small feet to a large map of the town pinned to the far wall. He peered closely at it for a moment.

"Here's Greentrees Avenue in Cotdene," his left index finger stabbed the map, "and here's where the girl was knocked down."

He pointed to a place about two inches to the right with the other hand.

"This is the Upton Road. The young lass had walked up from the shops and was crossing to get to her house on Cotdene Park Road. The car was found abandoned about here."

His hand moved further to the right.

"I see."

I made a mental note of the approximate positions, I had my own map of Northworthy back at the hotel and would check it when I got back.

"Thank you."

We resumed our seats at Sergeant Peat's desk. He looked preoccupied.

"You look puzzled, Sergeant."

"Hmm? I was just thinking about what you said a minute ago. Understand, Miss, that we didn't concentrate too much on the victim. We don't in a hit and run accident—we're more interested in who drove the vehicle and caused the death. In a murder," he said the word with a relish I found disconcerting, "we'd need to know more about them, the victim that is, their relations, friends and so on."

"Yes?"

"Well, what I'm trying to say is, there ain't a lot here," he indicated the sheets on his lap, "about the girl herself, but you mentioning dancing reminded me of what her mother told me when I interviewed her. Charlotte had been attending a local ballet school and had hopes of becoming a dancer when she was older. Funny that, with you asking like you did."

Funny? Hardly. A coincidence? Maybe. Or had Graham Smith, now calling himself Greg Ferrari, deliberately taken the same career path Charlotte Neill had chosen for herself in some strange attempt to expiate his sin? Well, it was possible. I might suggest it to KD. It was the sort of twist she liked.

"Thank you, Sergeant Peat."

I put my notebook away in my bag.

"Oh you're welcome, Miss. Makes a pleasant change to talk over old times with an attractive listener."

Assuring him I could find my own way out—poor young Liz might actually get some real work done once I'd left the building—I smiled and said goodbye.

My visit to Northworthy had certainly proved worthwhile, both from the point of view of a possible new case for KD and my own investigation into the JayJay murder. Proving that Greg Ferrari had once been Graham Smith might be trickier, though my earlier research had proved that it was surprisingly easy to change your name with few, if any legal requirements. I could, if I so wanted, start calling myself Hermione Hellebore or Tallulah Swindon-Wilts and I could even open a bank account or set up a business in those names. However, I couldn't apply for a passport or change the name on my birth certificate without it getting complicated and needing some legal advice—advice that Ferrari could well afford to pay for. The dancer had to be my chief suspect for JayJay's murder—now I just had to work out how he'd done it. I hurried past the abomination of the Arts Centre eager to get back to the Georgian, pick up my car and go home.

I packed my bag, paid my bill at reception, putting the receipt carefully away in my purse for KD to pay me back later, and drove out along the Upton Road towards Cotdene. It was barely six o'clock, still time to have a look at Greentrees Avenue and take a few photos. I had the map on the seat next to me, risking a look every time I pulled up at traffic lights—Northworthy doesn't believe in roundabouts except on the Ring Road—to make sure I didn't get lost. I could see what Sergeant Peat had meant about Cotdene being a rough area. It hadn't improved much in twenty years, that was for sure. The council houses which, from their design, dated back half a century or more, looked for the most part uncared for, their front gardens unkempt, playing host to old settees, fridges and, in one case, a burnt out car. A lot of the houses were boarded up. A parade of derelict shops had undergone similar treatment and was home now to winos, drop outs and illiterate graffiti artists.

It all looked very depressing but slowly, street by street, the condition of the estate began to pick up until, by the time I was within striking distance of my destination, there were real signs of regeneration. I drove round the corner into Greentrees Avenue, slowing down, taking a close look at the homes on either side. I pulled in towards the kerb intending to park up but then, with a gasp, shot out again, accelerating away in a squeal of tyres, face turned to the right. Instead of stopping and taking my hoped for pictures, I drove past the bright red Ferrari, and the tall, unmistakeable figure of its eponymous owner standing talking to an elderly woman on the pavement. I carried on, mind in a whirl, heart pounding against my ribs, possessed by a terror that caused sweat to trickle down my back until I'd calmed down sufficiently to discover myself driving in the wrong direction down the Upton bypass.

I pulled into a service station and got out of the car, legs buckling like two wet noodles. Inside the shop, thinking it a shame they didn't sell brandy, I asked for a coffee and directions to the motorway. My hand was visibly shaking when I handed over the money. Back outside, I looked carefully at the cars on the forecourt and the traffic speeding past but felt safe enough. It isn't easy to hide a red Ferrari.

Sitting in the car I drank the hot brown sludge from its polystyrene beaker hoping the caffeine would settle me. Knowing that I'd been right all along, my suspicions of the dancer proved, brought me no comfort nor any sense of satisfaction. Maybe I wasn't cut out to be a detective—I grinned to myself as I heard KD say, 'what would Agnes Merryweather do?'—because, right now, I just wanted to get away, to put as much distance as I could between me and Northworthy. And never come back again. I was twenty miles down the road and already on the motorway before I felt able to relax and stop checking my rear view mirror every few seconds.

Traffic on the motorway was light for a Friday evening. Making good time, I made a comfort stop at the first roadside place I came to after turning off the M1, rinsing my face in cold water and drying myself with the aid of a paper tissue and the hot air machine. I would call Jerry Farish as soon as I got home, I decided, but I could leave telling KD of my discoveries until tomorrow. Apprehending Jaynee Johnson's killer was the first priority, not solving a twenty year old hit-and-run, even allowing for the fact that the same person had committed both crimes.

Once back on the road I still kept a look-out for an Italian sports car but my earlier terror had receded as the distance from Cotdene had increased. A few cars passed me but the road behind was clear. Not far now from the turn off towards Crofterton. I relaxed and thought about Jerry Farish. I imagined he would move pretty quickly when I passed on my information. The long arm of the law would snake out to bring a killer to justice as his arms had snaked around my waist the other evening. I was so lost in my girlish, romantic fantasy I didn't realise my danger until the first bang came. Lurching forward in my seat, about to pull in to see what was wrong, the car was shunted again. A large truck filled my rear view mirror. Panicking, I put my foot down overshooting the slip road. It was only two miles to the next one but my old car was struggling. Cursing myself for relaxing my guard, I checked the mirror again. The truck pulled out and started to overtake. Who was driving? Who was doing this? I couldn't see clearly, hampered by trying to concentrate on the road and sneak quick glances up into the cab. Was it that bastard, Ferrari? How had he caught me up so fast? What a fool I was to have made those stops, I should have driven straight on until I was home. One hand gripping the wheel, I reached for my bag with the other, feeling inside for my phone. I screamed as the 7½ tonner, now nearly abreast, swung in towards me. I wrenched the wheel to my left just as I hit a button on my phone.

"Hello? Hello? Can you hear me?" I yelled as the driver's side wing mirror slid out of sight, crushed by the side of the truck. I was already on the hard shoulder and the truck came at me again, crumpling my door and the front wing.

"It's Verity Long, I'm on the Crofterton bypass. I'm being run off the road by a truck. It's …"

Too late I saw the parked car, hazard lights flashing, and stamped on my brakes. Nothing happened. Nothing was working, not the car, nor my brain, nor my legs and arms which now, in my hour of need, appeared to belong to someone else.

"Help, please help," I screamed hoping that someone, anyone could hear. Knowing my luck the call had probably gone straight to voice mail.

Acting purely on automatic, relying on my reflexes, I swung the wheel hard over to the left to avoid the parked car, shot onto the verge, over the brow of the embankment and down towards the Armco.

"Oh, God, now nobody will know about Greg Ferrari," was my last conscious thought before the crash happened and blackness descended.

Chapter 13

THE DARKNESS MADE IT HARD to see. Taking stock, I decided that either something had touched my hair or, and I wasn't totally happy about this option, there was a large spider on top of my head. For a moment I felt its hairy feet before realising it was someone moving my own hair off my forehead. Whoever did so stroked gently and tenderly. Someone, perhaps the same someone, it was hard to tell without opening my eyes and I didn't want to do that, whispered my name. I knew I was lying down and felt pain in my side and in my knee. Something smooth lay under my right hand, fabric possibly. The stroking continued and I let it, the constant rhythmic movement soothing and restful. I sensed someone bending over me, a lingering kiss on my forehead then my lips. I murmured briefly, I think, before the world went away.

A soft hand picked up mine.

"Mmmm. Kiss me. Kiss me again."

"Not a good idea, really," said a cool voice. "The Medical Ethics Board does tend to take a dim view of that sort of doctor/patient relationship."

My eyes slammed open. To my horror, a total stranger in a white coat stood taking my pulse. On the opposite side of the bed a young nurse attempted to stifle a laugh. Mortified, I did the only thing possible. I closed my eyes, pretended I wasn't there and let the darkness sweep over me again.

This time the kiss on my lips lingered. I opened one eye and just as quickly closed it again.

"I know you're awake, Verity. Stop pretending, my girl, and talk to me."

Damn! I'd been rumbled. I opened the same eye again and this time kept it open. Inspector Farish occupied a chair by the side of my bed, a hospital bed by the look of the sheets and metal frame and seeing him brought everything back. I opened the other eye and tried to sit up. Pain shot through me and I let out a groan.

"He killed her, Jerry, he killed that child all those years ago and she found out so he killed her and then he…" It all came out in one long stream.

"Hush, hush." His strong gentle hands touched my shoulders, forcing me back. "I know I asked you to talk but you're gabbling. Relax, Verity, take your time."

I groaned again, my eyes closing as he eased me back, the pressure of his hands forcing me to obey.

Gabbling, I thought as my head touched the pillow, I'm not gabbling. How dare he say I'm gabbling, I'm not, this is important; he tried to kill me, the man, he forced me off the road, he … he … who was he, it was important, he'd killed her, killed the other one, the man, he'd killed me …

A cool hand took hold of my left wrist. I glanced sideways, a nurse taking my pulse. She smiled at me.

"So you're awake, are you? Just take it easy. I'll get you something to drink in a moment. Are you in pain?"

"Yes, a little."

"I'll get you something for that as well. Do you know your name?"

"Yes."

"Which is?"

"Verity. Verity Long."

"And do you know where you are, Verity?"

I looked around at the bare, white walls, the bed with the curtains around it and the metal stand at one side with the drip tube that curved down into my arm.

"Er ... that would be a hospital, would it?"

I felt the warning pressure of Jerry's hand on mine but the nurse carried on, oblivious to my sarcastic tone.

"Good. You're in Crofterton General Hospital." She looked across at Jerry. "Ten minutes, don't overtax her," she said sternly. "She's lucky to be here, it was one hell of an accident."

She walked away, blue uniform rustling. I turned my head to face Inspector Farish. The nurse's intervention had given me the time to put my shattered, incoherent thoughts into some sort of order.

"Greg Ferrari ran me off the road, didn't he?"

"Somebody did, certainly."

"Yes, well, Greg Ferrari," I began, raising a hand to stop him when he tried to silence me, "killed a child, a child in a hit and run accident twenty years ago. Somehow, Jaynee Johnson found this out so he killed her too to stop her talking. Then he tried to kill me for the same reason. I've got names, dates ..."

He stood up and leant over me, one hand on the metal frame of the bedhead, the other over mine. Was he going away again?

"It's important, Jerry. Ferrari has to be stopped. You have to mpmf, mnf mmf."

I couldn't say any more for his lips covered mine in a warm soft kiss. I let them.

"What was that for?" I asked, when his lips left mine and he walked to the door.

He stopped in the doorway and turned round, half in and half out of the room.

"It was the best way I could think of to stop you talking." He smiled. "Besides, I enjoyed it."

His eyes held the promise of better things to come.

"Get well, Verity, I'll speak to you tomorrow. Your boss will be along shortly and the doctor says you'll be fine—although, in a day or so's time you will have a small garden bird for a while."

And with this cryptic comment he was gone.

By the time KD breezed in a short time later, wearing a big smile and a startling cerise pink jacket, so garish it hurt my eyes and threatened an instant relapse, I was feeling much better. I had occupied the time between the Inspector's departure and her arrival trying to make sense of everything I'd learned in Northworthy but mostly I'd been polishing the memory of that last kiss.

"How are you, my dear?"

KD plonked herself down in the chair vacated by Jerry Farish, spilling grapes and chocolates onto the bed.

"Do you know who you are, where you are and what happened? Oh, I've been so worried about you. You were unconscious for nearly twenty four hours."

If the Inspector thinks I gabble, he really ought to hear KD in full flow, I thought as I removed the bag of grapes to the relative safety of the bedside table.

"Yes, yes and I think so, thank you," I said, though I hadn't realised I'd been out of things for so long.

KD popped a grape into her mouth. Cerise pink lipstick, I noticed, presumably to match the jacket.

"I'm fine, KD, and I'm sorry that I've worried you. Thank you for coming. Now, please tell me what day it is."

"It's Sunday, dear, Sunday morning." She looked at her watch.

"Nearly twelve o'clock. You called me on Friday evening from the bypass, screaming and saying something about being forced off the road. I called the emergency services for an ambulance and the police, and then I had to wait. I would have been here earlier but every time I phoned the hospital the nurses put me off, said you weren't able yet to have visitors."

Sunday, already? So that explained why the nurses constantly kept checking that I wasn't in a coma. I dragged my thoughts back to what KD had just said. Every time she'd phoned, eh? Bless her, she really had been concerned about me.

"I came anyway, in the end. I couldn't stand being at home and not knowing how you were."

"How long have you been here?"

"More than an hour, I think. I saw your Inspector chappie just leaving as I came in and I've been pacing the corridors ever since. The nurse wouldn't let me in. She said you weren't to have too many visitors too close together."

I decided not to try and make sense of this, my brain wasn't up to it at the moment.

"Greg Ferrari killed the other Charlotte Neill," I told her. "The one in Northworthy."

"Please don't talk about it now, Verity. I wish you'd left it to the police, like I told you."

"But …"

"I wish you'd never found the wretched Neal case. I don't want you in danger."

"But …"

"I think I'm going to give up writing from old cases and go back to making it up. It will be much safer for all concerned."

"KD …"

It was no good. In this mood she was as unstoppable as an express train and just as dangerous.

"I'm not going to have my friends risking their lives. Agnes

Merryweather just isn't worth it. From now on I shall ... why, Verity dear, what's the matter?"

To my extreme annoyance I was crying. Salty tears ran down my cheeks, into my mouth, into my hair and onto the pillow. KD whisked out a handkerchief and dabbed at my face.

"But I'll be out of a job," I sobbed like a child. Unable to stop, I blubbered on. "You won't need a researcher any more and I enjoy being your researcher. I don't want to be only a secretary."

This was ridiculous. What had come over me all of a sudden? I made an effort to get a grip on myself.

"I'm sorry, KD."

"It's all right." She squeezed my hand. "It's all right, Verity. You're upset and emotional. And who wouldn't be after what you've gone through?" she added quickly, seeing the look on my face. "Just take a moment to calm down. I shan't be a second."

She left the room and I dabbed at my eyes. Goodness, what a fool I was making of myself. Upset and emotional, indeed! Well, maybe I was. I blamed whatever they'd put in the drip. Yes, that was it. It was the drug's fault.

KD returned in a business-like manner and sat back down. Whatever was coming, I knew she'd brook no argument.

"The nurse has just told me that, all being well, they are going to discharge you tomorrow afternoon, which in my opinion is far too soon but is good news nonetheless. I have arranged with her that they are to order a taxi for you, at my expense, and that you are coming to stay at Bishop Lea with me. No, don't say anything yet."

I hadn't been going to. Right now, I didn't feel capable of anything, let alone organising myself. Or, worse, fighting my employer. For the moment I was happy to leave everything to KD.

"You can't drive home. Your car is a write-off, anyway."

I groaned. Great! More expense.

"But we can see about getting you a new one later. You aren't fit to look after yourself so you can come to me for a few days until you are. Do you understand?"

Well of course I understood. I'd been in a car crash, not had a brain transplant. I nodded meekly.

"Yes, KD, and thank you."

"Pfft! And stop worrying about your job. We'll discuss this when you're home because I have no intention of losing you, Verity. Be very clear on that."

I smiled tremulously at her.

"Right. Now I'm going to leave you to get some rest. I'll see you tomorrow afternoon."

She pecked briefly at my cheek before sailing out, a one-woman marvel, prepared to take on the world.

KD often claimed that Bishop Lea was haunted by the ghost of the departed rock star who had once owned it and if she got up in the night for any reason—she meant her bladder—she would hear the spectral sounds of his music drifting through the darkness. Personally, I thought it far more likely that she had forgotten to turn the radio off before going upstairs to bed. Certainly, no such unearthly sounds had kept me awake the night before.

The taxi had dropped me off at Bishop Lea the previous afternoon and KD had insisted I go straight to bed. I hadn't demurred, I'd had very little rest the night before, finding it impossible to sleep in the hospital. The constant beep of monitors, ringing of alarms and interruptions by the nurse to take my blood pressure were hardly conducive to restful repose. Now I lay on the long, three seater sofa in KD's lounge covered with a fleece blanket and propped up by pillows, looking through my notes on Jaynee Johnson in a desultory way. I still ached all over as a result of the accident and Jerry had been spot on with his cryptic reference to a small garden bird. Noticing blue bruises developing nicely across my ... erm ... chest and down my left side in the shower that morning, I'd begun to appreciate the Inspector's warped sense of humour.

"You have a visitor," KD announced, carrying a huge bouquet of flowers into the room.

"Oh, how lovely!" I said catching sight of them. "And lilies! My favourites. Who sent them?"

"I did," said Jerry Farish, appearing from behind my employer and her armful of trumpets and greenery.

"That's very kind, Inspector."

"I also brought these."

He placed a box of Belgian chocolates on the small table pushed up against the side of the sofa.

"Why, thank you."

I fluttered my eyelashes at him before looking down, coyly. I love a man who buys me chocolates—especially of the Belgian variety.

"How are you?" he asked, pulling a pouffe closer to the sofa and sitting down on it.

"I'm OK, thanks, Jerry."

Hoping I looked wan and palely loitering, as the poet had it, I whispered his name softly. KD took the hint and left us, muttering something about finding a vase and water.

"Have you arrested Greg Ferrari?" I asked when she had gone.

He looked at me gravely.

"No."

"But why ever not?"

I pushed myself up on the pillows the better to berate him.

"Jerry, he killed that girl. I told you. And he tried to kill me. It was definitely him. You should have arrested him for that. You ..."

"Verity."

The voice was low, urgent. He placed a hand over mine.

"We can't arrest him. He's beyond our justice now."

"What?" Had they let him escape? Had he flown to some far-off place with no extradition treaty? What was the man blethering about?

I looked at him blankly.

"He's dead, Verity. Greg Ferrari was murdered three days ago."

"Oh, my God!"

I subsided, turning my face away from him and into the cushioned back of the settee.

"I'm sorry." He squeezed my hand, continuing to leave his own gently on top of mine.

I turned back to face him, seeing the pain in his eyes. Why? Was he blaming himself for this?

"What happened? How was he killed? Stabbed?"

"No." He shook his head. "He was found in his flat, a cable tie tight around his neck. The flat had been trashed, though whether he arrived home and found someone there, searching, or whether the place was turned over after his death we don't yet know. And I owe you an apology. You were right about the girl in Northworthy."

I nodded. Strangely I felt no satisfaction in the fact.

"We broke the news of Ferrari's death to his mother—the woman in Cotdene—and when we asked her about the hit-and-run, she admitted that Greg had been driving the car the night that Charlotte Neill was knocked down and killed."

Poor woman, I thought. Her son had brought her nothing but grief.

"We also think, agree rather, that he tried to kill you."

My eyes flashed.

"He did."

"Yes. His mother told us that he'd rushed off on Friday to see his cousin on the same estate. A cousin who owned a 7½ ton truck. But he can't have killed JayJay."

"What? Look, Jerry, I know it's a different MO this time." His lips quirked at my use of the term. I ignored it. What did he expect? I worked for a crime writer. "But he could still have stabbed Jaynee Johnson."

"She was murdered on the Sunday evening," he began in a patient voice, "the day before you found her."

I grimaced at the memory. He squeezed my hand again, it was getting to be a habit.

"I'm sorry, I didn't mean ..."

"It's all right. Go on."

"Well, Ferrari was in London that evening, in full view of several hundred people at an awards ceremony. He didn't leave until after midnight—by which time JayJay was dead."

"Oh."

My brain ran furiously.

"How long have you known this?"

And why didn't you tell me, I wanted to ask but kept my peace. He'd probably told me more than he should anyway.

He smiled.

"For a while. Like you, we made the connection between Ferrari and Mr Smith. Sergeant Harrison's a bright girl. Then we began a deeper search into his movements and his background."

"Was he drugged too? And how did the killer give Miz - whatever you called it - to JayJay?"

"Midazolam. No, he wasn't and Midazolam is soluble in water, so she probably drank it. It was a hot day, remember."

I nodded.

"I'm sorry about JayJay, Jerry."

It was my turn to give the sympathetic squeeze.

"Oh?"

"Well, I'd forgotten she was your friend ..."

"She wasn't," he interrupted firmly. "It's my job to find her killer but I hardly knew the woman."

He pulled at his lower lip, perhaps debating whether to continue. I remained silent looking at his face as if for the first time; the strong jaw, the brown hair curling over the wide forehead, his straight nose and dark, deep-set eyes.

"I met Jaynee Johnson only once at a civic function last

November. We exchanged no more than a few words, though, luck being what it is, that was long enough to get us snapped by some photographer who sold the picture to the tabloids. I presume that's where your friend Jim Hamilton saw it. And before you say anything …"

He held up a hand; I closed my mouth with a grin.

"… she wasn't my type. For all her modicum of intelligence, behind the make-up and hair dye she was a fairly ordinary woman underneath. Satisfied?"

"Satisfied."

I smiled, retrieved my hand from under his and picked up my notebook again. I flipped through the pages until I found the one on which I'd written the list from JayJay's diary.

"We're still left with two names unaccounted for. Spaniel and Dawn."

He nodded.

"Yes, the two that feature on dates closest to her death. Any ideas, Sherlock?" He grinned.

I stuck my tongue out at him.

"None at all," I admitted, looking down at the book again. "We've identified JB, Holly, Greg Ferrari and Candida …"

"Woh-oh, Candida."

KD's voice filled the room as she carried the flower filled vase to the mantelpiece.

"What?" She looked across at us. "I was only singing."

"Yes, we know. 'Candida' by Tony Orlando. She's named after it, apparently."

"No," said KD.

"Well, that's what she told me," I said.

"No, I meant, it wasn't by Tony Orlando, at least, not the first time it was released. It was by Dawn. Though they did become Tony Orlando and Dawn later, I'll grant you."

Jerry and I looked at each other. Was this what we'd missed?

"Dawn? Really?"

"Oh yes. Believe me, when it first came out, in 1970 I think, well before your time, anyway, it was by Dawn. Google would confirm the year."

"Why would JayJay have two different names for Candida Clark?" asked Jerry, voicing my own thought.

"I don't know. The first was hardly complimentary, though."

"What, thrush? I thought it was just a songbird."

KD guffawed loudly at the Inspector's innocence. I looked down unable to meet the gaze of either of them and unwilling to enlighten him. KD, bless her, had no such niceties.

"My dear Inspector Farish, Candida is the medical term for vaginal thrush, a rather nasty, irritating and persistent fungal infection. Believe me, JayJay was not referring to birds nor was she being complimentary."

I felt my cheeks turning as red as my hair and sank lower down the sofa in the vain hope that it would swallow me during KD's doctor-like explanation. Farish, however, remained unabashed.

"Nasty, irritating and persistent, eh? She really didn't like her, did she? Perhaps Jaynee found cause to change her opinion of the producer if she later referred to Ms Clark as Dawn. Unless," he turned to KD with a wicked gleam in his eye, "you know of any other embarrassing female conditions with that name?"

She gave him her best haughty stare.

"If I can think of any, Inspector, you'll be the first to know."

He left shortly afterwards, telling me to take care, stay out of trouble and behave.

"He doesn't know you well, does he?" remarked KD after he had gone. "Not yet," I replied.

I was working on that, though I didn't feel it necessary to tell her so. I leant back on the pillows, eyes closed, thinking about JayJay's riddles. Jerry had said nothing about not working on the remaining conundrum. Five down, one to go. Spaniel.

I was still scratching my head over the identity of the last remaining name on my list the following morning when the door bell rang. A moment or so later, KD walked into the living room with a large rectangular box.

"What have you got there?" I asked from my semi-reclined position on the sofa.

"It's for you. Something I ordered yesterday. Special delivery," she replied setting the parcel down on the coffee table at the side of the fire place while she fetched a paper knife from the desk.

"For me?"

She pulled a large book from the box and I groaned inwardly. I'd been 'recuperating' at Bishop Lea for nearly three days. Over sixty hours of KD clucking round me like a mother hen was beginning to grate. She had been very kind but I'm not one of those women who 'enjoy' poor health. With the exception of Jerry's very welcome visit, my boss had done her best to keep the world at bay. I hadn't seen a newspaper or any television since the previous Thursday and she had gone to quite inordinate lengths to keep the conversation off the topic of murdered celebrities. Yesterday, when I'd protested that I was bored and needed something to read, she had presented me with a new hard backed tome and said,

"You might like to read this."

"What is it?" I'd asked, picking it up and looking dubiously at the lurid front cover of sand, pyramids and a curvaceous blonde wearing a pith helmet and sitting atop a grinning camel.

"It's a new biography of Dame Freda Park by that dreadful woman Polly Tinker. My publisher has given it to me in exchange for a quotable quote to go on the cover of the next edition."

"Have you read it?"

"Oh yes. Freda Park was an amazing woman. A great adventurer and explorer and an inspiration to her sex. She led a truly exciting life. It's just a shame that the writer of that particular effort,"—she'd pointed to the unopened book in my lap—"couldn't write with the same excitement and panache."

"Is that going to be your 'quotable quote', then?" I suggested mischievously.

KG glowered at me over the top of her glasses.

"Certainly not. Polly Tinker might be seated on the same table as me at the next publisher's lunch and bore me rigid with the details of her forthcoming project."

"Is Freda Park still alive?" I asked, idly flicking through the photos in the middle of the book.

"Heavens no! She disappeared about ten years ago on an expedition to the Hindu Kush. She was over ninety at the time."

"It's a wonder she lived that long if some of these chapter titles are anything to go by. Danger in Darfur, Terror in Timbuktu, Bekkar and Beyond."

"You see! Bloody woman can't write for toffee."

I'd agreed with KD's assessment by the end of the first chapter.

That had been yesterday, and another book was not what I needed right now. I needed—no, wanted—to go home.

"Here we are. Especially for you."

KD carried the huge volume across from the table and placed it, carefully, in my lap. Her face was wreathed in smiles—it would be churlish not to appear delighted at the gift. I looked down.

"Oh."

'The Complete Encyclopedia of Crime', I read. 'Solved and Unsolved Cases From the Middle Ages to the Present Day'.

"It's my latest idea," explained KD from the end of the sofa. "There must be dozens of interesting cases in there for you to check out over the next few months."

Months? It could take years, judging by the thickness and size of it. I flicked through the pages. Arranged alphabetically, it covered everything from the A6 murder to somebody called John Young.

"According to the reviews it contains all the details we need for my stories. And, if we want more information, there's still the internet."

She's determined to keep me out of trouble, I thought, looking at her beaming face.

"Thanks, KD. Do you want me to get started straight away?" I grinned at her. "Seriously, this is going to prove a great help. Where did you find it?"

"Kristy Baker-Sanders mentioned it to me sometime last week, and after our conversation at the hospital ..."—she meant when I'd cried like a baby about losing my job—"... I thought you might find it useful."

"Oh, I'm sure I shall, thank you,"

"I said that I don't want to lose you, Verity, and I meant it. You're too good at your job for me not to take your concerns seriously."

She disappeared in the direction of the kitchen and, easier in my mind, I returned to my self-imposed task of finding JayJay's and Greg's killer.

"We are taking the rest of the day off," announced KD, coming back into the living room an hour later carrying a wicker basket covered with a cloth.

"We are?"

"Yes, you could do with a change of scene and some fresh air. I've made an executive decision."

"Well, OK, though I'm hardly dressed for it. Still, if you insist."

"I do. Bring your notebook and mobile, just in case."

That was more like it. Despite outward appearances and protests to the contrary, KD never switched off, never stopped being a writer. Ideas came to her in the most unlikely places and at the most inconvenient times; it was up to me to keep pace with her, to get everything down for later retrieval. Where she led I would follow. Mind you, I would draw the line at the bathroom door.

"Where are we going?" I asked, when we were in the car.

"You'll see."

KD turned the nose of the Range Rover towards Bellhurst and waited for a break in the traffic, peering to her right to make sure the road was clear before pulling out.

"We are going for a picnic," she said as she accelerated away from Bishop Lea. Behind us the automatic gates swung silently closed.

I checked my watch. Half past eleven, which meant an early lunch or a long drive. Just short of the outskirts of Bellhurst she turned right onto a minor road. With no idea of her ultimate destination, I relaxed and enjoyed the drive. The height of the Range Rover allowed me to see over the tops of the hedgerows to the patchwork quilt of the English countryside stretching away on either side. Green and brown squares were dotted here and there by the bright yellow flash of rape fields, like a Mondrian painting. A tall row of poplars shot past on the left, sheep ambled on a distant hillside, fields of torpid, cud-chewing cows gathered around the single sentinel left standing guard in their midst. I breathed a contented sigh.

"Nearly there," said KD a few miles further on, taking a left hand fork down a country lane. The road was rising, carrying us up an escarpment towards woods of beech and oak. We hadn't passed another vehicle in miles, which was just as well given the width of the Rover and the narrowness of the roads. Almost at the brow of the hill KD stopped just past a gate on the left.

"Shan't be a second."

I waited till she got out of the car and opened the padlocked gate as wide as it would go.

"Here, hold that, will you?"

She dropped a combination lock into my hand before reversing the Range Rover, rather expertly I had to admit, between the gate posts.

"Here we are." She switched off the engine. "Can you close and lock the gate, please, Verity. I'll make a start unloading the car."

I'll say this for my boss, when she plans a picnic she does it in style. None of this sitting on the ground getting grass stains on your clothes whilst sipping lukewarm fizz and nibbling a curled up sandwich. Oh no. The back of the car was packed with folding chairs, a collapsible table, blankets, rugs, a food hamper, two cool boxes, the wicker basket and table cloth she'd been carrying earlier and a wine cooler.

"You've forgotten something," I told her, surveying this baggage train of goodies.

"Oh?"

"Yes, the old fashioned wind up gramophone with trumpet."

She laughed.

"Damn! So I have. And I specifically told old Besom, the butler, to put it in the car. Never mind. We'll have to make do without."

She handed me two of the chairs.

"Just through there. Follow that path and turn right."

I did as I was told, catching my breath in delight at the view that unfolded beyond the thin screen of trees.

"Do you like it? This is one of my favourite places." KD came up behind me with the folding table and a holdall, the rug tucked under her arm.

I nodded. "I can see why. What a view!"

We stood on a grassy ledge on top of the escarpment looking out over the 'green and pleasant land' below.

"Thankfully, I know the man who owns it and he's more than happy to let me come here."

Which explains the padlock, I thought, as we battled with the furniture.

"I'll leave the food in the car for the moment."

KD shook out the rug before laying it on the grass and placing the table on the top of it. From the voluminous black holdall she removed a plastic bowl, a paper bag with salted peanuts in it and two tubes of potato based snacks.

"There."

She sat on one of the chairs and poured the peanuts into the bowl.

"How civilized. Damn, I've left the booze in the car."

"I'll go back for it," I volunteered.

She threw the car keys at me.

"It's in the blue cool box and the glasses are in the white cutlery bag. Bring the wine cooler, as well, will you."

I wandered off, leaving her to apply the sun cream she'd also thought to bring with her. Honestly, travelling with KD is like a planned military operation. She was wasted as a writer. She was a natural born logistics expert.

Seated at last, I poured two glasses of chilled mineral water before re-capping the bottle.

"Water, Verity? There's white wine in there as well."

"No, it's only just gone twelve. The sun isn't over the yardarm, yet."

She laughed, squinting upwards from behind dark glasses. The sun was almost directly overhead, well capable of shaking off the few, thin white clouds that streamed across the sky like strands of uncoloured candy floss. I munched on the snacks and washed the salt away with frequent sips of water. This was better than sitting in an office and I thanked my lucky stars for finding the job as KD's PA. I glanced across at her lying in the chair, eyes closed, wafting a Chinese fan in front of her face. The world seemed a long way away with the only sounds the buzz of insects and trilling, melodic bird song. All it needed was a babbling brook. Or maybe not. The sound of running water always makes me want to go to the loo.

"I think," KD muttered lazily, "Agnes Merryweather needs a place like this. Perhaps our missing schoolgirl," she turned her face towards me, "you know, the Charlotte Neal/Emily Whatshername, character, disappears on a geology field trip up here."

"No. You can't," I said. "That would spoil it. Don't bring death, murder and crime into this perfect place."

"Hmm. Maybe you're right. I could make it a special, thinking place for Agnes to muse in, though, couldn't I?"

"Ye...es," I agreed. "That would work."

"Get your pad a moment." She indicated the bag at my feet.

Reluctantly—I knew it had been too good to last—I did so.

For the next ten minutes, while I wrote it all down, KD described the surroundings—the trees, the fields, the view—in glorious words and phrases that brought it all to life for the poor future reader who couldn't sit here and see it for real as we did. Or, rather, as I did. KD managed the feat with her eyes closed in concentration.

"That will do," she said, sitting up and reaching for a peanut. "Lunch time."

I helped her carry the food hamper and wicker basket from the car. Hardly a starvation diet, I thought, pushing back the hamper's lid, and pulling plates from the holdall. Chicken legs, mini quiches, a film-wrapped bowl of salad, ham, cheese, olives, slices of ready buttered baguette. We could have fed the five thousand on top of that cliff. I poured more water for KD and a glass of chilled Chenin Blanc for myself, while she unloaded sauces, pickles and condiments from the bottom of the basket.

"Are we expecting guests?" I asked, looking at the still half-full hamper.

She giggled.

"Do you think I might have overdone it?"

My reply was merely a raised eyebrow. Nothing if not thorough, my boss. We ate in silence for a while. I took occasional sips of the fresh, flowery wine, its bouquet reminding me of honey and clover.

"There's a bowl of raspberry trifle under that plate of ham, for when you've got room for it." KD rose to her feet, shaking crumbs from her skirt. "I need the loo."

She glanced around.

"You mean you've got a Portaloo in the back of the car?"

I wouldn't have put it past her, but KD grinned.

"Nope, sorry. It will have to be the back of a tree."

She wandered off, leaving me to savour the wine and enjoy the rural peace and tranquility. I must ask her where we are, I thought, having got thoroughly lost on the drive.

"I think," she said, reappearing through the trees, "that we should make a habit of this. We could make it a summer of picnics."

"Sounds good to me."

I spooned trifle into bowls.

"There's a sweet wine, Sauternes, I think, to go with that if you want it."

"No thanks."

I shook my head. The wine I'd drunk already was making me feel tiddly. No point in overdoing it and making myself sick.

An hour later, we packed everything carefully away, stowed it all in the Range Rover and drove back to Bishop Lea. It had been a lovely afternoon, but tomorrow, I was determined I was going home.

Chapter 14

FTER A DETOUR TO A showroom for me to choose a new car, KD dropped me back at my flat the following morning. I unpacked my few things, opened the windows for an hour to air the place after nearly a week shut up, and then caught a bus into town. I knew my absence from the ABC would not have gone unnoticed and I wanted to reassure my friends of my continued existence as well as my continued need for a glass of Merlot.

"Verity! Ah, *chérie*! At last you are returned."

Only one table was still occupied when I entered the wine bar and Valentino had no compunction in telling the young couple who sat there, lingering over empty glasses, that he was closing. He turned the sign round on the door and gave me a big hug before racing off into the kitchens. I heard him call out to his brother and the rapid, excited words that followed before he reappeared carrying a tray with three glasses and a venerable bottle of the family's own *marc*. I hid a smile at this demonstration of the esteem and affection that the D'Ambreys still held for me. It wasn't everyone who was offered a glass of the precious grappa, made by their late father and cherished by all the family and the few others lucky enough to taste it.

"Come. Come and sit down."

Val carried the tray to one of the booths and had barely poured a small amount of the fiery liquid into each glass before Jacques slid on to the seat opposite me. He leaned across and kissed me warmly on both cheeks.

"*Salut!*" Valentino said.

We clinked glasses.

"I am so glad to see you, Verity." Jacques' dark, sardonic features surveyed me closely. "You are better now, yes?"

"Yes, thank you. The hospital released me into KD's care on Monday. How did you know? How did you find out about it?"

I couldn't imagine my boss coming into the wine bar to tell them. It isn't her sort of place.

"It was your friend the policeman. The one who is in love with you."

I coughed, pretending the strong spirit had caught my throat, but failed to hide my surprise.

"Oh, but yes. Did you not know?" said Val.

"I hardly think so, Val."

"Trust me. We Frenchmen can tell these things," he replied while, across the table, his brother nodded in agreement.

Not for the first time I wondered why the French are so convinced they are the only ones to understand love. I hurried to change the subject.

"What else did he want?"

"To ask questions, naturally. He said you had been in an accident. That somebody had been trying to kill you."

Jacques raised an interrogatory eyebrow. I nodded and let him continue.

"He wanted to know about your meal with Greg Ferrari."

"And who had been in the wine bar recently at the same time as you," put in Valentino beside me.

In other words, the same enquiries that KD had told me to make of Val. I took another sip from my glass.

"What did you tell Inspector Farish about my dinner with Ferrari?" I asked Jacques.

He rubbed a finger down the side of his thin nose for a moment before replying.

"Not very much. I could have told him what you'd eaten …"

I grinned, not only at Jacques' phenomenal powers of recall where food is concerned but also at my own memory of his chocolate mousse.

"…but I did not think that the Inspector desired to know your menu choices. He asked if you had left together. I told him that you had left first …"

"That's right." I interrupted. "Greg said he'd order two taxis."

"Non." Jacques shook his head. "While you were using the ladies' room, Ferrari asked me to call a taxi for you but then I see him making a call on his mobile and telling someone to come and pick him up."

"Oh. Do you know who?"

Jacques gave a shrug.

"It was a woman." Valentino supplied. "After he left the restaurant he came in here for a night hat …"

"A nightcap?"

"*Exactement.* Then this woman arrived and he left with her."

"Can you describe her?"

"Tall, perhaps late thirty or forty, yellow blonde hair. You know her?"

Val turned at my inarticulate sound.

"Yes. She works at the studios."

So Greg Ferrari had called his producer after I'd left, had he? Which led me to the obvious question.

"Was he drunk, do you think?"

Val gave a shrug while he considered this.

"Perhaps."

"He had not drunk much wine," Jacques pointed out.

And a thin Italian red, as I recalled, but I'd noticed him slurring his speech during the meal. Perhaps he'd been drinking before he'd arrived at the restaurant.

"Hmm." I ran a finger over my lower lip.

The boys remained silent, waiting for me to continue. Busy wondering if Greg always called his producer when he needed a lift home or whether he had again been in need of the same service she had rendered to him once that day, I sipped at my glass of *marc*. There remained the possibility of another as yet unknown explanation, of course, but Candida Clark's name had just shot to the top of my list of suspects. I really needed to talk to her again.

"You are safe now, Verity? Now this Ferrari is dead? Yes?"

Valentino had asked the question but both the brothers looked at me keenly.

"Oh, yes. I'll be fine now."

I smiled brightly, confidently, in an effort of reassurance but a killer still lurked out there somewhere.

"The good Inspector Farish," Jacques pronounced it Faireesh, "he will protect you, Verity."

Val didn't look convinced but I'd caught the laughter in his brother's eyes and didn't quibble. I just hoped he was right.

My hands were full of wet rocket leaves when the doorbell rang.

"Jerry! What a nice surprise! Come in."

"I'm not disturbing you, am I?"

He looked tired, hag-ridden and careworn and definitely in need of some TLC. I wondered if that was why he had come or whether he had more sinister motives for arriving, unannounced, on my doorstep.

"No, not at all. I was just making myself some supper. Please say you'll stay and join me."

Was it just my imagination or did he look relieved, less tense, less tight in the shoulders, at my invitation?

"I'd love to, thank you. What are we having?"

"Only omelettes and salad," I told him, putting the now dried rocket into a bowl. "With a selection of cheese, Cheddar, Stilton, Brie, for after."

"Great. What can I do to help?"

"You can open the wine to start with."

I pointed to the wine rack under the work surface.

"Any preference?" he asked, sitting on his haunches for a closer look at the half dozen bottles that constituted my wine cellar.

"Mmm. There's a Montepulciano, left hand side, top row, that should do nicely."

I cracked eggs into a bowl, whisking them with a fork until frothy.

"You'll find cutlery, plates and glasses on the dresser thing, behind you."

"The dresser thing?"

His glance travelled round the kitchen till he found it. I watched him as he laid the table placings with military precision.

"You weren't in the army, were you, Jerry?"

"Me? Good heavens, no!" He caught my glance and grinned. "That's what comes from growing up in a large family with only a small dining table."

I took some ham from the fridge along with the cheese to let it come up to room temperature and added lettuce to the salad. Then I reached the frying pan down from the shelf above the stove.

"So, to what do I owe the pleasure of your visit?"

I swung the pan in my hands for a moment. Jerry stared at it as if thinking I might use it to hit him.

"I just wanted to see you. See how the recovery was going. I phoned KD's thinking you were still there. She told me you'd come home already."

Already? I'd been at Bishop Lea for nearly four days, playing the part of the invalid. While it's nice to be pampered once in a while, I had begun to feel overly protected, wrapped up in cotton wool by KD's kindness.

"I'm fine," I reassured him. "I still get the occasional headache but that's no reason to lie, malingering, at KD's."

"Malingering? Hardly that, surely? It was a pretty nasty smash you had, Verity."

I shrugged and turned away from him, pouring eggs into the pan. A good omelette needs constant attention. Like a man, really.

I served his before I made my own, urging him to get started.

"You should always eat an omelette whilst it's hot."

I carried my plate to the table a moment or so later, glad to see him tucking in. We ate in companionable silence.

"Mmm. Excellent." He smiled in satisfaction as he finished the last of the eggs and ham. "Did Jacques teach you how to make such a brilliant omelette?"

He sat back in the chair, fingers interlaced over his stomach.

"Cheek!" I laughed. "I'll have you know that Jacques admits I make a better omelette than he does."

"I can well believe it, if that was an example."

I cleared the plates to the draining board and brought the cheese on to the table.

He picked up his wine—he'd barely touched it so far, but then he was driving—holding the glass by the stem, twirling it back and forth in his fingers, an action that reminded me of my employer.

"Do you enjoy cooking, Verity?"

I reached into the back of the cupboard for a packet of crackers to accompany the cheese before I answered.

"I don't mind it but it's more that I enjoy my food. I should have thought that was obvious," I said, putting a hand on my tummy and waist. In fact, I had lost quite a bit of weight after several days on hospital rations.

He ran an appreciative glance over my body.

"From where I'm sitting, I can't see anything I don't like the look of."

I blushed and sat down offering him a grape from the fruit bowl on the table.

"I take delivery of my new car tomorrow." I changed the subject. "Courtesy of KD."

"That's very generous of her."

"Oh, I shall pay her the insurance money when I get it, but, yes, she is very kind."

"She obviously makes a lot of money from her books."

"Well, I'm her PA not her accountant," I smiled across the table before cutting a sliver of Cheddar, "but I'm sure she does."

"Who says crime doesn't pay?" He laughed. "Maybe I should turn to writing."

"You could always collaborate with KD on your cases."

"Actually, I was thinking of a closer, more personal, collaboration."

His hand closed over mine, hazel brown eyes searched my face, hoping for… for what?

"I'll admit that the middle of an important murder enquiry is hardly the best time to fall in love …" he went on, hesitantly.

"Is that what's happening?" I asked, thinking back to my conversation with Val and Jacques.

"I don't know. But I'd like to find out."

I withdrew my hand. Confused, I left the table, moving our used plates and cutlery to the sink. I squirted washing-up liquid into the bowl before turning on the tap, watching as the contents bubbled and frothed—a pretty good description of my brain at the moment.

He pushed back his chair and came and stood behind me, hands sliding round my waist to hold me, hot breath tickling my skin as he buried his face in my neck.

"Verity, Verity," he murmured.

I could feel my body responding to his, to the brush of his lips on my neck, my throat. I tried to concentrate on the fact that I had my hands deep in soap suds.

"Jerry, this is too soon." I made an effort to sound brisk, matter of fact. "I've barely known you a fortnight."

"Two weeks, three days," he whispered, husky voiced, as his mouth caressed my neck, my cheek, my mouth.

Was the man keeping count? I thought only women did that. Reluctantly I pulled away.

"Tea towel." I pointed to a couple of hooks in the front of the work surface. "Pots. Dry."

"You're a hard woman," he said, sliding his arms, slowly, from around my middle and picking up the cloth.

I wasn't but, never again wanting to be hurt, after Rob had left me I'd built a barrier around my heart. The brickwork had started to crumble when I'd met Valentino but I'd buttressed it well and the wall had remained intact. Did I really want to demolish it now for a man who riled as much as attracted me? Besides, I had other preoccupations at the moment.

"I'm not, Jerry, believe me, I'm not. I just need time to sort my life out. I need to forget all about JayJay, car crashes, and Greg bloody Ferrari before I can think about other things ..."

I placed a freshly washed plate on the drainer.

"Did you fancy Ferrari?"

"No, I fu..."

I'd been about to lash out in fury at the question until I saw the twist to his mouth, the laughter in his eyes.

"His body, yes. Him, no. He was too busy fancying himself."

When we'd finished the pots I took him by the hand and led him through to the living room. He slid his arm round my shoulders as I curled up next to him on the settee.

"You know, Jerry, we've forgotten the book."

"The book?"

"Yes, JayJay's exposé. You remember, Holly told me she was writing a memoir."

"Mmm."

"So what happened to it?"

"Well," he muttered, in between kissing the top of my head gently, soothingly rather than lustfully like before, "There was a page of it under the bed in Willow Drive. Obviously missed by your eagle eye, Miss Marple."

"What?" I pulled away and turned to face him. He laughed.

"No, I'm joking. We found it in her safety deposit box at her bank."

"Oh! And?"

"Well, as a work of literary merit ..."

"Idiot!" I punched him, playfully, on the arm. "Did you find anything in it? Any hint who killed her?"

He drew my head back onto his chest, stroking my hair.

"She certainly didn't hold back. Vicious isn't the word for it, it's pure vitriol in places. And she'd been doing an awful lot of prying into other people's business."

"Mmm? Including Candida Clark throwing acid at somebody, perhaps?"

"How did you know that?" The policeman was back in his voice.

"Just something Holly told me. She overheard part of a conversation JayJay had with Candy without, I think, seeing the significance of it."

I thought back to my first visit to Silverton. According to Holly, JayJay had remarked on 'how disfiguring acid could be'. I'd thought at the time it was a strange way to describe spilling vinegar on a dress and that the presenter had implied far more by it than Holly had realised.

"And you never thought to tell me?"

"Well, you didn't seem to want my help."

I sounded petulant, even to myself.

"I didn't want you getting hurt," he said, quietly.

"And you never told me about finding the book," I pointed out.

"Touché." He smiled briefly before becoming serious again. "She also knew about Ferrari's hit and run and John Brackett's serial womanising."

"But that doesn't help," I cried. "We know that Greg could not have killed her and I hardly think …"

"No, Brackett's out of it as well. He's another one with a cast iron alibi."

He sighed but my thoughts had moved on.

"The bed, that's another thing. How had that got there? And who had a key to Willow Drive?"

I fired questions at him as if thrashing out a story with KD rather than discussing a real murder with the chief detective assigned to the case.

"Oh, the bed's easy. We traced the previous occupants who admitted leaving it there. They'd bought a new one and didn't want the trouble of getting rid of the old when they'd moved out." Shifting his position, he gazed at me sombrely for a moment. "But Verity, if this relationship between us is to develop …"

"Do you want it to?" I asked softly, suddenly aware that his answer was important. I needed to be totally sure of him before I let my defences slip.

"Yes. Haven't I made that obvious?"

"You've made it obvious that you want my body," I pointed out.

He shook his head.

"That's not enough. Yes, I want your body but I also want the rest of you, only you have to understand …"

"That you're a policeman and I'm not?"

"Exactly!"

He looked relieved, smiling at me like a physics professor whose student had finally grasped some abstruse but vital part of relativity. How typically male, I thought, to only see his own side of the argument.

"And you don't think that this might also apply to me?" I said.

"What might?"

"That I might want all of you. Including the bit that's a policeman."

"Oh."

I gave him a moment to let this sink in.

"And I have an enquiring mind, Jerry. I'm curious about things, that's why I do the job I do. Will you accept that," I saw him about to interrupt and hurried on, "if I also accept that I have to stay out of the job you do?"

He heaved a sigh.

"Fair enough. And if you do come up with any more ideas on this case, you will let me know?"

I nestled back against him.

"Of course," I reassured him before adding, "And will you keep me informed of your progress? As far as you can do, that is?"

He gave a sardonic laugh as his arm went round my shoulders.

"If I make any progress, I will, yes."

On Friday morning I woke with an impending sense of excitement. Unsure as to the cause, I didn't linger in my bed but showered and dressed quickly before wandering through to the kitchen for toast and coffee. Over breakfast I tried to analyse why I felt so restless and ill at ease. Was it my relationship with Jerry Farish? I didn't think so. I found him attractive and hard to resist. Soon, I promised myself, I would give up that particular fight. The problem didn't lie with my employer. KD had eased my earlier worries over my job and I appreciated the thought behind buying the encyclopedia. I appreciated even more her kindness in buying me a car and laughed out loud at the memory of our time at the showroom.

"That's the car for you, Verity."

She had pointed out a Citroen C1 at the back of the lot.

"It's such a lovely colour," she'd said, running a hand over the royal blue paintwork. "It goes with your hair and will really suit you," she'd added.

I didn't mind what colour of car I had. As long as it was cheap to run, easy to drive and got me from A to B then my boss could have bought a Ferrari, for all I cared.

Ferrari. I pulled myself up short, shivering at the name. Maybe the cause of my disquiet lay there, in the demise of a man with whom I'd had dinner little more than a week ago. I made more coffee, pacing around the kitchen while I waited for the kettle to boil, getting my thoughts in order. Strangely, I felt no compulsion to investigate the death of Greg as I had with JayJay. For all that I had met and had a meal with the man, somehow his death didn't touch me as much as finding JayJay's body.

Other than asking if I'd fancied him, Jerry had mentioned nothing yesterday regarding the police enquiry into Ferrari's death and I hadn't liked to question him about it. With two high-profile cases on the Inspector's desk, it was scarcely any wonder the man had looked so haggard and careworn when he'd arrived on my doorstep. I made the coffee, stirring the rich brown fluid in a desultory way as I thought about the murders.

My thoughts were interrupted by the arrival of the new car. Once the delivery driver had gone and the keys were in my possession, I phoned KD to let her know.

No sooner had I replaced the phone then it rang again.

"Is that you, Miss Long? It's Holly Danvers here."

"Oh, hello, Holly. How are you?"

"I wondered if you could call round and see me this afternoon, say, about three o'clock?"

Well, why not? It would give me a reason to go somewhere in the new car. I'd had a test drive and been shown where all the buttons and switches were—and which ones operated the lights, indicators, horn and so on—at the showroom the previous morning but the thought of having a tootle, without a car salesman sitting next to me or KD commenting from the back seat, was enticing.

"Yes, OK, Holly. You'd better let the receptionist know that I'm coming. Tell her I'm from *Oh Hi!* magazine."

I might as well use the same subterfuge as before.

"Yes, I'll do that."

Only when I put the phone down did I realise that Holly had given no reason for wanting to see me. I hoped she might have some new information regarding JayJay's death, though it was just as likely she wanted to know how I was getting on with my investigation and the answer to that was 'not very well'. So what was I going to tell her? I shrugged and picked up my bag, rummaging through the contents for my notebook but my searching hand failed to close around the familiar spiral binding. Frustrated, I upended the bag over the sofa, lip salves, pens, odd coins and a roll of peppermints cascaded onto the floor. So did the toy gun that my boss had pointed at me a couple of weeks ago. I went and put it in the desk drawer and only then remembered that the notebook was still in my case since my stay at KD's.

Walking back from the bedroom I flicked through the pages, looking for the list of questions I'd made about JayJay's death and the notes I'd made after Jerry's visit to Bishop Lea.

Who was Spaniel? Had Jaynee used it in a derogatory way or in a nicer, fonder manner? Clearing the clutter that now littered the settee, my eyes fell on a folded piece of yellow paper. Taking it to the bin I realised, just in time, that I held in my hand the Crofterton Dog Show programme. Eureka! This was just what I needed. I sat on the space that I had cleared, straightening out the creased sheets over my knee, mentally kicking myself for not having thought of it sooner, while I rapidly scanned the list of classes.

Oh!

There were seven types of spaniel. Seven! Hell's teeth! Damn stupid bloody JayJay and her stupid bloody diary. Why was nothing ever easy? Ah, hang on a minute, I thought as my fingers traced down the list in mounting excitement. After Clumber, Cocker and Field came King Charles, Cavalier KC, Springer and Sussex. Well, well, well, not so stupid Jaynee, after all. Quite clever, in fact, if I was right and Spaniel referred to Kenny Cameron of Mariner Productions.

I eased back with a satisfied sigh, thinking through the implications. I now reckoned I'd worked out all the names in JayJay's diary. Was I any further forward in knowing which of them might have killed her?

Was I heck as like!

Chapter 15

COMING OUT OF THE LIFT and crossing the foyer towards me, Holly looked fresh and young in her green slacks and white blouse. She looked so much like a sprig of lily of the valley, I could almost smell it. Her ginger curls formed a perfect aureole around her head like a saintly halo in a Russian icon.

"Oh, Verity, it's been awful," she confided, as we went up in the lift.

"Why? What's been happening?" I asked, glad to see we were back on first name terms.

"The police have been here, interviewing everyone and searching the offices."

She looked composed although I noticed a distinct redness and puffiness around her eyes. Had she cried for Greg Ferrari as she had for his co-star, I wondered.

"Tell me all about it in a minute." I said, aware of other employees passing us in the corridors, and I thought it best we weren't overheard.

Once in her office I looked around in amazement.

"Gosh, Holly. What have you been doing?"

The room was transformed from the drab but functional work

space I'd seen before, the furniture had been re-arranged, a new pale wood filing cabinet stood against one wall and her desk was clear of papers. A small indoor fern in a gaily coloured pot brightened the corner next to a coat stand.

"Well, my office looked like a bomb had hit it after the police search so I decided it was time for a clean-up," Holly explained.

"I'm impressed," I told her. "Your office is far neater than my own. You should see the clutter on my desk, for a start."

I laughed, but Holly looked to be in earnest when she said, "My mother always told me that cleanliness was next to godliness."

With nothing to say to that, I simply sat down and took out my notebook and pen.

"I suppose the police wanted to know about Greg Ferrari?"

"Yes, they did. I still can't believe it, first JayJay murdered and now Greg. Are you ..."

I held up a hand to prevent what I felt sure was going to be the inevitable question.

"No, I'm not investigating Greg's death, even though I met the man and had dinner with him."

Her eyes flared.

"I'm still trying to work out who murdered Jaynee, though it's more than likely that the same person killed both of them."

"So, if you find who murdered JayJay you'll have discovered who killed Greg as well."

In Holly's scheme of things, unmasking a killer was evidently all in a day's work. My day's work.

"Well, I have deciphered all the names in the diary you gave me."

Her face brightened.

I gave her the list without telling her the code words Jaynee had used for each name.

"I thought you said earlier there were six names?"

"Yes, but Jaynee had used two different codes for Candida."

"Well, that's suggestive isn't it?"

"Is it? What of?"

"Well, thinking about it ..."—she rubbed a hand across her forehead which showed she was doing just that—"... she might have used one name to start with, when they were friends, and another one later after they'd fallen out."

She smiled at this tortuous piece of logic which contradicted not only what she'd told me on my first visit, when she'd claimed the two women were friendly and had a good working relationship, but also the evidence in the diary where the uncomplimentary name appeared first.

"Well, maybe, Holly, but I still have no idea who killed her."

"Oh." Holly's face fell as her mouth drooped at the corners. "I felt sure that by now you would have cracked it."

Her relentless confidence in my ability to succeed where the police had so far failed was beginning to irritate me and my answer came out sharper than I'd intended.

"Well, I haven't. I'd hoped that you might have new information and that was why you called."

"Sorry." She shook her head sadly. "I phoned because I thought you'd be looking into Greg's murder and I wanted to tell you what had been going off here."

"And what has been happening here? You mentioned police interviews."

"They interviewed Candida and me. Separately, I mean. Candida was fuming afterwards."

I'll bet. The redoubtable Ms Clark would not take kindly to the sort of treatment Jerry Farish had doled out to me at our first meeting.

"Do you know why?"

Holly shrugged, a movement that once again gave me a glimpse of the little gold chain around her neck.

"She said it was inconvenient."

"Inconvenient? I should have thought Greg's death was more

inconvenient, wouldn't you?"

Especially for Greg, of course, though there was no way of knowing what he thought about it.

"Well, yes," she said doubtfully, pulling at her lower lip, "but she was due in the recording studios—she does have other shows besides *Star Steps*—when the police wanted to interview her."

"I don't suppose she was any more pleased when they did their search."

Holly's eyes widened.

"Oh, I'll say. She claimed they were being totally disruptive. They went everywhere, searching the place from top to bottom, all the offices along this corridor, the recording studios, editing suites, even the penthouse."

Her tone suggested surprise at this thoroughness.

"Did they find anything?"

Her brow creased.

"I think so."

"You're not sure?"

Either the police found something or they didn't. Drawing information out of Holly was like drawing teeth.

"Well, I only know what my friend Lauren told me in the canteen. She said they'd found a bundle of computer ties."

My eyebrows rose. At last she'd said something useful.

"And they found them," Holly went on in a tone that suggested deep significance, "in a cistern in the ladies' toilet."

"Really?"

My mind worked furiously but Holly appeared to be struggling with something, for the furrow was back on her forehead.

"Only ... I'd seen computer ties around the studios days earlier."

"You had? Where?"

She fidgeted in her chair before blurting out, "In Candida Clark's office."

My head was reeling when I left Holly's office a few minutes later. Intending to go straight home and think about the implication of the secretary's revelation, I wasn't best pleased to see a familiar figure advancing towards me.

"Oh! It's you again, is it?"

Candida Clark, legs wide, arms akimbo, blocked my further passage down the corridor.

"Bloody journalists. You're as bad as the police."

"Well, I…"

"So what is it this time? Greg Ferrari?"

"But I …"

She flung open her office door and jerked her head

"Well, you'd better come in, I suppose."

Never one to look a gift horse in the mouth, I followed her inside and closed the door.

"I don't know why you've bothered coming back, Miss, er …"

"Long," I supplied as she gestured for me to the chair opposite her. "Verity Long."

"You might just as well re-use the same load of rubbish as you've probably concocted for Jaynee bloody Johnson."

There was no attempt to hide the contempt in her voice this time. No crocodile tears for either of her so-called celebrities. I wondered what had caused the change. She looked different too, older and more haggard than she'd seemed a fortnight ago. The neat French pleat had gone and she wore her hair loose over the mandarin collar of her suit.

"I think my readers might notice if I did that. I thought you might be able to offer them a deeper insight."

All lies and flattery, of course, but it had worked before.

"Miss Long, I have a busy work schedule and there have been enough disruptions this week what with the police and your fellow journalists,"—she gave the word a sneer—"virtually camping out here. Just take what I said before about Jaynee and use that for your piece on Greg, will you?"

"Would that be the nice or the not-so-nice version?" I asked, provocatively.

She ran a hand through her hair, giving me a harsh stare before shaking her head.

"How quickly the vultures gather. Look, if you want the dirt on Greg, there are plenty here who will give it to you."

"He wasn't popular, then?"

"That depends on who you ask and how old they are."

That sounded intriguing but before I could ask the obvious question, she fired one back at me.

"Did you ever meet Greg Ferrari?"

"Yes, I had dinner with him last week."

A matter of hours after you'd had him over the boardroom desk, I thought, remembering the narrow escape I'd had in the penthouse suite. Candida looked at me in disbelief, one perfectly plucked eyebrow raised.

"You're a bit old for Greg's tastes, I would have thought," she said bitchily. "He liked them young, old enough to be legal, but otherwise as young as he could get. Did he try to have sex with you?"

I didn't quite know what to say to that. I could tell the truth, but, 'No, actually, he tried to kill me' seemed overly dramatic—even for a television studio.

"No."

"No? What are you? Another career virgin like Miss Goody-Two-Shoes down the corridor?"

I didn't care for the personal note that had crept into her questions and made an effort to get back on track.

"So what are you saying? That Ferrari had a voracious sexual appetite?" She nodded. "And that he preferred young girls?" Another nod.

All at once, I had a horrible thought.

"What? Like Holly Danvers for instance?"

"I can't give you names, if that's what you're after." She made a moue of distaste at what she, no doubt, considered journalistic prurience. "Suffice it to say that there are plenty of girls in Crofterton who came here in innocence and left in disillusion."

What a cracking quote! And what a shame I couldn't use it.

"And what about *Star Steps*? Will it continue?"

"Not without sponsors, it won't, and they've been falling over each other to pull out. It couldn't go on without Greg, anyway."

"Oh?"

"We could have replaced JayJay easily enough. D-list female celebrities are two a penny. We've got blonde presenters coming out of the woodwork. Dancers—and believe me, Greg could dance—are harder to come by."

Was it my imagination or did her voice catch when she'd said that?

"So you're going to miss him?"

"Oh, yes."

There was no mistake this time and, suddenly, Candy Clark was in floods of tears.

I almost rocked back in my chair as realisation hit me. Candida Clark had been in love with Greg Ferrari. Who would have thought the Iron Maiden could be taken in by a shallow, self-obsessed Lothario like Ferrari. I felt incredibly sorry for her. How love makes fools of us all.

On the drive home I tried not to think about what I'd learned at the studios. The Friday evening rush hour was in full swing and the traffic and my new car took all of my concentration. The Citroen had a higher clutch than my old vehicle and I managed to stall it twice before I finally reached Sutton Harcourt. Hanging my bag by its strap over a chair, I threw the copy of the Crofterton Gazette I'd picked up en-route onto the kitchen table and put the kettle on for a cup of tea. Drinking the hot, sweet brew—I still like sugar in my tea though I have long since given up taking it in coffee—I leafed through the paper hoping for up to date news on Ferrari's death. But six days after his murder, and with the police no nearer catching his and JayJay's killer, both of the stars had faded from the headlines. Instead, they had turned their attention to matters of more parochial interest and I gazed in sheer disbelief at this little gem:

'Leap-frogging Mayor Bruises Tomato'.

I wondered whether KD had seen it - and what her reaction had been, given her firmly held view of the poor quality of writing in what she referred to as the provincial press. I didn't bother to read the report of the fruit-damaging local worthy but turned over to be faced with this riveting snippet of local life:

'Dinner Table in Speed Record Hope'.

What? I laughed out loud. Clearly, my boss was right and we were fast heading for hell in a hand-cart. Then my eye fell on the name Kenny Cameron. A small piece in the 'What's On' column informed me that the CEO of Mariner Productions would open the Crofterton Summer Fête tomorrow at 2.00pm in Victoria Park. Good, I thought, tapping a finger against my lips. I had been wondering how to approach him to ask him about JayJay and his presence at the fête seemed like a golden opportunity. I would casually bump into him and ... and what? Demand to know if he'd killed JayJay and Greg? Not forgetting to ask what his motive had been, of course, because at the moment I could see no possible reason why he might want to harm either of them. Hmm, more work needed there, I felt. I got up from the table and began to prepare my dinner.

Afterwards, curled up on the sofa with a glass of wine, I went over everything I'd learned at Silverton Studios and what Jerry Farish had told me the previous evening. The more I thought about it, the more convinced I became that Greg Ferrari was the key to this whole affair. Maybe I'd been looking at things from the wrong angle. I took a sip of wine, got up and started to pace, backwards and forwards over the faded carpet. If Greg's death was nothing to do with events in Northworthy twenty years ago then who else had a motive to kill him? Whoever it had been needed an equally good reason to murder his co-star. The obvious answer was Candida Clark. I trudged around the living room, mentally listing the points against the producer.

One: She had loved Greg but he had rejected her in favour of younger women.

Two: Holly had seen the murder weapon—a bundle of computer ties—in her office prior to the murder.

Three: JayJay's intention to quit the show might not be reason enough to kill her, but threats of damaging revelations in her autobiography certainly could be. Especially if they showed a tendency to violence in Candida's past.

Four: She had the strength of character, and the resourcefulness, to be a killer.

Great! I could make out a strong case against Candy, so why did I still feel dissatisfied? Something must be wrong somewhere, something that didn't quite gel. I sighed. My mother always said I was hard to please. So, who else was there? I racked my brains for possible suspects. Holly? Well, hardly. Greg may well have seduced her but, these days, that was no motive to kill a man. Most girls would relish his advances, assuming they didn't throw themselves at him in the first place and besides, try as I might I could not come up with a plausible reason why Holly would also kill JayJay. Kenny Cameron seemed an unlikely candidate for either murder, though I would be interested in hearing what he had to say for himself tomorrow and, according to Jerry, John Brackett had a cast iron alibi.

Eventually, with my brain tired from working out all the permutations and my legs aching from all the pacing I'd done, I took myself off to bed. I pulled the thin summer-weight duvet over my shoulders and lay there trying to rest and put all thoughts about death and murder out of my mind. But sleep proved elusive. It must have been an hour later that I decided to give up the struggle and wandered into the kitchen for a nightcap, hoping a tot of brandy would help me into the arms of Morpheus. I pulled down the half-litre bottle of Courvoisier from the cupboard where I stored it and reached for a glass. A headline in the discarded Crofterton Gazette screamed at me as I did so. 'Promises Were Broken Say Angry Mums'. Could broken promises also lead to murder? I was beginning to think that they might.

The Rotary Club Summer Fête took place every year in Victoria Park in the centre of Crofterton. Beyond the elegant wrought iron bandstand and formal gardens that fronted on to the town, and separated from it by a wide pavement, lay the twenty or so football pitches that in winter played host to hundreds of bare-legged, red faced men and boys of the local Sunday League. Now a myriad of gaily-coloured marquees, tents and gazebos clustered around a large grassed area in the middle where the various events were held. It was an opportunity for local charities and voluntary organisations to show themselves off. Stalls for the Guides, Scouts, and St. John Ambulance Brigade, interspersed here and there with ice cream and burger vans, battled against the cries enticing the public to part with its money at tombola and win-a-teddy stands.

When I arrived Kenny Cameron was just finishing his speech and declaring 'the Crofterton Summer Fête well and truly open', though by the looks of things it had been in full swing for some time. I wandered around, my pace leisurely, my mind occupied not with the fun on offer but with darker thoughts. Determined not to open my purse, I relented and tried my luck at a bottle stall, run in aid of Macmillan Nurses. Naturally, from a large trestle table filled with every type of brandy, whisky, wine and liqueurs, I came away with nothing more than a bottle of nail polish. Green nail polish! Still, I didn't really mind, at least my money had gone to a good cause.

"Excuse me." A touch on my arm made me glance up. "It's Verity Long, isn't it?"

Well, well. Maybe my luck had changed. Instead of me thinking up excuses to approach the man from Mariner Productions, here he was accosting me.

"Yes, Mr Cameron. Hello again."

"It was you, wasn't it?"

"Me?" I looked at him stupidly. What was the man going on about?

"Yes, it was you that found her?"

"Yes," I replied quietly. "I found her."

To my surprise he put a hand under my elbow and steered me away from the crowds.

"Please, Miss Long,"—he kept his voice low—"I need to talk to you."

We didn't stop until we'd left the area set aside for the fête, crossed the pavement, and were into the formal gardens. He aimed straight for the first empty bench.

"Let's sit down a moment."

"Mr Cameron, what is all this about?"

I turned to face him, shocked to see tears in his eyes.

"Was she peaceful when you found her? Did Jaynee die peacefully, do you think?"

Disgusted by this prurient interest, I was about to turn away but those tears pulled at my sympathy gland, keeping me on the bench.

"Why on earth do you want to know that, Mr Cameron?"

He took a moment, during which he gave me a long, calculating stare, before replying.

"Can I trust you, Miss Long?"

"It's Verity, please, and yes, I would like to think you can trust me. Though it depends what it is," I added as an afterthought. Who knew what terrible secret this man wanted to confess?

"Jaynee Johnson and I were lovers. Oh, I don't just mean in the conventional sense..." He waved a well manicured hand, as if to indicate that I should dismiss all thoughts that he could be so banal and hurried on. "I mean we were in love. We were hoping to be married."

For a moment he looked so utterly bereft, so devastated, that I had to restrain myself from putting an arm around him.

"I'm so sorry."

"The week that Jaynee was supposedly missing,"—tears ran down his face—"she was with me in my cottage in Derbyshire."

So I'd been right in my guess that JayJay was in a love nest somewhere, though in the face of Kenny Cameron's all too evident grief, that thought gave me no satisfaction at all.

"Perhaps you'd better tell me all about it," I said as he took out a large handkerchief and wiped his streaming face.

Slowly, with many pauses while he struggled to control his emotions, I got the story from him. They had been seeing each other since March, originally to discuss the producer's plans for a chat show but soon discovered they had a lot more in common than the industry they worked in. Business meetings had given way to romantic dates, though the realisation that they were in love had come more recently and as a complete surprise to both of them—or so Cameron claimed. The week at the cottage had been his idea but Jaynee had gone along with it, quickly seeing the opportunity it presented for some free publicity.

"How did anyone know she was missing?" I asked.

"Oh, Jaynee arranged it with a reporter she knew. This chap was to start all the 'Where is Jaynee?' and 'JayJay is Missing' business in return for exclusive revelations on her return. We knew all the press hounds would pick up the scent and run with the story."

"Did the reporter know where she was?"

"Oh, no. He'd have been camped outside the place if she'd told him."

"And the exclusive revelations?"

"Originally that was going to be Jaynee leaving *Star Steps* and presenting the chat show. I persuaded her to change it to an announcement of our …"—his voice broke suddenly as he gulped back a sob—"…our wedding plans," he whispered.

"So when did you go up to the cottage?" I asked, trying to fix the timeline to the murder in my mind.

He rubbed a hand across his eyes and brow.

"We went up after she'd finished recording the show on the Monday." His eyes lost their focus as he thought back remembering, albeit sadly, the time he had spent with his lover. "We had a lovely week. The cottage is hidden in wooded hills above Matlock; it's a beautiful spot, ideal as a place to unwind. On the Thursday we went down into the town and I bought her an engagement ring. Was she wearing it when you … when you saw her?"

I closed my eyes in an effort to remember, picturing again that still figure, the pale hands as they lay at her sides.

"Yes," I said finally. "There was a ring on her left hand. A small diamond solitaire."

He smiled for the first time, taking a crumb of solace from the knowledge that the dead woman still wore that token of their love.

"Thank you," he whispered. "Thank you for that."

"But weren't you both scared that she would be recognised when you went into town?" I tried to focus on the practicalities.

"No. Jaynee took care of that with a brown wig and dark glasses. She was also very good at imitating accents so she didn't sound at all like she did on television."

Which at least showed forethought, if not actual cleverness, on JayJay's part. Once again I found myself forced to re-evaluate my assessment of the dead woman.

"And when did you return from Matlock?"

"We returned on Saturday 5th. Jaynee had an appointment on that day."

"Who with?"

"Hmm? I don't know. Why?"

I bit back the retort that leapt to my lips. I had to make allowances for the state the man was in. As gently as I could, I pointed out the obvious.

"Because whoever she was due to meet could have been the person who killed her."

"Oh! I suppose you're right. Jaynee didn't say and I didn't press her. I wish now I had."

"Did she say what the appointment was for?"

He screwed up his face in effort of remembrance.

"I think she said something about a friend moving, or something. I really can't remember."

"Have you told the police all this?"

"Yes, of course!" He had his feelings under control now, the handkerchief put away. "Miss Long, you still haven't answered my first question and you seem to be asking rather too many of your own. Just what is your interest?"

I scratched my chin with a finger nail. Well, it had taken him long enough to wake up to that fact and I had got a lot of information out of him. I couldn't grumble if he now clammed up.

"I'm sorry, Mr Cameron. The answer to your question is, that when I saw her, she looked composed and, yes, peaceful. I don't know how much the police may have told you ..."

"Nothing," he spat. "Well, nothing that I wanted to hear, anyway. All they did was ask me questions. Like whether she had low blood pressure ..."

"Did she?"

"Yes."

"Was it common knowledge? At the studios, I mean."

"Some people knew, certainly. Her secretary, her producer, and one or two others, I think."

He scowled and, aware that I risked alienating him, I went on quickly.

"Well, Jaynee was wearing a silvery-white dress and lay on her back on the bed. There were no signs of a struggle. As I said, she looked very calm, very …" I sought for the word I wanted but couldn't find it. In the end I settled for, "She looked at rest."

He gave a deep sigh.

"Oh, thank you. That's eased my mind."

Yours, maybe, but not mine, I thought.

"As for my interest …"

He looked up quickly. "Yes?"

"I want to know who killed her. I want to know who left her body in an empty house for some unsuspecting person, in this case me but it could equally well have been a young estate agent, to find. But above all, Mr Cameron, I want justice for Jaynee Johnson."

Even to my own ears that had sounded dramatic and I expected Kenny Cameron to burst out laughing at any moment. Instead he gazed at me sombrely.

"You're right," he said softly. "I'm sorry for my harshness."

I brushed aside his apology with a smile.

"Not at all."

"Thank you for your time and patience, Miss Long."

I sat on the bench and watched him walk away, then went home in thoughtful mood.

Chapter 16

After dinner, I took out my pad and jotted down what I'd learned from Kenny Cameron. I felt sure he had given me the last link in the chain of this investigation, if only I could put those links together in the right order. I re-evaluated last night's conclusions in the light of what he had told me, and realised that the pattern had shifted and now, someone else had been brought into the frame. Surprised, I once again paced the carpet while I thrashed out motive, means and opportunity.

When the last piece of the jigsaw finally fell into place the outcome was so obvious that I kicked myself. Well, I certainly had the answer now, didn't I? I might have had it long since if I hadn't been so fixated on that stupid diary, so hamstrung by my own prejudices and deceived by appearances instead of listening to what people actually said. I took a break to make myself another drink and then went over it all again, just to make doubly sure.

At ten o'clock, convinced and happy with my reasoning at last, I picked up the phone.

"Jerry? It's Verity. I know who killed Greg and JayJay."

"You do? Well done, Sherlock."

I ignored both the incredulity and the mockery.

"I'm serious. Listen ..."

I told him of my visit to Silverton Studios, I told him about my meeting with Cameron and, finally, I told him who had killed the stars and how. Then I told him why. At the end, he let out a long, low whistle.

"I see. Yes, I see."

"I don't have any evidence, though, Jerry ..."

"Oh, we'll find that—now we know where to look. Leave it with us."

For once, I agreed.

"Yes, OK. You'll let me know what happens, won't you?"

"Of course. Good night, Verity. Sleep well."

I put the phone down and headed for the wine rack. Back on the settee, I consoled myself with a glass of red and the thought that I had done the right thing although, Lord knows, it hadn't been easy. I shook my head. Verity, I reminded myself, means truth.

I allowed myself a lie-in the next morning and it was nearly eleven o'clock before I'd showered, dressed and had breakfast. I was just about to go and fetch a paper when the phone rang.

"Hello. Is that you, Miss Long?" came a breathless, agitated voice.

I had been so sure that it would be Jerry Farish, I nearly dropped the phone.

"Hello, Holly. Are you all right?"

"Oh, Miss Long, please help me. I'm so scared."

"Why? What's the matter, Holly?"

"Can you come round to my flat? It's 42, Beaumont Mansions. I've just had a phone call from Ms Clark."

I pricked up my ears at mention of the producer.

"Candida? What did she want?"

"She threatened me, Miss Long. She said I was an interfering do-gooder and it was about time she silenced me."

"What?" That was a bit blatant—even for the likes of the outspoken Candida Clark.

"And she said she was coming round here and, I thought, if you were with me, then she wouldn't be able to do anything, would she?"

"Go and stay with a neighbour, Holly," I said, trying to be practical in the face of Holly's rising panic.

"There's nobody in, Miss. Two of the flats are empty on this floor and my neighbour's out at work. Please come. I'm frightened."

"Holly, why don't you phone the police?"

"But what would I say?" she bleated. "They wouldn't believe me and it would be my word against hers. Besides, she could come back when the police aren't here."

There was a sudden loud bang from the other end of the line and Holly squealed.

"What is it? Holly? Are you there? Holly?"

But the line had gone dead and I was talking to thin air and the dial tone.

Damn. Damn, blast and set fire to it. I really didn't have any choice. A killer might strike at any minute. I fetched the toy gun from the drawer in my desk and dropped it in my pocket, picked up my bag and then called Jerry Farish.

"It's Verity. I've just had an hysterical Holly Danvers on the phone claiming Candida Clark has threatened her and is on the way to Holly's flat to silence her. I'm going round there."

"No! Don't you dare," he screamed. "Stotty and I are on the way and there's a patrol car already despatched. Leave it to the police, Ve ..."

I pressed the button and ended the call. "Leave it to the police"? I had left it to them and now see what had happened. Besides, there was no way I was staying out of it. I'd been involved from the beginning; it was only right that I should be there at the death. Just as long as it wasn't *my* death we were talking about.

I announced my arrival outside the block of flats with a squeal of tyres and a spray of gravel. There was no sign yet of the police and I listened in vain for the wail of a siren as I belted for the outside door.

My heart pounded as I ran up the stairs, fear clutching at my belly, breath catching in my throat, hoping I was in time to prevent another senseless death. At the top of the third flight I stopped, bent double, hands on hips, struggling to draw air into my aching lungs. I heard a thud from the floor above and forced myself upwards. At the top of the stairs the overpowering smell of 'Youth Dew' stopped me as effectively as a brick wall. I took a moment to steady myself and tried not to inhale. I knew I was being stupid, that I ought to wait for the police, but when had being stupid ever stopped me? I walked down the corridor to meet Holly Danvers—the killer of Jaynee Johnson and Greg Ferrari.

Outside Flat 42 I put my hand to the door and felt no surprise when it opened at my touch.

"Come in, Miss Long, we've been expecting you," said a cool voice.

In an ice-blue dress that showed off her hour-glass figure and matched her frosty manner, Holly Danvers slammed the door shut behind me.

"Do take a seat next to my other … guest. It's quite a party we're having."

Candida Clark sat on the settee, trussed like a chicken, arms tied behind her back, legs roped around her shins above her red stiletto shoes. Across her mouth like a great grey gash was a strip of duct tape.

With a push to my back Holly propelled me forward. My mind raced. Time, you need time, said my brain. Somehow I had to delay things until Jerry got here.

"Why did you kill Greg, Holly? Did you hate him so much?"

"No! I didn't hate him. I loved him."

"Nonsense. If you love a man, you don't put a computer tie around his neck and pull it tight. *She* loved him." I flung out an arm towards the woman on the sofa. "That's how I knew she didn't kill him. You did."

Holly picked up a wicked-looking carving knife off the table.

"He deceived me," she spat, eyes narrowing. "He said he would marry me."

I backed away as she took a step toward me.

"Is that why you slept with him?"

"I gave him my honour and he rejected me."

"You were a virgin, weren't you? And religious, too."

Around her neck she was still wearing the crucifix on its slender gold chain.

"Yes. He broke his promise."

So I'd been right about the motive, after all.

"But why kill JayJay?"

I inched further away, trying to put the settee between us.

"She tempted him. She lured him away. Just like that bitch, there."

She pointed the knife at Candida who flinched and moaned behind the gag.

"Did you know Jaynee suffered from low blood pressure?"

"She used to send me to the chemists for her prescription so, yes, I knew."

"So you got your friend to make you up as an old woman, put on a grey wig and went to view the house. Then you stole the key."

"Oh, haven't we been busy," sneered Holly.

"You even called yourself Mrs Smith. Did you know it was Greg's real name?"

"Of course. It would have been my name too."

She seemed happy to answer questions, so I pressed on.

"How did you get Jaynee to the house?"

"Oh, that was easy. I told her I'd moved and invited her to my house-warming."

"But she went missing. Weren't you afraid she wouldn't come?"

Holly shrugged. I hoped she wasn't getting bored.

"No. I knew it was all a stunt and that she'd show up."

"And the drug?"

"Ha! I offered her a cold glass of lemonade on a hot evening."

And Midazolam was soluble, of course. She'd made the whole murder sound horrifyingly easy.

"And the 'Youth Dew'? You said you didn't wear perfume but you were wearing Lily of the Valley at the studios the other day. Do you only use Estée Lauder when you want to murder someone?"

Holly sneered and took another, menacing step towards me. I scanned the room frantically for anything I could use as a weapon before remembering the gun in my pocket. Pulling it out I waved it in front of her.

"Stop right there, Holly, I don't want to have to use this," I said, sounding like a character from some awful 'B' movie. Holly laughed.

"You won't use it, and if I die I shall be reunited with Greg."

Maybe that explained the calmness, her coolness and indifference. Still brandishing the knife she moved closer to Candida, putting herself between us. How long have I been here, I thought? Five minutes? Ten? Surely Jerry must get here soon. Just keep her talking.

"Let's face it, Holly," I said, attempting to distract her from the terrified producer, "you were hardly unique, were you? Greg Ferrari would sleep with anything in a skirt."

As a distraction strategy it did have its drawbacks—my own imminent demise being one of them. Shrieking like a hell-cat, Holly ran towards me, knocking the gun out of my hand.

"You bitch! You interfering old hag!"

I bolted behind the settee and round the other side snatching a shoe from Candida's foot as I did so. The producer raised her tied legs in time to catch Holly and trip her as we played cat and mouse around the furniture. Without thinking, I launched myself on Holly's back, trying to stay clear of her right hand, and hammered the stiletto heel into her naked shoulder. On the settee Candida writhed and wriggled, her despairing eyes watching our every move, less concerned for my welfare, no doubt, than that of her £300 shoe. I jabbed the heel into my opponent's neck.

"You hypocrite!" somebody yelled. It might have been me. "You lying, scheming little bitch."

I grabbed for the wrist holding the knife while still trying to grind the stiletto through the flesh of her neck. Droplets of blood ran down onto the carpet. I tried to stay calm. I could win this battle if I could just keep on delaying her until the police showed up. I needed to stay one step ahead and out-think my opponent, not match her insult for insult. Perhaps it was the memory of how Holly had fooled me that had turned me into a screaming virago now. She squirmed underneath me. I lifted and repeatedly banged her wrist and hand on the floor but she held tight to the weapon. Then she bucked, throwing me sideways.

"Arrgh."

I rolled across the floor, desperate to stay out of her reach, and bumped into the occasional table, bringing down a large pottery vase which landed within inches of my head. I twisted to the left, taking my eyes off the frenzied girl. When I looked back Holly was already getting to her feet, ready to attack me again. Banging my head on the table legs had caused my vision to blur and from somewhere I heard a pounding, my blood probably, sounding loud in my ears. Holly made a step backwards, the better to come at me again, as I lay, groggy and confused, at her feet.

"Mmfmph."

Candida moved on the sofa, at the periphery of my line of sight. I daren't turn to look at her, Holly was too close. Suddenly she grabbed at my hair, lifting my head from the ground. I curled round, trying to kick at her legs. I couldn't see the knife. Where was the knife? I screamed as a particularly vicious tug left my hair in her hands instead of in my scalp. My head fell back with a thud.

A black wave swept over me. I felt myself weakening, Holly had nearly twenty years advantage in the youth and fitness stakes. I still couldn't locate the knife, the girl's hands were a blur as she pulled at my hair again. I scrabbled to lever myself up as she let go and my head hit the side of the table with a crash.

"Verity! Are you all right? Don't try to get up."

Was it Jerry? Had I passed out? Died, perhaps, and gone to heaven?

"Mmm. S'OK."

If that was my voice it sounded like the bleat of a new born lamb.

I opened my eyes. Through the blur, a uniformed female was untying the ropes from around Candy Clark's legs while the producer rubbed at her bruised, but free, arms. I didn't envy her removing the duct tape. It does so play havoc with one's super-gloss lipstick. I giggled.

I tilted my head to the right, grimacing as a wave of nausea hit me. Holly Danvers, hands cuffed behind her back, a sullen, defeated slump to her shoulders, stood subdued now in the firm grasp of Sergeant Stott while Jerry intoned the words of the formal arrest over her bowed head. Two more police officers stood by the wrecked front door.

Oh good, I thought, as darkness swept over me. The cavalry has arrived.

I can't have been out for more than a couple of minutes. When I came to I was on the sofa, a paramedic dabbing something that stung on to my forehead, Holly Danvers was being led off to a waiting police car and Candida Clark was nowhere to be seen.

"Candy ...?"

"Hush, hush. She's already in the ambulance. Do you think you can stand?"

I nodded, struggling to my feet, one arm held by the medic, the other by Jerry.

The medic crossed to the door.

"Two minutes, Inspector. The ambulance is waiting."

Jerry surveyed me critically then grabbed me, roughly, by the shoulders.

"You bloody little fool! What on earth did you think you were playing at, putting us both at risk like that?"

Both of us? I was the one who'd just gone ten rounds with a rabid Holly Danvers.

"And how, exactly, am I supposed to have endangered you, Inspector?"

"Just how clear headed and effective, how good at my job do you think I am when I'm worried sick about you?"

"Oh," was all I could think of to say.

"I told you to leave it to us. When will you ever listen, Verity? I want you to stay out of my affairs."

"And out of your life, I suppose."

I said it bitterly, aware that I'd blown my chances with him, but his reply took me completely by surprise. He pulled me to him, almost crushing me in his grasp.

"Oh, God, no. Anything but that, you little fool. I want you in my life, part of my life. But out of danger." He stroked my hair then pushed it back, taking my face in his hands. "I want to love you, make love to you and, when I've done that, I want to do it all over again. What do you think to that?"

Actually I thought I quite liked it. His voice had been harsh but the hands that held me were gentle.

"Hmm? What have you got to say to that?"

What indeed? I couldn't do any better than finish the way I'd started. I hazarded another line from *Casablanca*.

"Louis, I think this is the beginning of a beautiful friendship."

He laughed, liquid amber eyes locked on my own.

"Oh, Verity. You and your movie quotes. Come on."

Gently, a protective arm around my shoulder, he helped me downstairs to the ambulance waiting below.

I was sitting at my desk, idly musing on the outcome of the Jaynee Johnson case and wondering whether I would hear from Inspector Jerry Farish again when the telephone rang.

"Good morning, Kathleen Davenport's office."

"Hello," said an unknown woman's voice. "May I speak to Verity Long, please?"

"This is Verity."

"Oh, hello. I'm calling about the advert. The one in the Crofterton Gazette."

"Ye..es?"

For a moment my mind was blank.

"The one where you asked anyone with information about Charlotte Neal to contact you."

I snapped to attention, pulling my pad and pen towards me, thoughts of romance forgotten.

"Oh yes. Who is this?"

"My name is or, rather, was Kimberley Hughes."

I nearly fell off my chair. The friend whose house Charlotte had just left on the night she disappeared.

"I'm now Mrs Atkins and don't get over to Crofterton to visit my mum very often. She saved the advert out of the paper to show me."

Fascinating, no doubt, but I wasn't interested in her long winded explanation. I wanted to know what she could tell me about Charlotte and the night she vanished.

"Yes, Mrs Atkins. Do you have information about your friend?"

"Yes, yes I do." She sounded eager. Maybe she had something to get off her chest after twenty years.

"Look," she went on. "Could we meet? I'd really rather not discuss this over the phone.

"Of course. Where and when would suit you?"

"Could you come over to my mum's place? Say, in about an hour?"

I confirmed that her mum was still living on Conway Drive and assured her I'd be there.

"I'll be waiting outside for you," she said, and put the phone down.

KD was just sliding an omelette out of a pan, folding it over on the plate with an expert flick of the pan's edge. A crisp green salad lay ready on a side plate on the table.

"Cheese omelette?" she asked, putting the plate down and picking up a bottle of Montepulciano.

"It's tempting but no thanks. I've got to go out."

"Oh?"

"I've just had Kimberley Hughes on the phone. The friend in the missing schoolgirl case."

"Ah." She sipped her wine. "Will she know anything, do you suppose?"

"Only one way to find out. I'll be a couple of hours."

"That's fine. I'll see you when you get back. Oh, and Verity ...?"

I turned in the doorway.

"Be careful. Drive safely." She waved a forkful of egg in my direction.

"Sure thing, boss."

I left her to enjoy her lunch.

A tall, brown haired woman wearing a green summer dress and a white cardigan waited for me as I parked the car outside 122 Conway Drive. We shook hands but instead of turning towards the house she began to walk in the direction of the shops.

"I hope you don't mind," she began, "but I didn't want to discuss this in front of my mum. She's not well and ..."

"That's all right."

She led me across the road and through the waving sea of parched, sun browned grass towards the trees.

"I'm taking you to where the plot was hatched." She smiled at me. Then, seeing my baffled look, said, "Don't worry, that's not as sinister as it sounds."

"Well, I'll admit to being intrigued," I said.

I followed her along the path. Somehow I knew that our destination would be the old bomb crater. On the far side of the rim a large log had been placed on the stumps of two long-felled trees. Only when we were seated on this makeshift bench did Kimberley Hughes tell her story.

"First of all, as far as I know, Charlotte is alive and well, though I haven't had any contact with her for over a year."

"You've been in touch all this time?"

"Oh yes. I've always known, roughly, where she was. You have to understand that Charlotte had a very unhappy home life, her father was abusive, her mother too drunk to interfere or put a stop to it. She was desperate to get away."

"Really? From what I read they seemed like an ideal family."

She pondered this for a moment before she went on.

"They certainly convinced the police that they were doting parents and, with hindsight, they probably were very shocked at Charlotte vanishing like that. They convinced the press too," she added, scathingly. "But that year, 1990, in the May I think it was, Charlotte met a lad and fell in love. Well," she laughed, "it's what you do when you're fourteen isn't it?"

She stopped for a moment, her eyes unfocused and far away as she remembered her youth. I waited for her to resume.

"Anyway, this boy lived with his family on a canal boat."

Of course! That's how she got away unseen by anyone. I kicked myself for not having thought of it, especially given my recent too-close encounter with the canal's watery depths.

"How old was the boy? Did his family …"

"He was sixteen," she interrupted, "and, yes, his family knew of Charlotte's situation and were happy to take her and hide her if necessary. She asked for my help and swore me to secrecy."

I nodded.

"On the day she supposedly disappeared, we arranged for Charlotte to come for tea. Afterwards, I said we were going for a walk, but we actually got the bus to Crofterton. There's a stop close to a canal bridge about two miles from here and that's where Charlotte joined Adam. When I got home, about six thirty …"

"Six thirty? I thought she went at eight."

"Yes, it was all part of the plan. I called out to Mum that we were back, made a lot of noise and pretended to talk to Charlotte as if she was with me. Then, at eight o'clock, I opened the door and closed it again and told my Mum that Charlotte had just gone. That way the police and her parents would think she had disappeared much later and be looking in the wrong place at the wrong time."

"So, you took most of the risk."

She shrugged.

"I didn't mind. She was my friend and I wanted to help."

I mulled all this over. How wrong I had been about the case and how prescient of KD. I must remember to tell her.

"And Charlotte? Did she get a happy ending?" I asked.

Her face softened as she smiled and looked away from me, down into the crater.

"Yes, she stayed with Adam, married him two years later and had two kids a few years after that. They bought their own boat with help from his parents and are still together, as far as I know, still cruising the canals of England and Wales."

"I'm glad," I said. "And I'm glad you've told me."

"What will you do now that I have?"

She licked at her lips, holding her breath, a tiny flicker of fear in her eyes for the first time.

"Nothing," I assured her, suddenly realising she'd never asked why I had placed the ad. Why I wanted to know and was asking questions about the affair now, after twenty years had passed. Maybe the need to unburden herself had overridden such considerations.

"Nothing? You're sure?"

"Well, there's a retired policeman I know who'd appreciate the truth but he won't lose any sleep if he remains in ignorance. He told me his sergeant always said you knew far more than you were telling."

"The woman?"

I nodded.

"Yes, I suspected as much. In the end I just played dumb. I knew they'd never find her without my help."

I rose from the log.

"Thanks again for telling me. It will go as far as my boss, the writer, but no further. I promise."

"Thank you."

She smiled as we shook hands.

"I'm pleased I've told you. Twenty years is a long time to keep a secret."

I thought of the other Charlotte in Northworthy and silently agreed with her. Both Charlottes and Jaynee Johnson had been granted a form of justice, I reckoned. And in the end that may be the most that any of us can ever hope for.

The End

The stories in The Verity Long Mystery Series are all available as e-books from your local Amazon store:

Strictly Murder (The Verity Long Mysteries Book 1)

Organized Murder (The Verity Long Mysteries Book 2)

Scouting for Murder (The Verity Long Mysteries Book 3)

Married to Murder (The Verity Long Mysteries Book 4)

A Novel Way to Die (A Verity Long novella)

If you would like advance notice when new books are published, and absolutely no spam, please sign up for my mailing list:
http://eepurl.com/r0jRf

To find out more about me, and my books, please visit my website: http://www.lyndawilcox.com/

Please visit my Facebook page for more info about my books or to get in contact: https://www.facebook.com/LyndaWilcoxBooks

About the Author

Lynda Wilcox's first piece of published writing was a poem in the school magazine. In her twenties she wrote Pantomime scripts for Amateur Dramatic groups and was a founder member of *The Facts of Life*, a foursome who wrote and performed comedy sketches for radio. Now she concocts fantasy stories for older children (10-13) and writes funny whodunits for adults.

Lynda lives in a small town in England, in an untidy house with four ageing computers and her (equally ageing but very supportive) husband. She enjoys pottering in the garden where she grows brambles, bindweed and nettles along with roses and lilies. Oh! And slugs! Slugs that feed well on everything but the brambles and weeds.

Most of all, she loves to write — it gets her out of doing the housework. She also reads a lot and enjoys good food and wine.

45547364R00151

Made in the USA
Charleston, SC
27 August 2015